Praise for Teresa LeYung Ryan and
LOVE MADE OF HEART

"With raw, engaging dialogue as its narrative essence, *Love Made of Heart* dismantles the easy clichés of unconscious loyalties and entices us with searing honesty to journey through complex psychological realms with its female protagonist until we are left with a quiet appreciation of the truthfully tender."
—Lydia Kwa, author of *This Place Called Absence*

"*Love Made of Heart* is a book made of wisdom. Ryan writes of mothers and daughters, but the truth of her fiction strikes much deeper; beyond family, beyond gender, all the way to the fragile, universal heart."
—Frank Baldwin, author of *Jake & Mimi* and *Balling the Jack*

"In *Love Made of Heart,* Ruby's struggles to make peace with her life etch themselves deeply into the reader's own heart, so that you find yourself caring and wondering about how she is doing long after you've read the last page of her story."
—Carol Schaefer, author of *The Other Mother*

LOVE
MADE OF
HEART

Teresa
LeYung Ryan

KENSINGTON BOOKS
http://www.kensingtonbooks.com

KENSINGTON BOOKS are published by

Kensington Publishing Corp.
850 Third Avenue
New York, NY 10022

ISBN 0-7582-0217-2

First Hardcover Printing: October 2002
First Trade Paperback Printing: October 2003
10 9 8 7 6 5 4 3 2 1

Printed in the United States of America

In loving memory of six powerful women:

Rita Leung (the little girl known as Yun Yuet Kwai)
who was my lovely mom;
Yun Gim How (daughter of Lee Fong and Yue Shue Ngun)
who was my mom's mom;
Leung Tai Oy, who was my father's mom;
Carmen Ryan (the little girl known as Carmen Juanita Vacossin)
who was my sweet mother-in-law;
Lisa Craft, who taught me patience; and
Angie Hu, who taught me compassion.

ACKNOWLEDGMENTS

My deepest gratitude to the folks directly responsible for the birthing and presentation of this novel:

The critique group buddies—Evelyn Miché, Theresa Stephenson, and Olga Malyj.

Pamela Marsh Markmann for critiquing the "first" draft.

Kim McMillon for telling me to "walk the walk" of a writer.

Becky O. Breitwieser for editing a "young" manuscript.

Advisers Andrée Abecassis and Laurie Fox.

Mentors Frank Baldwin and Carol Schaefer.

Luisa Adams for encouraging me to "dig" deeper.

Martha Alderson for asking: "Where's your 'front story'?"

Susan Canale for giving me "the four-tissue" award when I really deserved it and not before.

Dr. Susan Thackrey and Maxine Hong Kingston for being the inspirations.

All the dear ones (relations, pals, coworkers, California Writers Club, old friends and new friends) who cheered me on; some even test-marketed for me.

All the Mrs. Nussbaums in my life.

The El Cerrito Fire Department.

The authors who generously gave their time to write quotes for the back cover.

Super-agent Stacey Glick of Jane Dystel Literary Management.

Dynamo editor John Scognamiglio and the talented folks at Kensington Publishing Corp.

Lou Malcangi for cover design; Libba Bray for cover copy; Jacquie Edwards for copyediting.

Linda Christensen for author's photo.

Flossie Lewis, Ph.D. for introducing the writer to new worlds.

Maria, my sister, for helping me remember the precious stories.

Lyle, my husband, for nourishing my heart, thus making me a brave storyteller.

CHAPTER 1

Fifty-One-Fifty

What have I done? I watch the uniformed police officers escort my mother from my apartment.

"Ruby! Don't let them take me away!"

My head is exploding and my chest hurts. But why can't I speak?

"Ruby, don't let them take me away! Ruby!" Mother pleads in Chinese this time. Whenever Mother is scared, she retreats to her native tongue.

Even though I know what I should be saying to my mother, the warm and gentle words stay in my mind but do not cross my lips. She must realize I am doing the right thing. Surely she knows I do not want to see her end up like Grandmother. Please don't end up like Grandmother.

I try calling out, "Mom, they won't hurt you," but the sounds do not come. What's happening to me? I must take deep breaths. Bracing myself against the wall, I pray this is no more than another bad dream.

Mrs. Nussbaum, the elderly neighbor from down the hall, steps out of her apartment. She's clutching Rashi, her Pekingese. "What are you doing?" she asks the officers. They do not answer her.

Mrs. Nussbaum looks at my mother and gasps, "Oh, my God!"

I put my hand on my throat and take another deep breath. The words won't come.

"Ruby, where are they taking your mother? What's wrong with you, Ruby? Answer me."

Mother looks over her shoulder at me. "Speak up. Tell these people to go away."

I must focus. The walls can't be swaying.

Turning back to the officers, Mrs. Nussbaum shouts, "Young men, where are you taking Mrs. Lin?" Rashi starts to yap as if to shout at the officers too. "My poor *bubbele*, don't be scared, I'm here," Mrs. Nussbaum consoles. I'm not sure whether she is speaking to her dog, to my mother or to me.

The senior of the two officers answers. "It's a Fifty-One-Fifty, ma'am. Please don't block the hallway. Everything is okay."

No. Everything is far from being okay. Fifty-One-Fifty is a police code for someone endangering her own life.

Mrs. Nussbaum, with Rashi still in her arms, reluctantly retreats into her apartment. Susan, the social worker, redirects my focus. "Ruby, I'll go with your mom. You stay here and wait for Dan. Okay? Ruby? Can you hear me?"

Through my tear-filled eyes, Susan looks as if she's standing behind a sheet of warped glass. My head is splitting.

"Here, use the banister. Your mom will be in good hands." Susan supports my elbow as we go down the four flights of stairs.

Reaching the lobby, she leads me to the stone bench. "Ruby, sit here and wait for Dan. He'll bring the car around, but it'll be a while. We couldn't find parking out front. All right?"

I nod.

Sitting here, nauseated and speechless, it seems like a disjointed dream to me, a dream that started two months ago.

CHAPTER 2

The Visit

It was the Saturday before my twenty-seventh birthday that my mother came to see my new apartment. I heard the doorbell ring three times. The clock on the bookcase said 11:00. How annoying. She was an hour early, as usual. Many times she said only losers arrive late and that Father was always late. Three to four hours late was his style. Late for our birthday celebrations. Late for Christmas dinners. Late for family events.

Mother entered with an alertness which told me she was going to inspect my new home. She seldom carried a purse. On that day, she had a large brown paper bag with her. The bag was folded over twice at the top. She plopped it down in the hallway.

"Very sunny," she said, as she marched straight into the living room. "You better close the drapes before you go to work or the sun will ruin that sofa. The fabric will fade. How much did you pay for it?"

"It was worth it. You know how I love brocade. Mom, look. Built-in bookcases."

She opened the French windows. "But you can't see the Golden Gate Bridge. Why have a view when you can't see the bridge?"

"Look, Mom. Sliding doors to separate the dining area from the kitchen and living room."

"All this space? For yourself? Why do you need all this space? Are you living with someone?"

"No, of course not. I just like to have a guest bedroom. Emily can use it when she visits. Plus, the second bedroom has a huge closet that I can use for storage. Out-of-town friends can stay here too."

"You're not a hotel." She walked away from me.

In my bedroom Mother slid open the closet door from the far end. "So many evening gowns, Ruby. Why do you buy so many?"

"They're uniforms. I wear suits for daytime and gowns in the evenings."

"Do they pay you, then? Fancy title, Manager of Special Events. But do they provide evening gowns? I bet not."

It's okay, I told myself, it's okay.

Mother slid the closet door shut and walked out of the room, looking for the kitchen.

"Working day and night. They're taking advantage of you."

"No, they're not. Do you know how many people would give their right arm to work at the St. Mark?"

She ignored me.

I saw her look of approval when she entered the kitchen. "New appliances," she said. Standing in the hallway, I breathed a sigh of relief that she had found no major fault with the apartment.

"Okay, Mom, let's go to lunch. A new place opened up last month."

She left her brown paper bag sitting in the hallway and said, "I'll come back for it later." By then I was curious to know what was in the bag, but I also wanted to be respectful. So I didn't ask.

~

In the lobby, we ran into Mrs. Nussbaum with her grocery cart. I held the door open for my neighbor. "Mrs. Nussbaum, the elevator *is* working today."

"Thank God. These bags are heavy. How are you, Miss China Doll?"

"I'm fine. And you?"

"Ruby, this is your mother?"

"Yes. This is my mom, Vivien Lin. Mom, this is Mrs. Nussbaum."

"Oh Mrs. Lin, you have such a sweet girl. Ruby is not like other young people—she's such a darling. You must be so proud."

"She's a good daughter," my mother said without smiling.

"I see where she gets her good looks." Mrs. Nussbaum touched my hair as a proud grandmother would have done.

"She doesn't get her looks from me. She has her father's face."

"I'm taking Mom to the new Chinese place. Can I bring something back for you?"

"No, dear. Thank you for asking."

Mother raised an eyebrow. Perhaps she didn't like someone else calling me "dear" or maybe I shouldn't have been chatting with a neighbor when she was supposed to be the center of my attention.

"Well, you have a good time, *bubbele*. A pleasure to meet you, Mrs. Lin."

Mother was already out the front door.

~

The new Chinese restaurant was four blocks away on Fillmore Street. I saw Mother crack a smile when we entered The Royal Garden. The dining room—decorated with green plants along the walls, the carpet with enough gold and red to suggest pageantry, the murals depicting Chinese pavilions—won her seal of approval.

"Pink napkins," she commented as we sat down.

Mother ordered our favorites. "Pot stickers, chicken with black bean sauce, honey-glaze prawns with walnuts, and garlic spinach," she told our starched-uniform waiter. One of Mother's golden rules was always to order enough food for the next day. "We want very hot rice. Not warm. Hot," she commanded. Then she dismissed the waiter by starting the conversation before he had finished writing our order on his pad.

"Ruby, how come you don't perm your hair anymore? I like it curly."

"I got tired of it. I like it this way."

"Let it grow. I like it long. With your oval face, you look better with long hair." She poured tea for us, first for me, then for herself. "Ruby, how much are you paying for that apartment? It's very beautiful, everything in the kitchen is brand new, but the landlord should cut the rent in half since you're just one person living in a two-bedroom apartment."

"Oh, Mom. It doesn't work that way," I sighed.

"They're thieves," she added.

"Mom. They are not. They pay for the water and garbage, and they didn't charge extra for the garage."

"Ruby, why should they charge for a garage? They know they're sucking blood already."

"Oh Mom. Please."

"Please what? Please don't worry about you? You're gullible. Your father is the same way. You take after him, don't know how to say 'no.' If I don't watch out for you, who will?"

I hated being called gullible. I hated being compared to Father.

"Mom, I think I'm getting a great deal, and I don't need a view of the bridge. I'm very proud of my new apartment."

"Proud," my mother mimicked. "How can you be proud of something you don't own?"

I pretended I didn't hear those words. I would have expected Father to say them, not Mother. Spending an hour together every two months had been the silent agreement between Mother and me. Just like an alarm clock, every two months I would feel the pang of missing her lovely face; but most of our dates ended up with my feeling as if I had failed once again to prove something to her.

"Mom, have you heard from Emily?"

"Your sister called me last week." Mother said it in a way to remind me that I did not call her often enough.

"So how's my baby sister?"

"Your sister is doing fine, I hope, so far away. There are plenty of universities in California. Why did she have to pick a school in Philadelphia?"

"But aren't you happy for her? I am. I wish I were getting my Masters. If I had to do it over again, I would have gone to college right after high school. But having had the taste of a paycheck made it so hard to go back—"

"If you had gone directly to college, you wouldn't have gone through that year—"

"Mom!" I held up my hand to stop her from finishing her sentence, knocking over my cup of tea. "That year is not important. I've erased that year."

The gray-haired woman at the next table looked at me as I blotted the spilled tea with my napkin.

Mother mercifully quit. "Well, you're going now. It's never too late. But I don't like to see you burning yourself out working a full-time job and going to school."

I scrunched my face at the woman from the next table and she finally looked away.

"I'm fine, Mom. I need to keep busy. Besides, not all the classes are intense. One class is actually fun. Greek Tragedies."

"What is Greek Tragedy? That's sick! You're studying tragedy? I hope your sister is not taking any nonsense classes."

"Mom, forget it. Just forget it."

The waiter came over with the pot stickers. He handed me a fresh napkin with a smile.

Mother's motto, *Never reveal your pain when someone hurts you— Don't give them the satisfaction*, rang in my head.

"I'm so proud of Em. Remember when she was in high school, she used to announce a new career every year?"

"Thank God she's not an actress! Do you know of any Chinese-American actress making it big?"

If Mom only knew that I have become a great actress.

"In my days, pure hard work was everything anyone needed to know. Your father and I would not have left Hong Kong if it were just the two of us. But we wanted all of you to get a good education. The sacrifices we made for you kids," she sighed.

I kept still. Usually I would have rolled my eyes. *There goes that speech again.* I waited for her to finish because I felt guilty that I had had to cancel our last lunch date. The flu epidemic hit our department. Three coworkers were sick. Then I got it two weeks later. Four months was a big stretch of time not to have seen one's mother.

"Thank God for immigration laws and President Kennedy," my mother continued. "In Hong Kong you were in the second grade. Your father didn't make enough money for one tuition, let alone three. We barely scrape by . . . *It's scraped, Mom. Say scraped. I'm gonna scream!*

" . . . We had to leave before John and Emily started school too. You were a good girl, Ruby, we didn't have to pay your tuition because you were Number One Student in the first grade. You would've been Number One in second grade too."

"What if I were Number Two or Number Three? Would they have given us a discount on tuition?"

"Who knows, who cares! You were Number One!"

"I miss Emily. Long distance phone calls can't replace the hugs. It's really strange, even though we're six years apart, I feel like we're twins. I can't explain it."

"You're a good daughter. She's a good daughter. But why can't she be happy here?"

I looked at Mom as she was eating. Her face had become so tanned. It must have been from going out every day. Perhaps if I visited her more often, as a good daughter should, the new lines on her face would not seem so pronounced. Though when she smiled, no one would guess she was fifty-two. She had the smile of a thirty-year-old. We could have passed for sisters, except she'd be the beautiful one. With her hair pinned up that way, she looked like a Chinese Eva Gabor, but I bet Eva would not have been so critical of her daughter. Why couldn't my mother be like the moms on television?

Half an hour later when the two of us had enough, Mother waved at the waiter. "Waiter! Waiter! Four boxes, and a big bag. Waiter! One more order of rice to go! Not a small bag, a big bag," she specified.

When the boxes, the large bag, the order of rice, and the bill arrived, she grabbed the bill before the waiter had a chance to put down the little tray. Our starched-uniform waiter was startled by Mother's quick movement.

I used to argue with her about who was to pay for lunch, by reminding her that I had a good job and could afford to take my own mother out. *But not today. Just let me outta here.* She smiled a big smile as soon as I said, "Okay, Mom, thanks for lunch." She scattered four one-dollar bills on the table for a tip. I stacked the bills neatly in a pile and she scattered them again.

"I want him to see four one-dollar bills, not just one or two. If they're stack . . . *It's stacked, Mom. Stacked.*

" . . . he'll come over, grab the bills, shove them into his pocket, and never know I gave him four dollars," she explained. She had a reason for everything.

"Mom, so much food, you take it home."

"No. It's all for you."

"But I eat at the hotel, remember? One of the perks."

"They don't have rice! This is good food. There are two meals here."

On the way home, we passed a flower stand where Mother insisted on buying me some chrysanthemums.

"I'll buy two bunches for you," she announced.

"One is plenty, Mom."

"Are you sure?"

"Yes, I'm sure."

She saw me looking at the roses. The yellow ones were breathtaking.

"Roses are pretty to look at, but they'll droop two days later," she said.

Mother was the generous type. But she will not pay fifteen dollars for a dozen roses when she can buy three bunches of chrysanthemums for the same price or less. How I wished that for once she would give me roses.

～

Back at the apartment, she took off her shoes. That was a cue that she wanted to stay for a longer visit.

The telephone rang. It was my coworker Marilyn. Her voice was raspy.

"Ruby, help. I'm sick as a dog. I can't go in like this. Please say you'll cover the Miller wedding tonight. I would've called Clyde but the bride's mother is obnoxiously picky, and everything must be perfect. Plus, they've booked twenty rooms. Please say yes."

"Of course I'll say yes. You rest up."

"Thanks, Ruby. You're a doll. Mrs. Miller won't miss me. She likes you. Remember you told her that *donna* is the Italian word for 'woman' and she said you could call her by her first name anytime?"

"I remember, Marilyn. If you need me to pick up some chicken soup or Chinese rice porridge, I'll be happy to do it."

"No, thanks. I don't need soup. Ruby, I owe you one."

I said yes to Marilyn because I liked her. Besides, any more time with my mother would have given her an opportunity to find fault with the apartment or harass me about the rent I was paying.

"Mom, that was a coworker asking me to sub for her. I better get going. The bride's mother is already there."

"You shouldn't answer the phone, Ruby, on your one day off. People take advantage."

"Help yourself to a cold drink, Mom, and the *TV Guide* is on the table," I said to her. "And don't worry about double-locking the door when you leave. The door locks itself as soon as you pull it shut. See you soon, Mom. You pick the restaurant next time, okay?" I added.

"A beautiful apartment and she's never home," Mom said under her breath as she shook her head.

I left her standing in the living room examining my framed posters of European cities. I knew she would check my cupboards as soon as I closed the door and make a list of what to bring me the next time she visited. In my haste I almost tripped over her large paper bag in the hallway. What could she have in that bag? A house-warming gift no doubt—a surprise that she would leave on the coffee table with a note written on a restaurant napkin to explain how thrilled she was when she came upon it at the store, probably at Merrill's Drug Store. Ever since Woolworth's closed its doors, Mother had done all her non-birthday gift shopping at Merrill's. Or, perhaps it was a birthday gift. But she hadn't said anything at lunch.

~

That evening, when I came home, I was startled to see the hallway lamp on. I heard sounds coming from the guest bedroom. The living room was dark. With my finger on the trigger of the mace canister, I called out, "Mom, is that you?"

She responded in Chinese, "Ruby. It got dark so fast. It wasn't safe to go home."

Strange—she hasn't spoken Chinese to me in years. I looked into the room and saw that she had moved the nightstand to the other side of the bed, closer to the window. The brown paper bag was folded flat. I understood then. The bag had contained a change of clothes, her yellow flannel sleeping gown which she was wearing, her grooming kit, her Bible, and her green slippers. I felt an ache in my chest. Half of me wanted her to stay, but the other half already envisioned what life would be like living with her. She turned down the bedding to let me know that she was retiring for the evening. We both said, "Goodnight."

I went to my room and sat on my bed for an hour thinking about how strange this event was, but I was not completely surprised. I was more relieved than surprised. Why couldn't she just tell me she needed sanctuary? Why the pretense? What she said about the night getting dark so fast and that it wasn't safe to go home was such a sad metaphor, under the circumstances.

~

When I was a girl, I envied those classmates who had divorced parents. Every year I made the same wish on my birthday. Not for new phonograph records, or for my acne to disappear, but for my parents to divorce each other. A divorce would have brought peace and quiet.

"Did you make your wish?" my mother asked every year.

"Yes," I answered with a nod each year. She never asked me what I wished for. I never told her. She would have hated me if she knew.

"Only evil women divorce their husbands," Mother said many times. More than anything, she wanted Father to respect her. I think Father wanted the same from her.

Just the year before while visiting Emily in Philadelphia, I found out she had made the same wish on all her birthdays. We were sitting in her living room eating leftover cake from her birthday party.

"I had wished for the same thing, Ruby. Every year," my sister confessed. At first we cried. I felt the tears stinging the corners of my eyes. Then we laughed over the fact that we could have gotten records and toys if we had made normal wishes like normal children. But ours was not a normal life.

~

There I was, sitting in my bedroom with my mother sleeping in the guest room. Ironically, perhaps, I was finally getting my birthday wish. When I had become old enough to talk to Mother as an adult, I had pleaded with her to leave Father. She would not listen to me. Why would she? I was her child.

Nothing more was said that night or at any other time. There were no heart-to-heart talks, no working out details, no discussing other options. She had simply moved in.

The next morning before I headed for work, I left Mother a set of house keys, my pager number, and the names of coffee shops and stores in the neighborhood. That night when I returned, I read the note she had written on a large napkin.

Ruby,

Thank you for being so thoughtful. I went exploring today. Don't worry about me. Pretend I'm not here. I don't want any fuss. I like the way things were—lunch date every two months. I know you're very busy. And don't call your father. He already knows I'm here.

Love,

Vivien

She had been signing her notes Vivien, instead of Mom, since Emily moved away to college. I wondered if it was an identity crisis. She used to love it when people told her she couldn't be my mother because she looked so young.

A feeling of relief came over me as I read the note. *We don't have to talk about it. It's done. She's here, safe with me.*

The Friday night after Mother moved in, I left her a note asking if she wanted to have breakfast with me the following day. Since Thursday had been my birthday, I was disappointed that she had forgotten. There wasn't a gift, not even a card, waiting for me.

The next morning I found her response written on another napkin. It was placed next to the loaf of sesame challah on the kitchen counter. Mother knew I was a creature of habit; I ate toasted bread to start the day.

The note read:

Ruby,

    Thank you for your invitation, but I prefer to sleep in, get my coffee and doughnut around 10:00, go walking, eat an early dinner. I've been sleeping twelve hours! I haven't done that since I was a girl. I must really need it. Anyway, you go about your routine. I'm fine. Lafayette Park is so clean. I go there every day. Don't work so hard.

Love,

Vivien

That was the first time she'd ever forgotten my birthday. She usually gave me a gift certificate from Emporium and a Hallmark card that had the words "Happy Birthday to a Wonderful Daughter" on the front and a poem inside. One day out of the year, she gave me recognition by signing her name to a dedication written by a greeting-card poet. I convinced myself that her moving in with me must have been extremely emotional for her. That would have explained the forgetfulness and the large amount of sleep. I told myself to be grateful that she wasn't nagging or criticizing my not being home enough.

To my astonishment, sharing an apartment with her became a painless arrangement for both of us. Mother did not have the financial means to live on her own, but she did have a modest savings account to pay for her daily expenses.

My lifestyle did not change after Mother moved in, and she never asked me to alter my daily habits. With my getting up at six in the morning, working all day, then going to class, or back to work for a special event, or to the library, I would not come home until ten o'clock or later. By then she was always asleep. Saturdays were my one day for any social life. I was gone from morning to night. Roommates who didn't see each other—what a dream.

A perfect setup, I thought. A roommate who keeps to herself and none of the inconvenience of who gets the bathroom first in the morning.

~

A month went by. Coworker Marilyn, in her way of thanking me for the Miller wedding, had volunteered to work for me that day. The first Sunday I'd had to myself in two years. What a treat. I had much studying to do. By late morning, I realized that Mother had not come out of her room. I knocked on her door. There was no answer. I turned the doorknob but found it locked from the inside. I knocked again.

"Mom, are you okay? Are you sick?"

"No," she shouted. "I'm sleeping."

"Sorry," I whispered, and went back to my studying. I would live to regret that day.

CHAPTER 3

The Truth

That was the beginning of my ignorance (or was it denial) of what was happening to Mother. Perhaps I was grateful for having been spared as solo-audience, forced to listen to Mother recount our family history. That gratitude kept me blind and careless. Every night in my half-sleep I heard the flushing of the toilet in the bathroom. I was living under the assumption that she was far from danger in my home.

It took me another month to suspect that something strange was happening to her. One Friday morning as I was leaving for work, Mrs. Nussbaum, who had taken Rashi out for his early morning walk, stopped me in the hallway.

"Ruby, your mother left? She didn't like the apartment?"

"No, Mrs. Nussbaum. She's still here."

"She's still here? I haven't seen her in over a month. She used to go out at ten every morning on the dot. I know because I could hear the door slam shut, ten o'clock every morning, but I haven't heard anything for weeks now."

"Are you sure, Mrs. Nussbaum?"

"Of course I'm sure. I have to know who comes in and out. Rashi and I are all alone in the building while you young people go to work. It was comforting to know your mother was there. When I didn't hear her coming and going, I thought she'd moved out."

"Thank you, Mrs. Nussbaum."

~

I went back to the apartment. As I approached Mother's bedroom door, I heard her voice from inside the room. I put my ear to the door. "Evil! You're evil! You're all evil! Evil!"

A chill ran up my spine. Softly I knocked on the door.

"I'm sleeping," Mother responded.

"Mom, are you okay?"

She didn't answer.

"Mrs. Nussbaum says you haven't been out for weeks."

"Tell her to mind her own business. I'm sleeping."

"May I come in?"

"No! I'm sleeping."

"May I come in for just a minute?"

"Ruby, it's okay. Everything is okay. Go to work."

I reached for the doorknob. The door was locked. I stood there for a few minutes, confused. I heard Mother moving about in the room. Then she read out loud from the Bible. She was reading the psalms in an orator's voice. My hand was shaking as I reached for the knob again. "Mom, I'm going to work, okay?"

"Good. Go to work."

~

I had to go to work. The hotel catering business did not tolerate any excuses, with the exception of a contagious disease. From the office, I called my friend who was a social worker.

"Michelle, my mom is acting weird. A neighbor says she hasn't left the apartment in a month. She's locked her bedroom door and won't come out. Plus, she's talking to herself in there."

"What's she saying to herself?"

"She's reading the Bible in a weird tone. She always reads out loud, but it's different today. Her voice sounded scary."

"I can give you names of a few psychiatrists, Ruby, but they'll ask you to bring your mom to them."

"She won't come out of her room."

"Here, Ruby, write these down."

~

I called the three telephone numbers. Their answering machines were on, all three of them. I left each doctor a message.

The first doctor who returned my call assured me not to worry. "It sounds like she's depressed and she'll snap out of it," he said with conviction in his voice.

The second doctor asked me, "Do you have insurance coverage?" He warned me about out-of-pocket expenses since most insurance companies did not cover psychotherapy. My head was throbbing.

The third told me I should call the police before I found myself charged with Elderly Neglect. As I hung up the telephone, I asked myself, *Elderly? Neglect? Me?* I had never considered Mother as being elderly.

Michelle called me in the afternoon. After hearing my discouraging report, she gave me another name and telephone number. "Ruby, I didn't give you this name earlier because I thought she had relocated her practice, but she hasn't. She's got a great reputation."

That name was Dr. Gloria Thatcher. She was the only one out of the four who expressed any genuine concern.

"Ruby, is your mother eating?" asked Dr. Thatcher.

"I don't know. A neighbor says she hasn't left the house in a month. We don't eat together because I work at a hotel. I eat my meals here. But I do store plenty of frozen dinners and canned foods. I'll check the supply tonight."

"Ruby, your mother could be dehydrating herself. I want you to call OMI. Ocean Medical Intake. This is an agency that sends out so-cial workers to conduct home-visit assessments. . . ."

"Thank you, Dr. Thatcher." I didn't want to hang up the telephone because the calmness in her voice made my headache subside.

"Keep me posted, Ruby, will you?"

"Yes, I will. You're very kind. Thank you."

It was already four o'clock when I called OMI; their answering machine's outgoing message said: *We are closed until Monday. Please leave your name and phone number, and someone will call you back.*

Oh God, not until Monday. I was going out of my mind. Perhaps Father could get her to come out of the room. What was I saying? He'd be the last person she wanted to see.

~

I went straight home after work to look through the freezer and the cupboards. Nothing had been eaten, as far as I could tell, except the bread on the kitchen counter. I checked Mother's drinking glass. Thank God! There was moisture in the glass. *At least she's drinking water*, the voice in my head was grasping for hope. *Bread and water. Oh, Mom, even prisoners eat better than this. Why are you starving yourself?* I took two more Motrin tablets to numb my headache.

I dialed long distance to my sister for emotional support. "Em, I don't know what's going to happen when the home-assessment peo-ple come. What if Mother suspects something already, and she leaves the apartment before they come?"

"Ruby, I'll fly out. Just say 'come' and I will. You know I will, don't you?"

"You have midterms coming up. I promise I'll call you if the OMI people feel that you need to be here too. I'm sorry that I had to burden you with all this bad news, but I needed a family member to tell me it's okay to have people come to evaluate Mom."

"Ruby, should I call Father?"

"I did already. I felt he had a right to know. He was incredulous. He said Mother must be faking it, pretending to be sick so that he would beg her to come back. Do you believe him?"

"Ruby, I'd believe anything. Did he use the word 'crazy'?"

"Yes, he did. He said, 'Your mother is not crazy, she's bored.'"

"If Mother is having a breakdown, it's because of him."

"I was relieved when he didn't volunteer to come over to help. He said Mom would crawl back to him in a few weeks."

"I've an idea, Ruby! Go tell Mom that I'm on the phone. She'll come out to talk to me. She yells at me for spending money on long distance calls. She'll come out."

"Yeah. That'll work."

I knocked on Mother's door. "Mom, Sis is on the phone. She wants to talk to you."

No answer.

"Mom?"

"I'm sleeping."

"She's calling long distance, Mom. Just say hi to her."

No answer.

I went back to my room. "Em, it didn't work. What am I going to do?"

"You're going to take a hot shower, then eat dinner. You hear me, Ruby? Don't fall apart, Ruby. One family member at a time, okay? I know you're Big Sister and you want to take care of everybody, but take care of yourself first. Promise me now."

"I promise. God, I'm so tired."

"Ruby, I'll call you tomorrow. Please try and get some sleep."

"I will, Em. Love you."

"Love you too. I'll send good thoughts. Now go take that hot shower!" I heard the distress in her voice.

~

That evening, I tried to entice Mom with food. "Mom, please come out and eat something. I ordered chicken with black bean sauce and pot stickers."

"I'm not hungry. Leave me alone, Ruby."

I had a horrible dream that night.

I'm sleeping in a guest room of a castle. It's a windy night. Wisteria is brushing against the windowpanes. The windows are reinforced and the door is made of iron. I am aroused from a deep sleep by a pounding noise. I sit up in bed. My eyes search the room. To my horror, I see that the iron door has become a wooden one. The knob is turning. There is evil on the other side. I scream.

That wasn't the first time I had that nightmare. The setting from dream to dream changes, but it's always the same theme. *I've got to stop these dreams.* After one of those I could never go back to sleep. This one made me tremble in a cold sweat. I went to the kitchen to get a drink of water.

While I was asleep, Mother must have come out of her room to eat some bread and use the bathroom. The Chinese food in the refrigerator was untouched. By Saturday she had stopped answering me through the door. Over the weekend, I heard her reading her

Bible, stopping at passages and enunciating the word *evil* over and over again.

~

Sunday morning I left her a note near the bread, asking her to page me if she wanted me to bring home a particular food. At work I performed my tasks like a zombie. I knew I had lost a client when she had to ask me twice to adjust the temperature in her meeting room. More Motrin tablets in the morning to dull the headache that I'd had since Friday and a pot of strong coffee helped me survive the day. Every few minutes I checked to see if my pager was still working. In case Mother had read my note and granted my wish, I wanted to be reachable.

That night, I brought home beef stew over rice. I knocked on her door. "Mom, I have one of your favorite meals, still piping hot." No answer. I left her another note by the bread. The next morning, I found my note crumpled in the garbage can.

~

At work that Monday the call from OMI came. I spoke with a social worker named Susan who had a kind voice; she explained about the home-visit assessment. The visit would take place Wednesday morning at nine. She advised me to go to work and keep whatever routine I could so that Mother would not be suspicious of me. "Sometimes unwilling clients do sneak away when they find out that we're coming," she told me.

The next two days felt endless. I could not focus on my work or my classes. Susan had stressed the point about keeping my routine schedule so as not to stir up Mother's suspicions. Both nights, I had sneaked home after work to check if Mother was out of her room, but she wasn't. The food in the refrigerator had been untouched. I'd quietly leave the apartment and go to class or back to work before returning home at the usual time.

Mother continued reading her Bible out loud every morning and every night. I had tried forcing myself to stay awake every night, hoping to get a glimpse of her when she came out of her room, but every morning I fell asleep. By the time I woke up, usually before dawn, Mother had already crept out to eat some bread and drink some water. How did she know when I fell asleep each night? I dreamed that she had underlined *evil* in red ink every time the word appeared on the pages of her Bible. I prayed for Wednesday to come.

~

Tuesday afternoon my boss called me into his office. "Ruby, sit down. How are you?"

"I'm fine, Chad."

"You don't look fine, Ruby. Just because I'm in meetings all day doesn't mean I'm not aware of daily operations. We can't afford to make mistakes in this business—you know that. I'm not saying your job's in jeopardy, Ruby, but you might as well know that headhunters call me every week. There are energetic people out there waiting to work for the St. Mark."

"What did I do wrong, Chad?"

"Mrs. Alexander was unhappy that you forgot to change the writing on the cake. It was supposed to be *Buon Viaggio,* not *Bon Voyage.*"

"I know, Chad. I was the one who told Mrs. Alexander about the Italian phrase when she said her daughter was going to Italy."

"Well, the point is you disappointed a client, a very important client I might add."

"I'm sorry. I'll call her to apologize."

"I knew you would say that, Ruby. To appease her, I had to offer dinner for four on me." Chad was about to continue, but his phone rang. He held up his index finger to signal me to stay.

I sat there thinking about what I would say to Mrs. Alexander. She had to be the most difficult client I'd ever had at the St. Mark. If only all our clients were more like Mrs. McKenzie. Mrs. McKenzie was a dream client—always courteous to us and considerate of time constraints. She liked calling me "Tall Blonde." She said I sounded like a tall blonde on the telephone.

Chad was off the phone. "Where were we, Ruby? Oh, yes. It's none of my business what my staff does outside working hours, but I feel like a father to you young people. You haven't been yourself lately. Is it boyfriend problems?"

"No, Chad. My mom's sick."

"Oh. Sorry to hear that. If there's anything I can do, you let me know."

"Thank you."

"Ruby, one other matter. I know you're not scheduled to work next Saturday, but I really need you at the Turner function. I want to show off my multicultural staff. Turner Senior wants to impress his Taiwanese clients."

"But I don't speak Mandarin."

"What's the difference? You're Chinese, they're Chinese. Just be your charming self."

Chad's telephone was ringing. "Chad Hamilton." He covered the mouthpiece. "Ruby, thanks," he said, winking at me. He swung his leather chair around to face the window. "Bob, how the hell are you?"

I walked out of his office with a splitting headache. I wished I could have told him to go to hell.

~

Wednesday finally came. Marilyn covered for me. I was up early and sat nervously until eight forty-five. Then I went outside to intercept the visitors before they rang the doorbell. I remembered Susan's warnings about not alarming Mother.

Of all days, the elevator wasn't working. I had stood there for five minutes before seeing the small note taped to the door, ELEVATOR REPAIRMAN HAS BEEN NOTIFIED.

Susan and her partner, Dan, were punctual. They were both calm. After writing down my answers to their questions, Susan asked me to coerce Mother to come out of her room.

I had spent hours the night before concocting a story to convince Mother that I needed to enter her bedroom. Here was the test. While Susan and Dan waited in the living room, softly I knocked on Mother's bedroom door.

"Mom, sorry to disturb you, but I need a file in the closet. I've looked everywhere, and then I remembered that I stored it in a box. I need it for work."

Susan and Dan both nodded, communicating to me that my excuse to enter the room sounded convincing. We all stood in silence. Mother did not respond. I heard a clicking sound. From the look on Susan's face, she must have heard it too. As I was about to repeat my request, I put my hand on the doorknob. She had unlocked the door! My heart was beating fast. I walked in while the two visitors stood by the doorway. Mother was in bed, with the blanket pulled over her head.

"Mom, why don't you get out of bed and enjoy the beautiful day?"

She did not answer. Susan nodded her head to let me know that it was all right to tell Mother we had visitors.

"Mom, because I've been worried about you, I've asked two nice people to come see you. They just want to ask you a few questions."

"Tell them to go away," she shouted.

My heart jumped. Susan and Dan walked toward me.

Susan spoke. "Hi, Vivien. Don't be angry. Your daughter was worried about you and asked us to come and see you. Please come out and sit with us."

"Go away. I am sleeping," she answered, in a less angry voice this time.

After more gentle prodding to get her out of bed but to no avail, Susan walked over to the bed and lifted the blanket. My head started ringing when I saw what Mother had become. Oh God! Mother had wasted away to skin and bones. She was in a fetal position facing the window, pretending to be asleep. Her yellow nightgown looked like a thin cloth draping a frail child. Dan went out to the living room to use the telephone.

I stood there feeling nauseous and hearing fragments of Dan's phone call. ". . . Dan Wong from OMI . . . need assistance . . . Fifty-One-Fifty . . . : S.F. General . . . female in her fifties."

I could hear Susan explaining to Mother that we wanted to take her to see a doctor. While still lying on her side, Mother answered Susan, "I don't need a doctor. I don't need anything."

Mother, I'm unable to speak, but please, please know that I had no idea you were doing this to yourself. Please read my thoughts, Mother. Can you hear me?

Two uniformed police officers came; in the hallway they spoke with Dan. *Why didn't Dan call an ambulance instead?* Both officers walked into Mother's bedroom, and said hello to Susan and me.

The officer who looked as if he'd been one for a long time said, "Ma'am, will you come out into the living room and talk to us?"

Mother did not respond.

"Sure is a nice day, ma'am. We just want to chat with you," said the younger officer.

Mother would not answer.

"Ma'am, do you know what day this is?" he added.

Tell them, Mother. Tell them it's October. Tell them it's 1985. Please tell them.

The older officer tapped her shoulder and said, "Ma'am, we'll have to carry you if you don't cooperate."

The younger officer looked at Susan and Dan. Without exchanging words, the two men in uniform lifted Mother so that she sat up. Mother did not look at me. She kept her head lowered. Susan picked up Mother's green slippers and gently put them on Mother's feet.

"Why are you doing this to me?" Mother finally looked up to speak to me. Her eyes had lost their sparkle. She was emaciated. Her shoulder-length hair was dirty and tangled.

I could not answer her with words. *Oh Mom! If you could see yourself, you wouldn't have done this. Why did you do it? Why, Mom?* Perhaps seeing my tears fall onto the hardwood floor convinced her that I loved her. *Why didn't I see this coming?*

"I haven't done anything wrong, Ruby. I'm not the one shouting disgusting words in the backyard. Arrest those people in the backyard, not me," she added.

"Ma'am, let's take a trip to the doctor's office." The officer who had tapped her shoulder earlier was showing his impatience.

"I'm not going anywhere, Ruby. I'm staying. You tell them to go away. I'm still your mother.

"Go away. My daughter did not invite you into her home." She directed this to the officers.

The impatient officer took out a pair of handcuffs.

"Officer, is that really necessary!" Susan was just as shocked as I was.

"It's for her personal safety. We don't want this to get out of control." He looked at my mother. "Ma'am, we're taking you to the hospital." He snapped the cuffs onto my mother's tiny wrists.

Mother pleaded in Chinese, "Ruby! No! No! Don't shame me like this, Ruby!"

It's a nightmare, Mom. We'll all wake up and everything will be fine. I closed my eyes for a second, but when I opened them again, I saw Mother, cuffed like a criminal, walk out of the bedroom in her slippers as the two officers ushered her toward the front door, with Dan and Susan following close behind.

~

Later, as a passenger in Dan's car, I felt a strange sense of relief that Mother was on her way to receive medical attention. *Oh God, she came to hide out in my apartment and I ended up neglecting her.*

Dan explained to me what would take place at the emergency psychiatric ward, but I heard only half the words. Something about an examination, Mother's rights, and drugs. He also apologized that there were no plainclothes police officers available to take the call. Being taken away by the blue uniforms and the shiny badges made it look like Mother had broken some law. That's why she'd said, "I haven't done anything wrong." But what did she mean when she said there were people in the backyard? There was no backyard.

Why didn't I insist that she open her door that Sunday? Why didn't I? What kind of daughter am I?

CHAPTER 4

The Same Crime Twice

That night after having spent the entire day at San Francisco General Hospital, I didn't get home until eight-thirty. I was grateful that the elevator was working. As the door opened at the fourth floor, Mrs. Nussbaum came out of her apartment.

"Ruby, I made a pot of chicken soup. Come in, dear. I promise not to ask questions."

I had wanted to be alone and normally I didn't like soup, but the way Mrs. Nussbaum invited me made me say yes. My last meal had been from the hospital cafeteria, and I didn't have much of an appetite.

Mrs. Nussbaum's little dog sniffed my shoes to greet me.

"Rashi, be a good boy and go watch *Wheel of Fortune*. Leave Ruby alone."

He obeyed.

Mrs. Nussbaum was well into her seventies but she still had a spring in her step. I followed her into the kitchen. Her baggy dress swished as she walked.

"You sit here. I'm going to give you some comfort food."

"It smells wonderful, Mrs. Nussbaum."

As she ladled the soup into a porcelain bowl, I felt warm inside.

"Here, Ruby. You eat up. I made plenty." She placed the bowl in front of me and started to walk out of the room.

"Mrs. Nussbaum, aren't you going to have any?"

"Don't feel you have to talk. I just wanted to make sure you had a hot meal after such a long day. I was worried about you."

"You're so kind. Won't you sit with me? I'd like your company."

"All right, dear. I'll have a bowl myself."

As we ate the aromatic soup in silence, I looked around the room. This was a big kitchen, with an old Wedgewood stove, plenty of wooden cabinets, yellow-tile countertops, and a yellow linoleum floor. I wondered why Mrs. Nussbaum's kitchen had not been remodeled as my apartment had been.

"This is delicious."

"My mother's recipe," said Mrs. Nussbaum.

I couldn't control myself. As soon as I heard *mother,* tears welled up in my eyes.

"I'm sorry, Ruby. I didn't mean to upset you."

"It's not your fault, Mrs. Nussbaum. I've had a draining day."

"I can imagine. You don't have to talk about it if you don't want to."

How can I talk about it? Maybe I'll wake up from this nightmare.

Mrs. Nussbaum's sympathetic stare made me uncomfortable, but her soup warmed me.

"This is good. I usually don't care for soup."

"Why?" asked Mrs. Nussbaum.

"Mother used to cook fancy soups, but she would pour the whole pot down the drain when Father made her angry. I guess that's why."

"That's too bad. Soup is good for you."

"I know. Strangely, I always crave it when I'm sick."

"Eat up, dear."

"They're holding Mother for seventy-two hours." *Why did I blurt that out?*

"Does your sister know? Have you called her?"

"I called Emily from the hospital. She wanted to fly out, but I told her there's really nothing we can do at this point. I think Mom's in good hands. I found out what Fifty-One-Fifty is. It's a police code that someone is endangering his life or someone else's. Do you believe it? Mom was starving herself."

"Your poor mother. When she comes home, we'll give her a welcome home party."

"No, Mrs. Nussbaum. I mean, thank you for the thought, but I can't ask Mom to walk into this building, not after what happened. To be taken out by police . . . she can never show her face again."

"The poor darling." Mrs. Nussbaum said it with compassion in her voice.

"I'm going to rent a house with a real backyard."

Mrs. Nussbaum listened intently.

"If she had a backyard, she could learn to garden. A house with a garden. Doesn't that sound wonderful?"

"She wants to live by herself?"

"Oh no. I'm moving out with her."

"Ruby, you just moved in three months ago."

"I know. I haven't completely unpacked. But I need to do this for Mom. I've got to. I thought about it all day. I'll make it work." *I owe it to Mom. She needs a real home. Why didn't I see it before?*

"Eat, dear. Eat."

I looked at Mrs. Nussbaum's gentle face. She must have been a knockout in her day. Her eyes still had a twinkle and even though her hair was gray, it was shiny and curly. Amy Irving, the actress, would probably look like Mrs. Nussbaum in another thirty years.

"If you know anyone who wants a beautiful apartment, Mrs. Nussbaum, will you put in a good word? The lease says I'm to pay all the rent that's due until the lessor finds a new tenant because I'm breaking the one-year contract."

"I'll miss you, Ruby."

"I'll miss you too. And Rashi."

It was nine-thirty when I left Mrs. Nussbaum's apartment with a large container of soup that she had packed for me. I felt warm and nourished. *But why did Mrs. Nussbaum keep on telling me I didn't have to talk about it? Was that her way to get me to spill my guts? I wonder if she'll tell the landlord that Mother moved in two months ago—they'll think I had planned for two people to live in the apartment all along.*

~

Back in my apartment, I felt a chill as soon as I closed the door. Having put away Mrs. Nussbaum's soup, I went into Mother's room to get her a change of clothes for the hospital. After stripping the bed, I sat in the antique armchair near the little writing table. I closed my eyes. Perhaps the whole day had been a dream. *But it's not.*

What if Mrs. Nussbaum turns me in to the authorities? She's the only one who keeps track of goings-on in the building. She's the only one who knows that Mother had been living here. If I am turned in, I'd have no one to blame but myself. How could I have committed the same crime twice?

Just like fifteen years before, how could I have been so heartless? I opened my eyes, closed them again, telling myself to forget, but it all came back to me and I couldn't fight it.

~

It was a Friday at two o'clock, a week before summer vacation, when Mrs. Pucinelli, the principal, came into our classroom. I thought she was going to announce some special activity since we were the sixth grade graduating class. But instead she called out my name and asked me to go with her. My heart was pounding. *What has happened,* I asked myself all the way to her office.

My answer was standing in her office. It was my father. I was terrified to see him there. He had never come to the school before, not even at registration. There he was that day, looking helpless as he muttered to me in Chinese, "Your mother is in the hospital."

I did not ask him any questions as we walked to the car because I was afraid of what the answers might be. A thousand thoughts rushed through my head. *Is she hurt? Is she dying?*

It was the first time I had visited a hospital. Up to then, I had only seen them in movies. Although the floors were clean, there was a strange smell—a mixture of Pine-Sol and something medicine-like. I knew that Father brought me along to translate complicated English for him.

I glanced at my father. He looked tired, more tired than I had ever seen. We were asked by the woman behind the desk to sit in the waiting room behind the big glass window. We sat in silence. It was just like the movie where Shirley Temple went from hospital to hospital looking for her father. In every face I, like Shirley, was searching for hope.

My hands were cold. My head was starting to hurt. I looked at the stark walls and even they seemed cold. A male doctor in a white robe and a Chinese woman wearing a gray suit came in to greet us. They pulled over two chairs for themselves. The woman turned out to be a translator, for which I was grateful since the tears began streaming down my face as soon as the doctor said, "Mr. Lin, your wife was hit by a car this morning." The woman gave me some tissues from her pocket. My head was splitting. ". . . intensive care," the doctor continued. ". . . four pints of blood. You can both see . . . but . . . unconscious right now." All this I heard in bits and pieces in English and in Chinese as the woman translated the events to Father.

The doctor escorted us down the long hallway, and we entered through double doors marked INTENSIVE CARE UNIT. We were led to a bed where a woman was hooked up to half a dozen long tubes. She had tubes in her nose and tubes in her arms. Underneath all the tubes was my mother.

Is this really Mother? I wanted to ask my father. I secretly watched him as he walked around the bed. For the first time, I saw my father cry. I was crying too. There we were, crying individually, separately. I wanted to hug my father, but the voice inside my head stopped me. If it was improper to look at one's father, then it certainly would have been improper to touch him. But I wanted to touch his hand, to let him know that I had already asked God to answer my prayer.

We stood there. We couldn't get close to Mother because there was a machine on each side of the bed. *I'm glad she's unconscious.* She would be scared if she was awake and saw all those tubes and the bag of blood hanging from the pole. The bag of blood frightened me the most because I knew that that was blood from strangers. My mother would never be herself again. She had other people's blood in her.

The doctor, who had left us earlier, came back to ask us to go home and come back the following day. He shook my father's hand. Before leaving, Father took off his new brown corduroy jacket and hung it over the chair near the wall. I wondered if that was his way of letting Mother know he would always be there for her. I felt close to my father at that moment, but I did not dare tell him so.

One week was left of the semester, so I went to class as usual. I did not tell anyone about what had happened to Mother because Father told me not to. "We do not want any sympathy," he said. *Are you ashamed of her?* I wanted to ask, but didn't. Father and Mother had said many times, "Bad things happen to careless people. They bring disaster to themselves."

Mother was taken out of intensive care a week after her accident, but the doctor told us she would have to stay in the hospital for six months. Her back had been broken in six places. On the telephone, Father told his aunt in Chinese, "She lost so much blood. . . . She lay there while assholes in their cars drove on without stopping. The son-of-a-bitch who hit her never even stopped to get help."

I never told anyone, but it was my fault. That morning as I was getting ready for school, my mother asked in Chinese, "Ruby, what kind of doughnut do you want today?"

"A maple custard, Mama," I answered with joy.

"Okay. I'll be back in five minutes. You can take it to school," Mother said as she closed our apartment door.

I packed my book bag and sat in the living room. Five minutes had passed. No sign of Mother. Ten minutes had passed. Still no sign of her. *I wonder what's keeping her?* Another ten minutes and still no Mother.

I went down to the sidewalk to look for her. Cars were zooming by in morning traffic. Mother had said many times, "It's a shame that we have a shopping center directly across from our building but we have to walk down two blocks to get to a crosswalk."

After standing on the sidewalk awhile, I walked back to the steps of our building to be at a better viewing position. *She'll be walking out of the mall any second now.* Still no Mother. *Should I go find out what's taking so long? No. Mother will be very angry if you go over there and she comes home and can't find you.*

I saw Ben, the parking attendant from the Italian restaurant, run across the street. *He must be getting doughnuts too.* Father said Black people like to eat sweets. Everyone in our family liked to eat sweets, but I didn't say that to Father.

I went back upstairs to get my book bag. I had decided not to wait for my doughnut. *Mother probably forgot. She's grocery shopping instead.* As I turned the corner from our home I thought I heard a fire engine siren.

Why didn't I cross the street to investigate? If I had, she wouldn't have lost so much blood. I could have seen her from where I stood, but I didn't look around. I should have looked up and down the street. "Ruby, you don't pay attention to what's around you. Life is not a straight road," my mother had warned time and time again.

I also found out later that Ben was not running across the street to get doughnuts. He was running to a telephone to call for an ambulance because he had seen Mother lying on the street in the middle of eight o'clock traffic. It was not the siren of a fire engine screaming when I turned the corner from our home. It was the siren of the ambulance that Ben had summoned. All summer long I asked God why I didn't see her lying there. Perhaps if I had gone down earlier and seen her . . .

If I had really looked, I could have saved her sooner.

The next day after work, I went straight to the hospital to see Mom. She beamed when she saw me standing outside her room. Nurse Shirley, who had let me into Ward 7-C, brought in a second chair for me.

"Your mom is doing well," she said before leaving the room.

"Mom." I hugged her frail body.

"Sit, Ruby. You don't have to work tonight?"

"Marilyn is covering for me."

Whatever drugs the doctor had given her were working like magic. My mother was sitting up and chatting as if the Fifty-One-Fifty had not happened.

"I've been looking out the window all day, Ruby. See. Down there is the courtyard for employees. It's too cold, but people still go outside to smoke. Look."

"Mom, did you eat anything today?"

"I had oatmeal this morning. Dr. Leu says soft foods for a few days. He says I can have regular food by Saturday. Did you know he is Vietnamese? He told me. He speaks a little Chinese."

"He seems very nice, Mom. I'm meeting with him tomorrow."

Mother's face turned into a mask of gloom. "Why? Don't talk to him."

"Why not, Mom? I want to know what his treatment plan is."

"I don't need a treatment plan. You're busy. I'll tell him you're busy. Don't waste your time." Mother got up from her chair. "I don't like it here."

Nurse Shirley returned just in time. "Vivien, here's your dinner."

Mother's gloom did not change. I knew it was time for me to leave.

"Mom, I'll see you tomorrow."

Nurse Shirley put down the tray on the little table. "Vivien, you have a very pretty daughter."

Mother did not respond.

"Mom, I'll see you tomorrow."

"Bye." That's all she said. If only she had looked at me—to let me know that she had forgiven me.

Nurse Shirley escorted me to the double doors. "Your mom will be okay. Don't worry."

"Thank you, Shirley." As soon as she closed the door behind me, I broke into tears. Avoiding the stares from passersby, I turned around to face the double door. I silently read the sign in big black letters:

PSYCHIATRIC WARD

AUTHORIZED VISITORS ONLY.

RING BELL FOR ADMITTANCE.

Despite Mother's objections, I kept my appointment with Dr. Leu the next day. It was one-thirty and it looked as if most of the patients were in their rooms because only a few were meandering in the hall-way. The aroma of hospital food filled the air. Nurse Shirley told me Mother was with a social worker.

Dr. Leu was a slight man in his late thirties. He had a Daffy Duck-type voice but his demeanor was calm and reassuring.

"Ruby, are your parents divorced?"

"No. Why do you ask, Doctor?

"Your mother told me she didn't have a husband."

"Mother left him two months ago and moved in with me."

"Will you ask your father to telephone me? I want to meet with him. Your mother doesn't want to answer our questions. Perhaps your father can tell us when your mother first showed signs of her ill-ness."

"I'll call him this afternoon, but I don't know what good that'll do."

"I just want to ask him what he knows about your mother's child-hood and early adult years."

"I'll call him. But she's not moving back with him. I've already started looking for a house to rent. My apartment is too small. I want to give her a garden. Dr. Leu, why was she starving herself?"

"I don't know, Ruby. I'll try to find out. Do you have siblings?"

"Yes. A sister in Philadelphia."

"Any brothers?"

I didn't want to answer. It was always so awkward.

"No brothers, Ruby?"

"Yes, one, but we haven't seen him since he left home many years ago. Father drove our brother away. He drove all of us away. It just took Mother a lot longer." *Why didn't she leave him and take us with her when we were still little?*

"Ruby?"

"Huh?"

"Can you help me by writing down your mother's history, everything you know about her? We'll use it as soon as you can provide the information. The evaluation team meets every morning to review patients' progress."

"Of course. I'll start on it right away."

"Your mother is doing well, considering what happened. She can eat solid foods tomorrow. She can't go home yet. The judge has extended the three-day hold another seven days. At the end of the ten days, the judge will review the case again."

After our meeting, Dr. Leu led me to the patients' living room. Mother was watching television. She smiled when she saw me.

"Hello, Dr. Leu," she greeted the doctor.

"Hello, Vivien. It's good to see you smiling."

Mother grinned like a child. Dr. Leu left us.

"Hi, Mom. Dr. Leu is right. It is good to see you smiling."

But her heart-shaped face was gaunt and her eyes had lost their brilliance.

"When am I going home, Ruby?"

"When Dr. Leu thinks you're strong enough."

"But I'm strong now."

"We'll talk to Dr. Leu, okay? He knows what's best."

"He's so kind to me."

"Yes, he is, Mother. Everyone here has been kind."

Grateful for her docile mood, I did not strike up any more conversation. We watched the sitcom, *Three's Company*, together. The last time we had watched television together had been more than a decade ago. I swallowed hard and fought back the damned tears.

CHAPTER 5

Why Can't We Live Together?

Emily and I had been taking turns calling each other since Mother was taken away to the hospital.

"Hi, Em. Mom is doing well. Her doctor, the nurses and the social workers, they're all so nice. Dr. Leu says Mom is manic-depressive and paranoid."

"Poor Mom. I called her this morning. She sounded like a little kid."

"I'd much rather have her this way, not angry, not punishing herself."

"How are you, Ruby? I wish I were there to pull some weight."

"You are pulling weight. Listen, Em, I need your help. I need for you to write down your impressions of Mother's behavior when you were living at home. The doctor wants to know when Mother first showed signs of her illness. Dr. Leu asked me to call Father, and I did earlier. But I won't be speaking to that man ever again."

"What did he do this time?"

"He said, 'Your mother would be fine if she would just listen to me. She has too much time on her hands.' You know how his voice gets on my nerves. 'Why don't you tell your sister to come home where she belongs so that you two girls can get a bigger place, let your mother keep house, cook meals? I'm willing to take her back, but my doctor told me I cannot take any more stress. Also, Ruby, don't let these American doctors tell you your mother is crazy. They have nothing better to do than to label people as crazy.' "

"He doesn't believe in mental illness, Ruby. Neither does Mom."

"I know. They think it's some sort of crime to have a breakdown."

"Plus, it's a tabooed subject. Remember Mother used to talk about someone at the 'Napa Crazy House'? She said people who go in never come out."

"Another reason why I hate talking to him. . . . The way he says *Daughter*. I have a name. But he always calls me *Daughter* to remind me that I'm the oldest and I'm supposed to fulfill obligations."

Emily sighed. "I think I know why Mom finally walked out on him. It slipped out today when he called me. He had to file for bankruptcy. He's broke, Ruby."

"I'm glad he's broke. Fuck. I'm not making sense."

"Ruby, you're tired."

"Em, I go to bed exhausted and I wake up exhausted."

"Be good to yourself, Ruby. Hear me? How are the girls?" My sister always knew just the right thing to say. She was referring to our dolls, the ones we played with such a long time ago. The dolls survived our childhood, and they were sitting on a shelf in my bedroom. Emily had given me her doll for safekeeping when she moved away.

"The girls are fine. They're mischievous as ever," I laughed.

"It's good to hear you laugh, Ruby."

"I shouldn't though. Life's a big mess. I didn't study for my midterms. The chance of getting A's—down the toilet."

"I'm sorry, Ruby."

"I know it's only night school, not like getting a master's, but damn. It'll mean acing the finals in order to get C's for final grades."

"C is a passing grade. Don't feel bad, Ruby. Kiss the girls for me. Have them give you big kisses for me, okay? I'll fax you some notes on Mom tomorrow."

"Okay. Sweet dreams, Em."

"Sweet dreams, Ruby."

Even though I told Emily not to fly out and miss her classes, deep down I was hoping she would come, if only for a weekend.

～

The day I found a house with a garden to rent, Carole, the property manager of my apartment, called. "Ruby, I have good news. I explained to the owners of the building about your circumstances, and they waived the penalty for terminating the lease. We'll just prorate this month's rent and return your security deposit."

"Who are the owners?" I asked. "I want to send them a thank-you letter."

"There's no need, Ruby. They're an old couple. They like their privacy. I'll express your gratitude to them."

Every little thing seemed to make me cry. *Who are these kind souls? What have I done to deserve such kindness?*

～

Mrs. Nussbaum and Rashi came to my door the following morning. She had an odd-shaped package wrapped in foil.

"Ruby, I'll be away for three weeks. I want to say goodbye now. You take care of yourself."

"I will, Mrs. Nussbaum."

"Here, Ruby, take this. You can freeze what you don't eat." She dropped Rashi's leash and handed me the package. It was heavy.

"Ooh, it smells like a roasted turkey?"

"You have a good nose."

"Please, Mrs. Nussbaum, please come in."

"No, no. I have to walk Rashi and you have to go to work."

"I'll miss you, Mrs. N. You've been so kind. I don't know what to say."

Rashi wagged his tail.

"Yes, Rashi, I'll miss you too."

With a turkey between us, Mrs. Nussbaum and I hugged cheek to cheek. Then she picked up Rashi's leash and started for the elevator. Turning back, she said again, "Take good care of yourself."

She and Rashi got into the elevator and the door closed.

To think I was suspicious of Mrs. Nussbaum's intentions. Why is it that good people never seem to stay long enough?

~

At work, I asked Chad for two days off. He was on his way to a meeting.

"Chad, Marilyn says she'll cover for me. I need a day for the move and another day for my mom when she comes home from the hospital."

"Two days, Ruby, without calendaring them first?"

"I couldn't have, Chad. This all happened so fast. Marilyn will cover for me."

"What can I say? Next time, please calendar it. I don't like my staff traipsing off and . . ."

Marilyn was calling me from the outer office. "Ruby, you have a phone call."

"Thanks, Chad," I said apologetically.

He walked out of his office.

Marilyn stopped me in the hallway. "You don't have a phone call. I just wanted you to get out of there. I heard what he said."

"Thanks, Marilyn. You're great."

"So where are you and your mom moving to?"

"A house in the Excelsior District. It's really nice."

"I'm glad, Ruby. Let me know when your mom goes home, okay?"

"Okay, Marilyn. Thanks again."

"Anytime."

I felt extremely fortunate that she had become a friend. If I had known Marilyn in high school, she would have been one of the girls I idolized. Five feet seven without heels, rosy cheeks all the time, big eyes, and she was blessed to look good in any hair color. That month she was a redhead.

~

The psychiatric team had recommended that Mother be given a few more days of supervision on her medication. She had been uncooperative in her counseling sessions, refusing to answer questions asked by doctors and social workers. Upon receiving Dr. Leu's report, the judge at the hospital extended the ten-day hold another five days.

Two days before Mother was released from the hospital, the furniture movers had transported all my belongings to the new home. The one-story house, complete with a garage, washer and dryer, formal dining room, a fireplace in the living room, had a garden that kept a gardener busy one day a week. I felt that a guardian angel was watching over me.

My fantasies of Mother going to gardening classes gave me hope that life with her would be peaceful. My wishful thinking also included the new landlord lowering the rent as soon as Mother provided horticultural care. Yes. I had it all figured out—Mother with a hobby—perhaps even some volunteer work. She'd be happy with her new life. I would see to that.

The morning of Mother's release, Dr. Leu reserved a few comments for me. "Ruby, I'm prescribing these two pills for your mother. One is for depression and the other is for paranoia. She must take them every day after dinner. Also, I have arranged for her to see a doctor once a month. He's a psychiatrist who will refill her prescription. Do you have any questions, Ruby?"

"Do you think this will happen again? Mother trying to starve herself?"

"I don't know, Ruby. Your mother promised me she would not do that again. But when a person is sick, they forget about their promises. Your mother doesn't like to answer questions. I've tried every day. The social workers have tried every day. She looks at the floor when she doesn't want to answer us. The notes you and your sister gave me were very helpful. Your mother has been through much tragedy—the war, losing both parents, being an orphan. She has seen starvation at an early age."

"This isn't the first time Mother has used food to express anger and defeat, Dr. Leu. I've seen her pour full pots of soup down the kitchen sink when Father came home late, sometimes three, four hours late."

"Is it possible for you to go home for dinner? Give your mother a reason to cook for someone she loves."

"I can do that. I can run home after work, eat dinner with her, then go to class or back to work. I'm also looking into volunteer work for her. She has no friends, but she'll have some if she's involved in clubs. And, the house I'm renting comes with a garden. Cooking, socializing, gardening. That should keep Mother busy."

"Ruby, I must advise you not to push your mother into any activity that she doesn't want to partake in. Please keep in mind that your mother comes from a different world. Her ideals are not the same as yours. The concept of happiness is not like yours. Her generation is bound by duty and obligations. Don't expect her to be what you want her to be."

"I just want her to be happy."

"You are a good daughter. Your mother is very proud of you."

"She is?"

"Your mother told me how hard you work, since you were a little girl, being Number One Student in school."

"Oh that. I think the message of working hard was drilled into us as kids. That was the only thing my father knew. I just want Mom to know she deserves to be happy."

"Perhaps your mother doesn't know what happiness is, Ruby. I have seen patients come back to the hospital nine, ten times, and every time their loved ones pray that perhaps this will be the last time. Perhaps this time, Mother, Grandmother, or Uncle would make the change. Mental illness is not recognized in many cultures as a real illness. And don't expect her to talk to any psychiatrist. She keeps the past in her mind. She will not talk about the pain because she would not know where to begin. She was brought up to endure life, not to enjoy it. If *you* need to talk to someone, Ruby, there are support groups."

"Thank you, Dr. Leu. I don't need support groups, but thank you anyway."

~

At the age of eighteen, I had sworn that I would never move back home with my parents. Who would have guessed that one of them would move in with me.

Mother seemed pleased with the house I rented. The day she came home from the hospital was like a holiday. She was excited, opening and closing cabinet doors, finding nooks and crannies, and rearranging the furniture in her bedroom. She used Lysol to wipe down the whole house.

"Lysol kills the worst germs," my mother announced.

"They should hire you as their spokesperson, Mom," I teased her.

Every night I ate Mother's home-cooked dinners except when I had to oversee an event at the hotel. The nights that I had class at seven o'clock, there was just enough time for me to rush home, swallow dinner, and dash off to school. Dr. Leu was correct about giving Mother a reason to cook for someone other than herself. I wanted her to feel needed.

"Mom, this is delicious."

She served pan-fried pork chops, *bok choy*, and rice.

"Remember when you were a little girl, this was your favorite dinner?"

"Yes, Mom. Remember you used to serve pork chops with a fried egg over rice?"

"Don't laugh. I didn't know American people ate eggs at breakfast time only."

~

In my solitude, I thanked the heavens that Mother's medication had stopped her hallucinations. She no longer heard voices and she had stopped reading the Bible out loud. She was much calmer. Another big change was that she showed more tolerance for people and she dropped the haughtiness in her attitude. She said *please* and *thank you* to waiters and waitresses the few times we went out.

Bliss ended too soon.

One evening after dinner, Mother cleared off the table without first taking her two pills. I followed her into the kitchen. "Mom, don't forget to take your pills."

"They make my mouth dry and I don't like taking them."

"But Mom, Dr. Leu said you're supposed to take them every day after dinner."

"Dr. Leu? Dr. Leu is not here."

We argued that night. Mother was among those who denied their mental illness. She said she could not forgive me for what I had done—that I had called strangers to take her away to a place where crazy people walked up and down the hallways all day long.

"How could you?" she asked me. "How could you call the police like that?"

"Mom, I just hope you'll do the same for me if I should ever get so sick that I would want to hurt myself."

I knew she was not listening to me because before I could finish the statement, she added, "Dr. Leu was kind to me. But I did not like the place. Not one bit. They had only one television set. A young man hogged the set and he watched Channel 7 all day. He was so drugged he didn't know what he was watching, but he wouldn't let anyone change the station. Putting me with crazy people. How could a daughter do that to a mother?"

"I did what I had to do, Mother," I said, raising my voice.

"It was humiliating to be taken away by policemen and the neighbors were looking at me as if I were a criminal."

"I'm sorry, Mom. There were no plainclothes police officers to take the call, so they sent uniformed officers. How many times do I have to say I'm sorry?"

"Who would believe my firstborn would have me arrested for not eating?"

I felt the lump in my throat but I did not cry because Mother would have interpreted my tears as an admission of guilt. The acid churned in my stomach as I counted to ten in my head.

"Mother, if you don't take your pills, then we cannot live together."

"Ruby. You take the pills. When did you decide to give me orders? You think just because I'm living with you that I'm no longer your mother?"

"I'm late for class, Mom."

I walked out as she started washing the dishes, mumbling to herself,

"Coming home to yell at me. . . . That's what she learns from school."

~

The following nights, Mother purposely displayed her untouched prescription bottles on the kitchen counter.

A week had passed.

"Mother, let's try to make this arrangement work. You take your pills and I leave you alone."

"I told you I don't want to take the pills."

"They're good for you."

"How do you know what's good for me? Having me arrested was good for me?"

"You used me. You were starving yourself in my home, making me the guilty party. I could have been charged with Elderly Neglect. That's punishable by law. Did you know that, Mother?"

"I didn't use you, Ruby. You let other people use you, just like that year in San—"

"I can't believe you, Mom. I give you a nice home and this is what I get?"

"Yes. It is a nice home. You're never here. Just like your father."

"Don't say that. I hate it when you say that. I'm nothing like him."

"You are exactly like him, Ruby."

I stormed out of the room, slamming the door behind me, just as I had done a thousand times as a teenager, except this time I felt a pain in my chest. *I am nothing like him,* I screamed in my head.

As if I were being punished, my nightmare visited me that night.

Working late at the hotel, I'm in the basement where the vault is kept. I hear steady footsteps behind me, but when I turn around there's no one there. Continuing down the hallway, I hear the footsteps again. A man's heavy footsteps. Louder and closer. I run towards the vault. There's no way out.

~

A week later on Thanksgiving Day, I brought home a turkey dinner from the hotel. Mom and I ate in silence. Emily called to say she had to stay in Philadelphia over the holidays, something about an internship. *How I wish she were here.*

December was a busy month at work, with clients and their company parties, our year-end reports, and strategy meetings for the new year. One evening Mother announced, "I'm not celebrating Christmas."

"That's fine, Mom," I answered. I agreed with her. There was nothing to celebrate about.

Worrying about my mother, I called the one person who made an impression on her.

"Dr. Leu, Mother has stopped taking her medication and she's not going to her appointments. Isn't there anything you can do?"

"Ruby, I would if I could. Your mother has her rights. No one can force her to do anything she doesn't want to do."

"What's going to happen, Dr. Leu?"

"I don't know, Ruby. Will you call me and keep me informed? I'm concerned for your mother and for you."

~

In so many ways she was like a girl. When curly hair was popular in the 70s and I slept in rollers every night, Mother also wanted curly hair. She had talked me into curling her hair every night before she went to sleep. She said, "Oh, Ruby, you do it so neatly." I performed the task every night for two years until one night I yelled at her for being helpless and told her that I would never again roll her hair. The next evening, like a little girl who'd found out she could tie her own shoelaces, she ran into my room excited. "Ruby, look! I did it. The whole head under thirty minutes."

When she made up her mind to do something, she did it with zeal. Perhaps she would find the same enthusiasm for psychotherapy. I was determined to find a compassionate healer for her. She hadn't talked to male doctors. She would talk to a female one. I convinced myself of that. I called Dr. Gloria Thatcher, the one who had referred me to the OMI home-visiting service. I could still hear her gentle voice over the telephone.

On the Saturday of my appointment with Dr. Thatcher, I fantasized about how Mother would have a chance to talk about her mysterious childhood at the orphanage, her fears about becoming a woman, and her turbulent marriage to Father. Just as in the movie *The Three Faces of Eve*, Mother would remember the events that had scarred her and by remembering, she would overcome the pain, find answers, and start a new life. At the end of the movie, the character that Joanne Woodward portrayed found a happy life for herself. And so would my mother.

Sitting in the small waiting room, pretending to read a news magazine, I broke into a sweat when I saw a figure standing in the doorway.

"Ms. Lin? I'm Gloria Thatcher." Her physical appearance reminded me of Gloria Steinem, except Dr. Thatcher had shoulder-length wavy brown hair, and she wore a long flowing skirt and a loose-fitting jacket. We exchanged hellos. As I followed her down the hall, I watched her skirt sway from side to side.

Her office did not have a couch. I was relieved I did not have to lie down and study the ceiling. The fact that the building was a Victorian home converted into offices would make staring at the ceiling a tremendous strain on my nearsighted eyes. I sat in a wing chair facing her.

Dr. Thatcher put her feet up. Her footrest resembled a sewing basket.

"Ms. Lin, how is your mother?"

"Please call me Ruby." *How can I let someone older, and a doctor too, call me Ms.?* "She's not going to her monthly appointments and she's not taking her medication."

"Perhaps she's feeling some side effects from her medication. Can the doctor adjust the dosage?"

"She's complaining of 'dry mouth,' but she won't tell her doctor."

The tiny digital clock on the round table between Dr. Thatcher's wing chair and mine said 2:02.

"Ruby, normally I don't take notes in our sessions, but for the first session I will need some personal history. Is that all right with you?"

"Of course," I answered.

"Let's start with age, place of birth, number of siblings."

"Mother is fifty-two. She was born in China and she has no siblings."

"I mean you, Ruby. Your personal history, not your mom's."

"You want to start with mine first?"

"Yes. Because if we're to work together, I'll need to know you better."

I couldn't believe it. She thought *I* wanted to be her patient.

"Dr. Thatcher, there's been a misunderstanding. I want you to treat my mother."

Dr. Thatcher leaned forward. "Ruby, I cannot take on a new patient this way. Your mother needs to decide for herself if she wants to see me."

"Oh." I was still processing her response.

"What about you, Ruby? Have you thought about therapy for yourself? I would like to work with you if you're interested."

My heart sank to my stomach.

Dr. Thatcher saw my confusion. It was on my face, the way I looked down at my hands. "You don't have to give me an answer now. But I will need to know by Tuesday. A patient of mine has asked for a Saturday slot, but I would reserve it for you if you want it. I know you have to go to work weekdays."

"Thank you. You're very kind."

"Also, Ruby, I won't bill you for this session. You're the first client who has interviewed me on someone else's behalf." She said this with a smile as she rose from her chair. Walking me to the door, she added, "I hope to see you again, Ruby."

"I'll call you, Dr. Thatcher. Thanks again."

~

At home when I told Mother I had found a female therapist who was gentle and caring, she raised the volume of the television set. The following Saturday, I dragged my body to my two o'clock appointment with Dr. Thatcher. I had called her on Tuesday. *How did I get into this mess? My mother should be doing this, not me. I'm rolling her hair again.* Was I supposed to learn a few psychiatric tricks and help Mother indirectly?

~

The first few weeks, I acquired phrases such as *dysfunctional family, pushing my button,* and *suppressed anger.*

At home, it wasn't easy transferring my new knowledge to Mother. We were hardly speaking to each other. I continued going home to eat with her. Every night I sat waiting for her to take her pills, and she was probably waiting for me to stop dropping hints about the sessions I was attending on Saturdays.

Just as I had resented curling her hair, I resented going to therapy on her behalf. I came down with a cold on three Saturdays and missed those sessions.

Home life had become unbearable. Not only did I fail in giving Mother secondhand therapy by sharing what I had learned from Dr. Thatcher, I had slipped into denial about Mother's physiological need for medications.

Mumbling to herself had turned into following me around the house with stories about how she was the good wife.

"I deserved a better life. I gave him three children and he thanked me by beating me. Ruby, I never raised my voice to him. Not once. I always spoke softly."

"Mom, stop it. Please stop it. I was there. I don't want to hear it."

"I never raised my voice to him. Always a good wife, while he fraternized with his lowlife friends. I never raised my voice to him."

"STOP IT! Why are you doing this to me?"

"I was a good wife. I did nothing wrong."

I ran out of the house, jumped into the car and drove off. But I didn't know where to go—I just drove. I got onto Highway 280, then Highway 1. Signs for Pacifica flashed by me. I couldn't see any other cars winding through Devils Slide. The Pacific Ocean, wild and merciless, raged in the darkness. At Montara I looked down at the fuel gauge; it read one-quarter tank remaining. I turned around.

Mother was asleep when I got home. I dreamed that she had cornered me in the kitchen, giving me an account of what Father did to her. *STOP!* My own scream woke me from the dream. *If you don't stop having these dreams, you'll go insane.*

~

The next evening when I came home from work, dinner was nowhere in sight and Mother was in her room. She was angry with me, no doubt. I went to class.

The following evening, there was dinner on the table. But Mother was waiting for me like a wounded lion.

"Ruby, what's the purpose of you coming home for dinner only to run off again?"

"I have class, Mom. I come home for you. Dr. Leu said you would—"

"Dr. Leu? What does Dr. Leu know? I'm not your slave. I cook a nice meal and watch you eat it like it's a burden."

"I appreciate your cooking, Mom. But I can't be late for class. As it is, I have to rush."

"Just like your father. Always rushing."

"Mom, don't say that. Don't compare me to him."

"Just like him. Never home. Treated me like a slave."

"Mom, you're not a slave. I thought you liked to cook."

She took her plate of food into the kitchen. I heard the grinding noise from the garbage disposal. She had trashed her uneaten dinner. I looked at my watch. Twenty minutes to go across town for my class.

"Mom, I'm going to class. Please eat dinner."

She did not answer me.

Driving to class, I thought about what she'd said. How I hated her for comparing me to the man who beat her. How I despised her for allowing him to perform violence on her body and John's, and making Emily and me helpless bystanders.

~

The following evening without class or a night event at the hotel, I brought home fixings for a stir-fry dinner. I thought that if I cooked dinner, then I could convince Mother that I wasn't treating her like a slave. Feeling frustrated that I had to cut the vegetables into bite-size pieces, I went into defense mode when Mother walked into the kitchen. We both waited for the other person to say hello first.

"I'm making stir-fry. Would you like to set the table?"

"Let me do that. You don't know how to cut vegetables."

"I know how to cut the damned vegetables."

"Don't swear at me. I'm not here to have you swear at me."

"Mom, why don't you go watch television, and I'll let you know when dinner is ready."

She used to say that to me when I was a girl. Every time I begged to help her with dinner, she would send me away, adding, "You'll learn when you're married."

She took the lid off the rice cooker and stirred the contents with a wooden spoon. Then she tapped the spoon six times to shake off the rice before putting the lid back on. My headache was starting.

"Do you know how many pots of rice I've cooked in my life, Ruby? Millions. I cooked and cleaned. I carried heavy laundry to the Laundromat. He never helped me, Ruby. I did it all alone. I raised the three of you all alone. He never helped."

"Mom, can we not start that again? Let's eat dinner and watch some television." I was regretting having bought green peppers. I was not enjoying slicing them.

"Start what? I'm not starting anything. I'm telling you that I was a good wife and your father was the one who yelled and hit me. He used to come home late and hit me for no reason. I never raised my voice to him, Ruby."

"MOM, STOP IT!"

"You're yelling at me now, just like he used to, for no reason at all. You are just like him. You look like him."

"STOP IT!"

"I never raised my voice to him. He beat me for no reason, Ruby." Mother's face was inches from mine.

"If you don't stop—" I had turned the point of the knife toward Mother's throat.

"HA! You want to kill your mother? Your father would like that."

I screamed, feeling the pain in my chest. The knife fell into the sink. I ran to my room, locked the door, turned on the stereo to drown out the noise in my head and sat up most of the night so that dreams would not haunt me. *Please, someone help me.*

~

The next day, as a criminal would plead his case to the judge, I confessed to Dr. Thatcher.

"Dr. Thatcher, something horrible happened last night."

"Is your mother all right?"

"I threatened her with a knife. She wouldn't stop repeating over and over again about Father beating her. I need help, Dr. Thatcher."

Dr. Thatcher got up from her wing chair to hand me the box of tissues. "Would you like some water, Ruby?"

"No, thanks. I took some Motrin already."

"Have you called your mother's doctor?"

"The last time I called him, he told me about patient rights, and that there's nothing he can do."

"Call him anyway, Ruby."

"Why can't life be like the movies? If I were Joan Crawford, I would have no trouble making my mother take her pills. "

"Ruby," Dr. Thatcher sighed with a smile. "You're not Joan Crawford. You are you. And you know you cannot *make* your mother do anything that she doesn't want to do."

"I know. Just wishing. Like wishing Emily would come home."

"Have you told Emily that?"

"No. She'd have to drop everything."

"Let Emily decide for herself, Ruby. If you want your sister to be here, tell her. Remember—ask for what you want."

"Okay. I'll ask."

"Now, what led to last night's incident?"

CHAPTER 6

Is It My Destiny?

Dr. Leu was right. I was trying to control Mother's future and it backfired. To avoid any further violent scenes in the kitchen, I wrote Mother a note to apologize for my actions, and also to tell her that I would not be home for dinner the entire week. I was just as angry as she was. Not knowing how to handle a crisis by thinking through the steps, I severed verbal communication with her, and avoided being home even when I didn't have class or evening events at work.

In one week, I had a valid reason to have Mother hospitalized again. She had not eaten in three days and that was enough cause to have the home-assessment team pay us a visit. The social workers were not Susan and Dan. They were new faces, yet Mother complied and went to the hospital with them. Go figure that! However, this time it was to Langley Porter Hospital, not San Francisco General. A whole new set of doctors, nurses, and social workers reviewed my mother's file sent over from Dr. Leu's office.

I believed Mother wanted to be away from me as much as I wanted to be away from her. We couldn't stand each other anymore.

Helen, the social worker, found a board-and-care home in the Sunset neighborhood for Mother. Kirkham Street was only two blocks from a commercial district. Mother would be near coffee shops and Chinese delicatessens. This living situation would provide her with a bedroom, three meals a day, and supervision with medication. Helen said the caretaker, Molly, was a caring woman.

"But, Helen, my mother can't afford it. And my salary isn't enough to pay for two rents." I heard the selfishness in my voice. *Maybe I can go back to a studio lifestyle and cut down on expenses.*

"I'll find out if your mother qualifies for disability income, Ruby. I'll get started right away."

"Thank you, Helen." *Manager of Special Events—and I can't even help my own mother.*

~

I was grateful that Dr. Thatcher was in my life. She listened whenever I told her about my nightmares and her calmness made me feel safe.

"Dr. Thatcher, how long does this work take? I mean, what's the average stay for your patients? Six months? A year?"

"I cannot give you an answer, Ruby, because no two patients are alike. People come to me for many reasons and with varying goals. Some patients have been with me for years. Then there are patients who have specific issues to work on, and they come and go, and come back again."

"I'm a fast learner. Do you think six months for me?"

Dr. Thatcher smiled, just the way my U.S. history teacher smiles when a student asks her an off-the-wall question.

"Let's take one session at a time, Ruby. Tell me about your week."

Walking out of her office, into the open air, I watched the fog veil my beautiful city. I felt cold and empty, like the tall buildings in the financial district on a Saturday afternoon.

~

Out of the blue one evening, Mrs. Nussbaum called me. "Ruby, I ran into Carole, our building manager, and I asked her for your telephone number. How are you? How's your mother?"

"I'm okay, Mrs. Nussbaum. How are you? How's Rashi?"

"We're both fine, dear. We miss you."

"You're so sweet. I haven't properly thanked you for everything you've done. How about a lunch date next month? I have to find an apartment before the month ends."

"An apartment? Why?"

"Long story, Mrs. Nussbaum. Mother is living in a board-and-care home. There's a good chance that she qualifies for disability income so that I won't be financially responsible for her. But I can't afford paying rent on this house—they make me pay for everything, including garbage and water."

"You're a lucky girl, Ruby. The one-bedroom unit on the third floor is vacant. You remember the nice fellow who lived there, the one with the bald spot. He always wore sweater vests. You know, the schoolteacher?"

"Oh yes. He moved?"

"He accepted a position in Los Angeles. Such a nice man, he was."

"Mrs. Nussbaum, are you saying that the apartment hasn't been rented yet?"

"Carole said she was still reviewing applications. You call her. Do you want me to call her for you?"

"I can't believe this. Do you think I'll have a chance; after all, I did move out and cause her inconvenience."

"Inconvenience! That's how they make money. You call her."

"Okay, Mrs. Nussbaum. I'll do it right now. Thank you so much. You're my guardian angel."

"Get off the phone, and you call her."

~

Sitting in my wing chair the following Saturday, I felt melancholy and Dr. Thatcher sensed it.

"What are you thinking about, Ruby?"

"Do you remember the show, *The Twilight Zone?*"

"I know of it."

"In one episode, this couple found themselves trapped in a town that looked like their home town, but nothing was real. There were no other people; just fake buildings. Almost the entire episode, they desperately tried to find out where they were. As the camera sweeps upward towards the sky, you can see two giant children playing with their model town, complete with model landscaping and model buildings. The two people were just playthings for these children. The fate of the two adults was predetermined. That's the way I feel right now. Like some pawn on a board and someone else is determining what to do with me."

"Why do you say that, Ruby?"

"A normal person would be happy that she'll have a great apartment. It's not the two-bedroom one, but it's just as nice. It's in a beautiful old building and Mrs. Nussbaum is wonderful as ever. I should be happy. Why am I not?"

"What's happening at work?"

"Nothing new. Same old demanding clients with their fancy parties and phony talk. I'll scream if I hear *honey* one more time. I hate people calling me *honey* when they have no right to call me that."

"You're not happy with your job?"

"I hate my job, Dr. Thatcher. People tell me I'm good at it. I'm good at being charming to people I don't know."

"Hate is a strong word. Have you thought about leaving?"

"Maybe hate is not the right word. I like work. I like having responsibilities. I'm extremely fond of my coworkers. And I like most of my clients, especially Mrs. McKenzie. She's my favorite."

"What would be your dream job, Ruby?"

"That's easy. A place where I'm appreciated. A place where I feel good about what I'm selling. Or what kind of service I'm providing. To be my own boss. To have something to call my own."

"Tell me more, Ruby."

I spent the remainder of the session talking about why I left other jobs. How I wished I had the courage to leave the St. Mark.

~

Visiting Mother at her board-and-care home was no joy either. We were alone in the living room. Molly was out back folding laundry.

"Ruby, they put another person in my room. I have to share my room with an old woman."

"It's a big room, Mom. There was an empty bed when you moved in so it's no surprise, is it?"

"She snores. Loud."

"Oh, I'm sorry. Can you ask Molly to give you another room?"

"What's the difference? She'll just put me with someone else."

"Someone who doesn't snore," I tried to soothe.

"She's loud," Mother repeated.

"Why don't we pick up some earplugs for you today? Merrill's has—"

"Don't waste your money. I won't wear them. They're not comfortable."

"How do you know, Mom? Have you tried them?"

She ignored my question.

"What's the use? They all snore. They all stink."

"Mom, your housemates don't stink."

"How do you know? Have you used the bathroom?"

"Do they use Lysol?" I thought if they used Lysol, then conditions wouldn't have been intolerable.

"I don't know what they use. I'm not their maid."

"Mom, let's go get some lunch."

It was more of the same over lunch. Mother complained about the housemates, Molly, and even Molly's daughter for listening to music.

When I dropped her off, she asked if I wanted to go shopping. I lied and said I had to take care of some business. The truth was I couldn't stand her complaining, even though I wouldn't have liked to sleep with someone who snored.

I called Molly the next day to tell her about Mother's unhappiness. Molly told me she had already asked Mother if she wanted to change rooms, and Mother's answer had been 'no.' *What more could I do?*

What kept me sane that weekend was a *Leave It To Beaver* marathon on television. This and other sitcoms had saved me from my childhood; it would save me again. Why couldn't my mom be like June Cleaver?

~

One day at work, I was in the "baby" ballroom when I came upon a notepad on a chair. An attendee of the conference must have dropped it. I looked inside the pad to see if there was a name written on the cover but there wasn't. So I took it to my office. At my desk I was about to call the client who had booked the baby ballroom when I suddenly realized I had seen that notepad before.

The spiral binding jabbed my finger as I picked up the little pad. And as if in a dream, it all came back to me.

~

I was thirteen years old. Mother and I were in the kitchen. While she wiped off the vinyl tablecloth, I stared at the new coat of yellow paint that was already chipping.

"I hate women," Mother said in Chinese.

"Then do you hate me, Mama?"

"Of course not, don't be ridiculous. Anyhow, you are not a woman. You are my daughter. You're a girl."

"Do you hate men too, Mama?"

"Men. Women. I hate them all."

"My teacher says I'm a woman. She says a girl becomes a woman when she starts her menstrual cycle."

"Why don't teachers concentrate on history, science and math and not talk about foolish things? Telling girls they are women! That's wrong! You are a girl until you are married."

My mother sighed disapprovingly. To change the subject so as not to further agitate her, I reached into the gray tin box in front of me. "I'll look for your address book, Mama," I said with the voice of obedience. Underneath our visas and birth certificates was a yellowed photograph.

"Who is this?" I asked Mother.

"Put it back in the box," she snapped. I took one more look at the woman in the aged photograph before doing so.

"You're very lucky to have a mother," my mother continued, in a softer voice. "My mother died when I was seven years old, and I was placed in an orphanage in China. I spent six years in that place."

"Is this your mother?"

My mother ignored me. She went on to say, "My father died in a plane crash and my mother starved herself to death because she loved him so much."

I opened my mouth to ask more about Grandfather, but Mother

snapped again, "Have you found that address book yet?" She looked at the wall clock. It was nine and Father was still not home.

I was supposed to look for her address book in the gray tin box. The little book with the spiral binding contained the handful of addresses of her relatives here in America. She wanted me to address the four Christmas cards she had bought for them. They all lived in Mississippi, a place too far away for us to ever visit.

"Found it!" I waved the book in my hand. The end of the spiral binding jabbed my finger. "Ouch."

Mother's voice was gentle and sweet now. "You write so beautifully, Ruby. I want you to write the addresses on the envelopes, and inside the cards write 'Dear Uncle and Aunt' at the top, and sign the cards for me."

My mother never took a course in management negotiations, but she certainly knew how to be persuasive by using those arm-twisting words, "You do it. You do it so beautifully."

That night in my room, I tried to remember the woman's face in the yellowed photograph. That must have been a picture of my grandmother. Mother was so vexed with me that I did not dare ask what Grandmother's name was. Anyway, in our family, children were not supposed to ask questions. It would have been disrespectful to ask. Children were not allowed to ask about their elders' names. It was enough to call them by their appropriate titles.

I went to bed thinking about my grandmother. I closed my eyes and imagined her. In the photograph she was standing straight with her arms at her sides. She had round eyes. Her short black hair was parted in the middle and tucked behind her ears. She had a clean face and a solemn look.

It was eleven o'clock and everyone, including Father, had gone to bed. He had come home, telling Mother he'd had to work overtime.

Without turning on any lights, I went to the kitchen and took the photograph out of the gray tin box and sneaked it to my room. Under the bedcovers I used my miniature flashlight to study the woman in the picture because I did not want to wake my sister who shared the room with me.

I was hypnotized by the photograph. I thought of the rhyme "Monday's child is fair of face" (that would be my mother), and "Tuesday's child is full of grace," then that is what I'll call my grandmother. Grace.

I switched off the flashlight and tucked my grandmother's picture under my pillow. I looked over at my sister's bed. I saw the outline of her head, half covered by her blankets. As I drifted off to sleep, I thought about the fact that my little sister was seven years old, my mother's age when she was placed in an orphanage.

~

That was the first time I was able to remember an incident with such detail. After calling my client to tell her I had found a notepad and that I would leave it with Lost and Found, I wrote down everything I had remembered for my next Saturday session.

That night I had to oversee a party at the hotel. A film studio had finished their shooting and the producer decided, last minute, to throw a bash for his crew. What a wild bunch. Champagne by the case. The young actress who played the lead walked around expecting everyone to grovel at her feet. Innocently, I had insulted her when I went around the room asking people to point her out to me so that I could deliver a telephone message to her. She gave me the once-over look as I handed her the message. "My agent," she said, instead of "thank you." Then she, in her see-through white dress, walked away as if I were her servant.

I didn't get home until two in the morning. Exhaustion brought on a bizarre dream.

I'm walking up a hill to get to the gray stone building at the peak. The building stands alone, looking like a fortress. The sun is setting and the wind is picking up speed. Tall grass is all around—it must be at least four feet high. As I turn back to see the distance I've traveled, I detect movement in the grass. I see a figure in a sheer white gown. From the movements, I suspect it is a woman, about five feet tall, slender. Her meager garment flutters in the wind as she scurries down the hill.

Is she a ghost? Is she my imagination? I feel a chill running through me. In a few seconds, I lose sight of her. What is she running from? Why didn't she use the path? I stand there watching the swaying stalks of grass. After walking over to the spot where she had walked, I see the crushed blades of grass. I did not imagine her.

Convincing myself that it's safe to proceed, I continue my climb up the hill. I'm determined to find out what is happening. My heart is beating fast and I'm shivering. I tell myself that once I'm indoors, I will be comforted.

The sun has recently set. The stone building before me seems deserted. There is no knocker. The door is ajar. As I step inside, I begin to feel weightless. My feet barely touch the cold concrete floor. I follow the left corridor into an area where Chinese men and women in green uniforms travel in different directions. No one seems to notice me. They pass by me without acknowledging my presence. They appear to be hospital workers delivering meals to rooms. I hear two female workers whispering to each other in Chinese.

"She ran away this morning," the taller one says.

"It's getting dark. She'll come back to get out of the cold," the other worker casually responds. "They're all crazy. Did you hear about the one

who starved herself to death? Her husband died in a plane crash and she starved herself, leaving a daughter behind. The little girl is in an orphanage. Lord knows what's going to happen to that wretched thing."

"What a selfish woman, to leave a daughter behind," the taller one sneers.

"She's not selfish!" I shout at the two women but they cannot hear me. I realize that they also cannot see me. "She's not selfish. You might have done the same thing." I try to reason with them, but to no avail. They cannot hear me.

I continue to glide down another corridor, feeling even lighter than before. This corridor is dark. I use my hands to work my way down the hall. The walls and the floor feel colder here. Seeing light from the room at the end of this hall, I begin to move like Spider Man. At the entrance, my body becomes completely weightless and I float into the spacious room. The walls are stone. The floor is stone. Four male workers, wearing the green uniforms, hover over a rectangular structure. No one is talking. I'm still invisible to these people.

I float a little closer toward the stone structure—a frail young woman is immersed in water. The four men work in unison. Two men are lifting the woman by her upper arms; the other two men are lifting her by the legs. The four lift the woman out of the water and dunk her again and again. A sheer white gown is on a hanger behind the tub. It's exactly like the garment the woman had been wearing—the woman running down the hill. I feel the coldness of the room penetrating my body.

The first sound I hear comes from the woman in the tub. "Oh, it's so cold. Oh, it's so cold. Please stop. I'm not crazy. I'm not crazy." Hearing her cries, I fall to the ground. Picking myself up, my feet touch the cold floor.

To my horror, the four workers are now looking at me. I'm no longer invisible to them. As they drop the woman into the cold water and come *towards me, I flee from the room and tear down the corridor. Pushing aside everything in my path, I make my way to the front door.*

Once outside, I run down the hill as if I am being hunted. The moon is bright, giving me sufficient light. The woman's moans are ringing in my head.

I awoke from that dream in a cold sweat. My sleeping gown was soaked. I looked at the clock: 5:20.

~

That Saturday, I read my notes of the memory flash to Dr. Thatcher, and told her about the creepy dream. "I remember Mother once telling me that she visited an insane asylum in China. She saw a woman crying in a cold-water treatment. Mother said, 'A dunking in cold water was the way they calmed the crazy people.'"

"What a horrible memory for your mother."

"Dr. Thatcher, I'm not so sure I like these memory flashes. Well, what I mean is they're okay, but I don't like the dreams."

"Ruby, you've been working very hard and, from what you tell me, not getting proper rest. The subconscious was playing with reality, fantasy and memories."

I knew Dr. Thatcher had the tools to help me unlock the door to the past. But just like going into an attic that has not been cleaned for decades, I was afraid of what I would find in mine.

"Ruby, are you okay?"

"Yes, of course."

"You might want to try to give yourself some quiet time before retiring for the evening."

"I'll try," I answered with a confirming nod. I was lying. Where would I find time to try it, with my schedule? But I couldn't have answered Dr. Thatcher differently. I wanted her to like me, and I wanted her to think I was sensible. I looked down at my hands.

"What are you thinking about?"

"You don't suppose Mother was talking about her mother in the asylum, do you?"

"I don't know, Ruby. Perhaps you can ask your mother when you feel that you and she are both ready to discuss it."

"Do you see a pattern, Dr. Thatcher? First my grandmother, now my mother. Will I be next?"

"Patterns can be broken, Ruby."

CHAPTER 7

Looking Chinese

Mother continued to be aloof at the board-and-care home. Molly assured me that my mother was taking her medication every night. Mother still refused to talk to the psychiatrist, but I was grateful she was going to her monthly appointments. The doctor had changed her prescription to a new drug that had fewer side effects than the one she had been taking.

With my learning new ways to talk to her, I felt like a child trying to impress an adult, but stumbling at every word.

"Hello, Mom. How's everything?"

"It's very boring here. The other people are old people. Old and sick people. I'm the youngest one in the house."

"The youngest and the prettiest."

Mother was not amused. "You don't have to come visit, Ruby. I know it's out of your way."

"But I want to visit. I asked Molly to recommend a good restaurant and she said The Chinese Crane is nice. Let's go there."

"I'm not hungry, Ruby. You go."

"But I came all this way to take you out."

"Don't waste your precious time, Ruby. I know you're a very busy girl."

"I didn't mean it that way, Mom."

"It's okay. You go and eat. I'm staying here to watch *Perry Mason*."

I didn't even try to persuade her to change her mind. I was thankful that she had released me from my duties of being a good daughter.

"Bye, Mom." I hugged her as she stood there with her arms limp at her sides. She still had the power to make me feel irresponsible.

No sense in my going to lunch alone. Even though Dr. Thatcher was on vacation and I didn't have a two o'clock appointment, I couldn't think of a place to go. So I went to work. In the lobby, I heard someone calling my name. It was one of the Taiwanese guests from the Turner function the year before.

"Hello, Mr. Hwang. How are you?"

"You remember me, *Luby*. A good *memerly*. How much does my buddy, Chad, pay you for having such good *memerly?*"

I hated people calling each other buddies when they hardly knew one another.

"Are you here to visit us, Mr. Hwang?"

"No. My son is here. He's helping me with business matter."

"How nice. Well, I'd better get some work done. Nice seeing you again, Mr. Hwang."

"*Luby,* wait." He follows me into the elevator. "*Luby,* are you *mellied?* I see no wedding *ling.*"

How I hated that question. How I hated the answer. "No, no time for that."

"A *pletty* girl like you? Not *mellied?* My son, thirty years old, successful, *vely* handsome. How about I take you two to dinner tonight?"

"Oh, I can't Mr. Hwang. Thank you for the invitation."

"Why not? I don't take 'no' for answer."

"I really can't. I'm working tonight."

"Then *toomalow* night. My son, he's here for two weeks."

I hated to lie, but what's a girl to do? To say 'no' to an old Chinese man's invitation to meet his son would be an insult to his name. So I lied. "I can't, I'm seeing someone."

"Oh. Why you not say so? I know a *pletty* girl like you have a boyfriend."

If you say pletty *girl one more time, I'm going to throw up on your shoes.* The elevator door opened. I was safe from further conversation.

"Bye, Mr. Hwang. Nice to see you again." One last lie.

"Bye, *Luby.*"

The next two weeks, I kept a low profile in the hallways—in case Mr. Hwang and his son happened to cross my path.

~

I told this to Dr. Thatcher and she laughed at me. She has a way of showing her appreciation for humor, which is one of the many reasons why I liked her.

"Ruby, why didn't you want to meet his son? He could have been a nice man."

"He could have been. As a matter of fact, for two weeks I found myself sneaking a peek at every handsome Asian man in the hotel. But I would never date one."

"Why not?" Dr. Thatcher asked with a smile.

"I don't want to get mixed up with anyone who might turn out to be like my father. And I'm not just talking about the violent nature."

Dr. Thatcher listened.

"He couldn't say 'no' to people. He had no problem saying it to Mother, but to other people, especially his aunt, he couldn't do it.

This was the aunt who had sponsored us to come to America. She said on the application she had to agree that if Father couldn't find work, then she, being the sponsor, would have to support us, the whole family. Father said we had a big debt to repay. 'If it wasn't for my aunt, we would be starving in Hong Kong.' That wasn't true; we did not starve. We came to the U.S. because of the public school system. 'No matter if you're rich or poor, your children can get an education here,' that's what Father's aunt had said.

"Mother said to Father, 'She filled out a damned form for us. Someday, we'll do the same for her if she needs us to sponsor other relatives. Your aunt is using you, and you can't see it.'

"Every weekend that first year here, Father, Mother and all of us kids, went to visit this aunt so that Father could repay the debt. You know, by helping her around the house. She was a widow and her grown children cared less about helping her.

"After a year, Mother was fed up. Father said his aunt needed his help. Mother yelled at him, 'She also needs a man to sleep with! She says it's lonely in a big bed. Why don't you help her with that too!' Mother got a bloody lip for saying that. How I hated him, Dr. Thatcher. This aunt used to brush against Father's sleeve while handing him a drink, or she'd go behind him and give him a quick shoulder rub after he 'performed' a day of labor for her.

"The day my parents fought over this woman, I watched my mother swallow her tears. She had no mother to run home to. Even Samantha Stephens, from *Bewitched*, remember that show? She had a mother to fly to. Imagine! A witch who could have turned her enemy into a toad was still running to her mother for comfort. Remember Endora?"

Dr. Thatcher nodded.

"Many times Endora turned Samantha's husband into worse things than a toad. Everyone needs a mother. My mother had no one."

"Your mother was very sad, Ruby. And you saw that."

Suddenly I didn't want to talk. We sat in silence. Then Dr. Thatcher spoke.

"Your father, even though a very important figure in a child's memory, was only one Chinese male role model. Weren't there others?"

"Yes. There was Kristie's uncle. Kristie was my best friend. Her uncle was a freeloader. Kristie's mom couldn't kick him out because he was her husband's older brother, and you'd never kick out someone older."

"How about younger role models?"

"There was one, but he was a jerk too. They were all jerks. No. Those were not the profiles of men I would consider as husband material. See why I wouldn't care to get mixed up with Chinese men, Dr. Thatcher? Now, Uncle Bill, from the TV show *Family Affair,* who adopted his orphaned nephew and nieces; Uncle Bentley from *Bachelor Father*; the Cartwright brothers from *Bonanza*, Adam, Hoss, and Little Joe—those were great men. They knew how to treat women and children. They were strong, yet gentle."

"Ruby, the men you're describing are fictional. They're not real men."

"I know. But writers create characters based on real people. I've seen men like them, wonderful men like my high school science teacher and the boss I had a long time ago. When I fall in love, he'll be someone wonderful like them."

~

Feeling guilty that I was avoiding my mother, but also feeling hurt that she didn't express a big desire to see me, I invited Mrs. Nussbaum to lunch instead. She would not make me feel either of those emotions. I really should have offered a lot more than lunch, what with her telling me about Mother hiding in my apartment, being kind, but not meddling, and for bringing me good luck in returning to this building.

I took her to The Decadent Eatery. They had fancy burgers, gourmet salads, and outrageous desserts.

"I could have cooked something at home, Ruby."

"No, Mrs. Nussbaum. What kind of 'thank you' is that if you have to cook for me?"

"I love to cook. Herman used to say I cooked better than his mother and his mother was a darn good cook."

"Your soups should be patented."

"You're such a dear. Why don't we split a little something here, go back to my place and I'll feed you there?"

"Mrs. Nussbaum, you're so funny. Here, check out the menu."

"What a menu," she exclaimed.

"I'm getting the chicken burger with roasted peppers and a Caesar salad. Doesn't that sound good?"

"I'll get the Primavera pizzetta. What I can't eat, I'll bring home to Rashi. He loves pizza and that's the one thing I don't make at home."

"He eats pizza?"

"He's a good eater." Mrs. Nussbaum waved at a waiter.

After giving the young man our order, Mrs. Nussbaum asked him for a cup of hot water.

"Hot tea, ma'am?"

"No. Just a cup of hot water. Thank you."

When the cup of hot water was delivered to our table, Mrs. Nussbaum dipped her silverware into the water and dried it off with her napkin. I would have died of embarrassment if my mother had done that, and she has. Watching Mrs. Nussbaum perform her ritual made me realize that other people have idiosyncrasies too.

"I know this is a fine restaurant, but I always want to make sure. Silverware gets handled and you never know if the person who set the table is sick. I'm a silly woman."

"You're not. You're a kind and wonderful woman."

Mrs. Nussbaum and I got to know each other a little better that afternoon. I told her about Mother, how she was orphaned in China, how we came to the States. . . . In turn she told me that, except for in-laws, she was the last of her family. She has made many new friends here, most of them she met through the Jewish Community Center.

When we returned to our building, we found the elevator out of order.

"Come on, Ruby. We'll take it slow. I can walk ten miles and back, but these old knees are not made for stairs. Come on, dear, one step at a time."

Mrs. Nussbaum used the railing as we climbed to the third floor. She was in better shape than I was. We said goodbye. I stayed on the landing and watched her climb the last flight. When she turned the corner I couldn't see her anymore. I waited until I heard Rashi greet her and she closed her door. *She would make a wonderful grandmother.*

~

Feeling good about having my own apartment and having Mrs. Nussbaum as a neighbor, I also felt blessed that I had found Dr. Thatcher.

"Dr. Thatcher, I had a dream three nights ago."

She walked over to her rolltop desk and took out a pad and a pen. After sitting down, she looked up, and smiled. That was her cue for me to start talking.

"I'm living in the hotel. In the basement. I had a huge room with a high ceiling. Instead of wallpaper, beautiful gowns cover all four walls. Anyway, it's nighttime and I just got home from having worked upstairs. After bolting the door and looking up, I see that Mimi, the doll from my childhood days, is suspended on the transom. Her eyes were closed, like she's sleeping. It was just her head, no body. Under her sweet face is a pair of hands. They look like my hands, clasped. Like in a prayer. I wasn't scared of Mimi's head because Mimi could never scare me. But the hands did. What were a pair of hands doing there? I felt a damp draft in the room. Mimi's eyes opened as if to warn me that there was someone on the other side of the door. Then the hands moved. I screamed."

Dr. Thatcher looked at her notes. "In the dream, Ruby, you're living in the basement?"

"Yes, but it felt like a cold, damp castle."

"What do you think of this symbol?"

"I spend so many hours at work, it does, sometimes, feel like I'm living there. And parts of the St. Mark feel like a castle."

"What about the hands, Ruby?"

"They were my hands and they were trying to warn me too, like Mimi's eyes."

"You felt threatened in the dream. Is there any reason for that concern in your life?"

I sat back to show Dr. Thatcher that I was giving her question serious thought. I knew what the threat was, but I was not about to tell her. I had made up my mind to forget about that year. And I planned to do just that.

Dr. Thatcher spoke. "It was a painful childhood, Ruby."

Dr. Thatcher's gentle words made a dull ache in my heart. I looked down at my hands. Teardrops fell on them. Dr. Thatcher handed me the box of tissue. The room was quiet.

"Ruby, do you still have the doll?"

"Yes, she sits on a shelf in my bedroom next to Emily's doll."

"You're healing the little girl inside. Perhaps the hands were there to protect Mimi."

Those words made me smile.

~

The next two weeks were super busy at work. I had to cancel my date with Mother and she wasn't happy. When we finally got together for lunch one Saturday, she had a proposition for me.

"Ruby, will you move out with me? I promise to take my pills and go to the doctor."

I almost choked on my food. "Move out, Mom?"

"Yes. A house like the other one. It doesn't have to be big."

I had to come up with an excuse fast. "My lease, Mom. I signed a lease."

"Oh," she said, and lowered her eyes.

I had lost my appetite.

"I'll pay for the penalty in breaking the lease," she said calmly.

I was tongue-tied. I took a sip of my tea.

"You don't want to move out with me?" she asked, with a voice of a girl.

"Mom, what does your doctor say? If it's a matter of not being happy with the current situation, perhaps we can find another board-and-care—"

"No need to find another one. They're all the same."

"They can't be. Let me call the social—"

"Don't call the social worker. Then Molly will think I'm a trouble-maker."

"You're not a troublemaker, Mom. You want to be somewhere else. What's wrong with telling the truth?"

"The truth? The truth is you don't want to live with your mother. Why don't you call your father and tell him that? That would make him very happy."

"Why would I call him? I never talk to him." I was raising my voice.

People from the next table were looking at us. Mother had turned her head away from me.

We walked out of the restaurant holding our lunch in bags-to-go.

Dropping her off, I said, "Mom, I'll call you."

She ignored me and walked up the steps to the board-and-care home. My head was hurting and my stomach was churning. I ate my lunch in Dr. Thatcher's waiting room.

I spent the session telling Dr. Thatcher about my unpleasant lunch date with Mother, and I heard myself going down my list of pros and cons for living with her. There were six cons and one pro. The pro was that Emily could make one phone call to us instead of making two.

~

At work, Clyde, a fellow catering manager had broken his leg while running down the stairs to answer a demanding client's page. Marilyn, who was a blonde that month, and I went to see him at the hospital.

"Clyde, you're not in show biz. Get it? Break a leg?" I was trying to be witty.

"I get it, Ruby. I get it." He adjusted his hospital gown.

"I think he's faking it, Ruby. He's after the doctors," Marilyn teased, as she hung her brown corduroy coat over the back of the chair.

"With my luck, they'll all be women," Clyde moaned.

"What a pessimist," I said. "Don't all moms want us marrying doctors?"

"Not my mom. She says we need a financial adviser in the family. These damned gowns." Clyde was pulling the neckline. "First a broken leg, then they want to choke you."

"At least you're skinny," Marilyn teased again. "The back flap of the gown won't expose your bum."

"Sexual harassment. Ruby, you heard it," Clyde pleaded.

"She cares about you," I said, with a giggle.

"So, let's talk business," Marilyn proposed. "When you come back to work, we want you to be off your feet. If there's any running around, page us. That's our offer. Take it or leave it."

"You better take it, Clyde." I winked at him.

"How can I refuse two lovely, caring ladies?" He winced. "Ooh, drugs wearing off."

The nurse came in as Clyde was about to ring the bell.

"Time for your pills," the nurse announced.

"Bless you, Ms. Nightingale." Clyde winced again.

"We'll leave you alone, Clyde. Gotta go back to work." Marilyn picked up her coat.

"Bye, Clyde. Take care of yourself. Looks like you're in good hands," I said.

"Bye, ladies. Thank you. I'll call you."

~

I had a psychotic dream that night.

I'm sitting on a hospital bench, overhearing a conversation between two nurses. "She passed away last night," one nurse says to the other. In the next clip of the dream, I am again sitting on the same hospi-

tal bench, overhearing another conversation. However, this time it's between a doctor and a nurse.

"A young boy and a young girl this time, and the police are here, questioning everyone," says the nurse. "They took a brown corduroy jacket for evidence," she adds.

In the third clip of the dream I am nervously sitting on the hospital bench when I see a police inspector stopping in the hallway to talk to a group of hospital staff. "I have reason to believe that the man is somehow connected to the woman, perhaps to the two kids as well," says the inspector. He's showing the staff a piece of paper. "Has anyone seen this woman? Please call me if you see her. And above all, do not let her go into any patient's room." The picture is being passed around.

As the inspector puts the photo back into his breast pocket, he looks up and his eyes meet mine. I get up to run out of the hospital, and he runs after me. I hail a taxi and order the driver to head for downtown. At a red stoplight I jump out of the taxi like a fugitive and run the rest of the way, but I don't know where to go. I dash into a building and get into a glass elevator. As the elevator ascends I see the inspector in the lobby, stopping people and questioning them. A woman points at the elevators. He looks up and barely scrapes into another elevator as its door closes. I push the button marked 36. It's the highest floor. The elevator door opens and I am inside a lavish restaurant with a panoramic view of the city. I scramble for a place to hide. I can hear his footsteps—closer and closer.

"I must not let him catch me," I say to myself. I run toward the large windows and look down thirty-six stories. I will NOT let him catch me.

I woke from the nightmare with such horror that I turned on all the lights in the apartment and triple-checked that my front door was locked. How could anyone go back to sleep after a dream like that?

~

The following Saturday, I retold the dream to Dr. Thatcher. I didn't have to read it from any notes—it wasn't a dream I would ever forget.

"Dr. Thatcher, in the dream, there was reference to a brown corduroy jacket. My father used to wear a brown corduroy jacket. Look, I'm getting goose bumps saying the words. I'm a murderer. How could I do that to my family? I killed them."

"It was a dream, Ruby. Thoughts and actions are not the same. It was subconscious. It was a horrible dream."

To my surprise, Dr. Thatcher did not analyze the dream the way she did with all the others. I suppose the symbols were all too obvious. To think I had killed, even if it was a dream. I just hope I had committed each crime with tenderness, like giving them an overdose of morphine. Having visited Clyde at the hospital played a number on me. A bad one, at that.

"I remember plotting to end our misery, by putting crushed sleeping pills in everyone's drinks. Or leaving the gas stove on while we were all asleep."

"The little girl was trying to stop the violence and the pain."

We sat in silence for a long while. I looked at the hem of Dr. Thatcher's skirt. It draped softly over her crossed ankles.

"Ruby?"

"Huh?"

"Do you know how to meditate?"

"No."

"When you leave today, I'll lend you some books, okay?"

"Okay. Why do you think I need to meditate?"

"It's very important that before you go to sleep that you're not rushing around. You need to prepare the body and mind for rest. Try to give yourself at least half an hour of quiet time. No chores. No problem solving. Just quiet time."

"I'll try it."

I took home the books which Dr. Thatcher had lent me. That night after perusing both of them, I decided that meditation was not for me. On the following Saturday, Dr. Thatcher did not ask me about the books, so I didn't tell her about my lack of interest in meditating. Besides, what I wanted to talk to her about that day deserved the full fifty minutes.

"Dr. Thatcher, I'm really grateful to you that I've gained long-term memory. But can we not talk about my childhood so much? I don't want to dwell in the past. I'm an adult now with adult problems."

"We do talk about current situations, Ruby. However, so much of how we deal with situations comes from how and what we were taught as children."

My face told Dr. Thatcher that I wasn't thrilled with her answer.

"Would you like to talk about your mother?"

"No. Actually, yes. I've been thinking about taking a break from her. She's still hounding me about moving out with her. I'm dreading our next date. We haven't scheduled one yet, and I'm already dreading it."

Dr. Thatcher sat forward. "Because you are my patient and I care about what happens to you . . . If you're telling me that you need time out from your mother in order to sort out feelings, then do it for yourself."

Her response didn't make me feel any better about my decision. I really wanted a break from her as well. Considering the candidates, I chose to break away from Mother.

Dr. Thatcher's lips were moving. "Every Saturday in this . . . you can pretend . . . and you can say to me what . . . want to say to her. This room is . . . punching bag . . . the child within."

I nodded. The rest of the session was a blur.

~

For six months I did not call my mother. I sent her notes wishing her well, making up excuses that my work was hectic, or I was sick, or my classes were demanding. I was never a good liar. Saying I was sick in a note was enough to make myself really sick. So lying to my mother had in fact given me a solid excuse to miss several appointments with Dr. Thatcher.

But I couldn't stop thinking about Mother. It was safe to think about her, as long as I didn't have to see her. I thought about the time she took me to Woolworth's to buy gym clothes for me. She looked at the price tag. Then she counted the bills in her purse. I remember feeling the tug in my heart, wishing I were old enough to work and pay for the purchase. Why didn't the school issue gym clothes, since physical education was compulsory?

That day, Mother bought me two outfits. "You'll sweat in one, we'll wash it, hang it to dry while you wear the other one. We cannot afford three."

"That's all right, Mother," I said with gratitude, knowing that Mom would scrimp on food purchases the next few weeks. Instead of buying five pork chops that afternoon, she bought four to exclude herself. That night I felt too guilty to eat dinner so I told my mother that eating meat aggravates acne and that I wanted to become a vegetarian.

~

During those six months, I did call Molly routinely to check up on Mom. Molly told me how Mom showed her my notes and cards, how she bragged about my being a good daughter. The more Molly told me, the more I disliked myself.

It was also during those six months that Emily finally came for a visit. I felt resentful that she had not flown out sooner, but I remembered what Dr. Thatcher said: "Always wondering 'what if' is no way to live your life." After all, my wish was to see my sister. So excited about having her home, I cleaned every room in the apartment. If I were to analyze the situation, then I'd say her visit was most timely, because at least Mother would get to see one of her daughters. *Let's see how fast Mom will drive Emily crazy. Oh God, I can't believe I thought that. If only I could shut off my brain and stop this tug of war.*

To my disappointment, my sister announced prior to her flying out that she would be staying with her girlfriend. Upon arrival, her telephone message lacked her usual warmth.

"Hi, Ruby. I'm here, at Stacey's. I can only stay until Friday. Saw Mom this morning. Taking her to a movie and dinner later. Can we have lunch on Friday? Call me. Bye."

It was already Wednesday. Three days. *She whips into town, avoids me, has fun with Mom, while I've been torturing myself with guilt.*

Friday, Marilyn covered for me so I was able to drive out to Stonestown to meet Emily.

My stomach was in knots when my sister floated into the restaurant at one-thirty. She looked like a model for The Gap in her blue jeans, stretchy top, and an oversized white shirt worn unbuttoned. All my trepidations vanished when I saw her running over after spotting me. We hugged so hard her sunglasses fell from her head.

I ordered what I called the college girl meal—a cheeseburger with fries and a Coke.

"I'll just have a slice of pecan pie," Emily told the waiter. "I had to eat lunch with Mom," she explained to me.

I was annoyed again. *Stop it, Ruby. She's here to see Mom. Be thankful for that.*

"How's Mom? Does she look okay to you?"

"She looks great. Her place is nice." My sister drank her glass of water in one gulp.

"She doesn't like her roommate. Did she complain to you?"

"No. She didn't mention it. I met Molly and her husband. Nice couple."

"They're good people. Em, what did Mom say about me? I mean, did she ask about me?"

"She knows you're busy. She's got all the cards you've sent all lined up on her dresser."

"I should be ashamed of myself, Em, but I can't see her right now. I'm afraid I might blow up at her, and I don't want to put her through that."

"Ruby, I'm sorry. About not coming sooner. Are you mad at me?"

"No."

"No?"

"Not mad. Disappointed. But then, I wasn't telling you the truth when I said I had everything under control. I thought you would blame me for letting it happen in the first place—the Fifty-One-Fifty."

"No, Ruby. That never entered my mind."

"Then, I thought you were paying me back for what I did, you know, when I ran off to San—"

"No. No. Ruby, how can you think that?"

"I'm sorry, Em. For what I did that year. Maybe it's because I haven't forgiven myself, so I assume you haven't forgiven me either."

"Forgive? Forgive you? I couldn't help my big sister when she was . . ." Emily was crying.

"Em." I hugged her. "It's okay. Don't cry. It's all behind us now. Here, Em." I handed her some tissues.

"Do you know why I didn't jump on a plane when you called me about Mom months ago?" Emily dabbed her eyes. "Mom. In a psychiatric hospital. I couldn't face it. Then you told me she wasn't taking her medications and flipped out again. Ruby, I didn't want to see Mom like that." Emily took a sip of water from my glass. "I'm afraid of mental illness. There. I've said it. The thought that it might run in the family gives me the creeps. I was so thankful when you said you didn't need me out here."

"I was lying. I wanted your moral support, but I really thought you had lost respect for me, for not being more observant with Mom."

"Ruby, I thought you'd lost faith in me!" She let out a big sigh. "Even though I wasn't here in person, I was doing my best to be supportive—"

"I know, I know. I would have gone off the deep end myself if we didn't talk so much on the phone. You know what, Em? It was luck of the draw. If I were in Philadelphia and you were living here, Mom would have moved in with you. I know you would have dealt with the situation if you had to."

"Thanks for the vote of confidence, but remember I was always the little sister. I never had to take care of anyone. I've been feeling guilty about that. That's why I decided to stay with Stacey. She's also a little sister. We can commiserate with one another about stuff we had to hear, like 'Why can't you be more responsible like your sister?'"

"I know it's not all easy street being the baby of the family."

"Did I tell you Stacey's aunt went through an ordeal like Mom, but everyone in her family stood by her as if she had a physical ailment?"

"Wow, good for them. School doesn't prepare us for it. High

school Psychology is one thing, but seeing your own mother taken away is brutal. People can see that a broken leg needs to be repaired, but there's a stigma with mental illness. It's sad, isn't it, that some people walk around with damaged psyches and don't know it. But look who's talking—a woman who hasn't seen her mother in four months."

"Ruby. Confession. I moved three thousand miles away for good reasons. I had to, for my own sanity. Sure, Mom brags about her baby girl away at school, but I'd bet you if I lived here she would glom on to me. When you were away that year, she actually tagged along when I went out with friends. At first it was fun, she paid for everything. But that got weird, fast. We couldn't talk in front of her. Ooh, she was pissed when I told her my friends felt uncomfortable hanging out with someone's mother. She didn't talk to me for a month!"

"You never told me that."

"You had enough to deal with."

"Poor Mom, she had no friends. It's the saddest thing, to have no friends."

The waiter came over with our food. "More water?" he asked. We both nodded.

"Hey Big Sis, thanks for being brave when Mom needed you."

"Hey Little Sis, thanks for being here."

Our waiter brought over a pitcher of water. We drank a toast to our mother's health.

"Em, how about splitting a chocolate milkshake?"

"Okay." My sister had a twinkle in her eye just as when she was five, ordering a soda at a restaurant. "I remember my first milkshake and the plastic straw shaped like a pretzel. It was a strawberry milkshake. You made it for me."

"I made milkshakes? I don't remember that." *I really don't remember.*

"You sure did. You used a whole carton of ice cream, and we drank until our stomachs hurt."

"Hmm. How old were you, Em."

"Four, I think. I also remember the first time I ate candy. I was two."

"Wow, Little Sister. You can remember as far back as two? I remember our room in Hong Kong. Five people in one room. Talk about too close for comfort. But that's all. Can't remember much more than that. Isn't that weird? It's a blank prior to age seven."

~

After lunch, we walked a bit and talked some more before saying goodbye. I hated to see her go, but that night I thought about everything we had said to each other and fell sound asleep.

~

At work one afternoon, our chef asked me to look at a special request from a client. Chef Pierre was a real French chef, imported from Paris. He indulged me by letting me practice my French with him.

I was standing outside the kitchen waiting for him when I noticed the empty sacks in the bin. I picked up one to see what it was used for. The sack had the imprint 50 LB. CAPACITY in four-inch letters. Just as the day I had found the spiral notebook, seeing the sack brought back memories of an incident that happened when I was only nine years old.

~

It was a warm Saturday afternoon in June. Mother was preparing for a trip to the Laundromat.

"Mother, may I go with you?" I begged, in Chinese.

"Yes," she said with a stern voice.

She stuffed the dirty clothes in a huge Navy bag that a relative had given her: 50 LB. CAPACITY was imprinted on the canvas. A week's worth of dirty clothes, towels and bedding from a family of five was no light load. The bag bulged and she could hardly draw the string tight. I looked at the heavy bag and wondered how my mother could lift it.

My mother was a petite woman. "Height: five feet and zero inches; weight: ninety-five pounds." That was how the nurse at the clinic had described Mother at her first physical examination the week before. I was there to translate for her.

The Laundromat was eight blocks away and we walked. Mother gave me the box of detergent to carry. After walking two blocks, Mother already seemed tired. In the middle of the third block, she dropped the bag. The bag stood upright against a building and Mother began to fall. As I reached for her, the box of Tide slipped from my hand. Detergent spilled on the sidewalk. I caught Mother by the elbow while she braced herself on the bag. She leaned on the heavy sack for what seemed an eternity. Her face had lost all color and beads of sweat covered her forehead.

I couldn't speak, as if my brain had stopped functioning. The sun was beating down on us and I felt nauseated. When Mother finally stood up and took the bag into her arms, I was still dumbfounded. I picked up what was left of the box of detergent and followed her. My voice came back when we were two blocks from the Laundromat.

"I can carry it the rest of the way, Mama," I said in Chinese.

"You are not a slave. So don't ask me to treat you like one! Don't you know you will be doing this one day?"

"Why won't you let me help you?" I asked in silence. *"I won't be a slave. I just want to help you,"* I begged, without uttering a word.

That afternoon when all the clothes were out of the dryers and

Mother had folded them, she filled the canvas bag almost to the top. She then walked over to the vending machine and bought a plastic bag—that was the first time she'd paid for a bag. Mother put the last two stacks of clothes into the plastic bag and gave it to me to carry.

Walking home, she stopped and said to me, "Don't tell your father what happened. I don't want him to worry. Do you hear me?"

"Yes, Mama," I answered.

A block from home Mother put down the heavy bag and turned to me. I thought she had decided to let me carry it. She looked at me with tenderness. "I want you to get good grades and grow up to be somebody."

~

". . . Ruby." "*Bon jour, mademoiselle.*" Chef Pierre was calling me. He had a large platter in his hands.

"*Bon jour, Pierre. Ça va?*" I asked him.

"*Très bien, ma petite.*" Pierre put down the platter.

"Pierre, you rang?"

"*Oui.* Your client, Ruby. She telephoned me."

"Ugh. These clients. They're supposed to call me and not bother you."

"It's okay. But I want to tell you what she wanted, and you can charge her extra."

"Which client, Pierre?"

"Miss McKay. She says her mother, long ago, she made a *gelée.* No, Jell-O, a Jell-O mold, with chopped meat, and she wants me to make one."

"You mean an aspic? Is that what she wants, Pierre?" I had seen one in the movie, *Dinner at Eight.*

"*Oui.* In the shape of a fish." Pierre used his hands to show me how big the mold would be.

"Okay, Pierre."

"She tells me to write something on the mousse. You charge her extra."

"Sure. What does she want on it?"

"Happy Mother's Day to a Wonderful Mom!"

"Oh. I didn't know it was going to be a Mother's Day party. I thought it was a birthday party."

"*Ma petite*, Mother's Day is in six weeks."

I nodded. "Oh. *Au revoir*, Pierre."

~

Walking back to my office, I felt like a heel, if a woman can be called a heel. Here was this Ms. Greta McKay planning a big party for her mother, and I hadn't seen my mother in six months. Having thought about it all afternoon, I picked up the telephone to call her and arrange to take her out on Mother's Day. She sounded pleased. I was a nervous wreck just dialing the number. If one could measure guilt with a cup, then mine was running over.

Chapter 8

The Little People

"Dr. Thatcher, I'm going to see Mom after all, on Mother's Day."

"That's great, Ruby. Does this mean you're ready to re-establish contact?"

"Well. Let's see how I do on Mother's Day."

"One step at a time, Ruby. Your mother is probably very excited about seeing you."

"I suppose. Dr. Thatcher, I had a dream last night."

She picked up her pad and pen.

"I dreamed a few nights ago that Emily and I were hiking near a mountain. It was a gorgeous day. Clear blue sky. Green lake reflecting the lush growth. As we were about to head back to our campsite, we both heard a rumbling sound. We looked up and saw giant boulders slipping from their positions. In a domino effect, the boulders came tumbling down the mountain towards us. Emily and I were standing about ten feet apart from each other. The boulders crashed down in both directions, as if some evil power had directed them to aim for us individually. I ran to Emily and the two of us joined hands as we fled to lower ground."

"What happened after that, Ruby?"

"I woke up."

"Have you and Emily ever gone hiking together?"

"No, that's why it's so strange that in my dream, I created this beautiful landscape. It seemed so real."

"What do you think of when you see boulders?"

"Rocks. I like all kinds of rocks. I think of foundation, stability, solidness. Is that a word?"

"Most people think of family as being a foundation."

"Wow! You're right. But these boulders were chasing us and trying to hurt us."

"Yes, Ruby. Your family did hurt you and Emily and your brother."

"Isn't the mind a scary thing? To dream up something like that— boulders, and hiking, and Emily and I running in the same direction, but our brother nowhere in sight."

"Dreams make us see what we sometimes don't want to see when we're awake."

"Well, I'm definitely calling Emily tonight to tell her about this one."

~

That afternoon, I took down the two dolls from my bedroom shelf and wiped their faces with a damp towel. We bought the dolls when I was ten and Emily was four. As I straightened out their bonnets, which covered their bald heads from too many hair brushings, I remembered the day when Emily and I first saw them.

It was Christmastime. Our parents started celebrating Christmas after we came here from Hong Kong, two years before, because they wanted to give us what American children experienced. We also celebrated Chinese New Year's Day on the lunar calendar which usually comes around in February on the Christian calendar. One thing was certain: we always knew exactly what presents we would receive on both holidays. On Chinese New Year, we would get the traditional red envelope containing cash. Our parents gave us each a crisp ten-dollar bill, which was a lot of money in 1968.

For Christmas, to ensure our satisfaction, Mother would take us to the store, and we were to pick out the one thing we had wanted all year.

So, a week before Christmas, Mother, Emily and I went to the giant Woolworth's on Market and Powell to do just that. Our brother John stayed home, as usual. He had written on a piece of paper what he wanted and we were to get it for him. Mr. Robot.

The smell of popcorn and pizza filled the air as we walked through the glass doors. Eating pizza at Woolworth's was a treat. For ninety-nine cents each one of us got a piping hot slice of pizza and a cold soft drink. The pizza crust was thin, salty and crisp. It had become another tradition—to stand at the Woolworth's counter, eating pizza and watching the hotdog racks rotate.

That day I ate fast, so Emily and I could get down to the real business at the toy department.

"Wipe your hands," Mother said in Chinese.

Emily was still eating her double-scoop Strawberry Heaven on a cone, and Mother was still enjoying her pizza, but I was ready to shop.

"Mama, can we go ahead?" I asked in Chinese. "I'll make sure Emily finishes her ice cream."

"Go. Be careful. Watch your little sister."

Since it was crowded, I let Emily walk in front of me so I would not lose sight of her. She had her ice-cream cone in her right hand as she raced toward the escalator. A man wearing a tweed jacket and carrying a huge package with both hands was about to run into my little sister. I opened my mouth to call out Emily's name, but suddenly, she turned around to see if I was following. The man's elbow became a magnet for her scoop of strawberry ice cream. Emily and I both froze where we stood, watching the man, oblivious to the accident, and her scoop of Strawberry Heaven walk out the store. I forced Emily to eat the incriminating evidence—the empty cone. I felt like the ringleader in a James Cagney movie. "Let's scram," I told my little sister.

In the toy department, where the shelves were abundantly stocked for Christmas shoppers, I felt discouraged that perhaps I would not find anything suitable. After all, at the age of ten, I was no longer a child. Emily ran from aisle to aisle, pointing to the toys she wanted. "Stop running," I ordered her. "I'm supposed to watch you." She pulled a tea set and a necklace off the hooks.

"Put them back. You can pick one, just one," I reminded, in a softer voice.

My little sister obeyed me. We found a pyramid of Mr. Robots. Mother came around the corner. "There you are," she said. She took down a dozen Mr. Robots before settling for one. Our mother would never buy anything if the box was dented or scratched.

Emily was looking at the miniature cosmetic kits when I spotted the dolls at the end of the aisle. On a shelf sat a doll with short brown hair and round brown eyes. She wore a blue dress with a lace collar. Her mouth smiled sweetly. I wanted her. As I stood there thinking of a name for her, Emily came over and cooed, "She's pretty. I'm buying her." My sister was looking at the same doll. Emily was standing on tiptoe and taking the doll off the shelf. "She's pretty," she said again, and she walked off to find Mother. I stood there in shock.

Father had said many times, "Older siblings must dote on the younger ones; the younger ones must obey the older ones. These rules will ensure harmony." I have often wondered who made up the rules.

From where I stood, I heard Mother speaking to Emily. "She's lovely. How much is it?"

Knowing that I could not be so cruel as to take from my sister what she wanted, I looked at the other dolls. Then I saw another one. She had blue eyes and her hair was blonde. She wore a red dress. I think older siblings in every Chinese family know the meaning of 'the second choice.' But by the time we stood at the cashier's line, I had fallen in love with the doll in my arms. It didn't matter she was second choice. She was mine.

At home, we wrapped the dolls and Mr. Robot in Christmas paper and hid the boxes under our beds. Even though we had selected our own gifts, we were not allowed to play with them until Christmas Day. Every night before going to sleep, Emily and I pulled up the bedding to see if the boxes were really there, counting the days before Christmas. I wondered if John did the same.

It must be a phenomenon that all American children wake up early on December 25th. It was five in the morning when I heard my sister's pitter-patter on the cold floor. "Is it time yet?" she whispered.

Before I was able to answer, she was already pulling out our presents. What could I do but help her? Quietly we unwrapped the boxes, pulled out the cellophane windows and loosened the dolls' arms from the backboards. When we set the dolls side by side, I realized the only difference between them was the color of their hair and eyes. Their other features were identical. "They're sisters!" I exclaimed.

"My doll's name is Pebble," Emily announced. My sister was a big fan of *The Flintstones*. The Flintstones had named their baby, Pebbles (with an 's'). "What's your doll's name?" my sister asked me.

"Mimi. She's French."

"Is Pebble French too?" my little sister wanted to know.

"No. She's from Bedrock."

"Who's older?" Emily asked.

"Pebble is, but just by a few minutes. We found her first, remember?"

We both took our dolls in our arms, climbed back into bed, and pulled the blankets over ourselves, all four of us.

Pebble and Mimi became an extension of Emily and me and, in turn, we became the little parents. When Emily started school, we'd come home every day after class and talk to our little girls.

My sister spoke in her Pebble voice. "Mimi got on the giant slide today."

"Weren't you scared, Mimi?" I asked my little girl.

"No. I'm never scared," answered Mimi.

"You're brave!" cheered Pebble.

"Time for dinner," Emily announced. She had made spaghetti with her colorful rubber bands. After feeding the girls, we, the parents, would brush their hair, change their clothes, and tuck them in with good-night kisses.

Those days, we were a happy family.

~

One day, Father came home in a foul mood. He turned on the living room lamp, and found it broken. Mother was grocery shopping. John, Emily, and I, with Mimi, Pebble, and Mr. Robot, were all watching the *Yogi Bear Show*.

"John!" our father called out.

I knew what was about to happen. I took Emily and our girls into our room.

"I didn't do it," our brother cried. His voice trailed into the bathroom.

Then we heard Father's heavy footsteps following John's. "I didn't do it," our brother's voice pleaded. The door slammed shut. Emily and I tucked the girls into bed and we sat on the floor, covering our ears. But we couldn't cover the sounds of the bathroom door shaking as if Father were leaning his weight on it as he took his belt to John.

Later the whole apartment was quiet. We heard Father going into the kitchen. I thought my heart had stopped. Our brother's cry, *I didn't do it*, rang in my head. Emily took Pebble out of bed. "Pebble wants to talk to Mr. Robot," she said to me. I nodded.

"Wait, Emily. Take Mimi. She wants to go too."

My sister walked out with a doll under each arm. Afraid of what I would see in John's eyes, I stayed in our room. My little sister was brave. I was not.

CHAPTER 9

Who Takes the Blame?

Mrs. Nussbaum had fractured her ankle at her Senior Citizen Exercise Club. A neighbor had told me, so I went up to her floor and rang the doorbell. Mrs. Nussbaum took awhile getting to the door, but I could see she was happy to see me.

"Come in, Ruby."

"Hi Mrs. N, I'm on my way out, but I wanted to see how you were doing."

"This will teach me to wear proper shoes. I thought I could save a few dollars by wearing my slip-ons to exercise. I'll heal. Now that I'm hobbling around in a cast, I'll just get fatter and fatter."

"You're not fat."

"I'm fat all right. I used to weigh a hundred and two."

"Oh, that's way too thin," I said. "I know you have plenty of friends, Mrs. Nussbaum, but since I *am* in the building and I'm great at running errands, I want you to add me to the 'call list.' Please promise me you'll do that."

"You're a dear. I'm stocked for months. Old people like me are always prepared for disasters. Rashi needs his walks, but Olga and Ida, bless their hearts, volunteered to take over."

"Isn't there anything I can do?"

"There is one thing, Ruby. With this cast, and crutches, and now with the rain, I won't be going anywhere for awhile. Would it be all right if I kept your telephone number next to the phone, just in case?"

"Mrs. N, you can keep more than my home number. I'll give you my work and pager number, and I don't want you to hesitate using it because I can zip back here in no time."

"Thank you, Ruby. Now go on. I've kept you long enough. You'll be late."

"I always give myself plenty of time to get to my two o'clock appointment. Take care, Mrs. Nussbaum. I'll check on you later."

~

I was five minutes late for my appointment. Dr. Thatcher's office door was open and she was writing at her desk.

"Dr. Thatcher, sorry I'm late."

"Hello, Ruby."

"My neighbor, Mrs. Nussbaum, fractured her ankle. I was at the health food store trying to find something, a nutrient, something. But I couldn't find anything appropriate. I found products to help build healthy bones. But it's too late for that."

"You're very thoughtful, Ruby." She closed the door behind us and we took our seats.

"She's really thoughtful. I think she's the oldest tenant in the building."

Telling Dr. Thatcher about Mrs. Nussbaum turned into talking about my grandmother and my mother.

"I'm envious of my girlfriends who have 'cool' grandmothers. I used to fantasize about having one. I even made up a personality for her."

"What was she like, Ruby? Your imaginary grandmother."

"She was a cross between Myrna Loy and Katharine Hepburn. She would definitely bake cookies, plant flowers, and most of all she would talk straight talk. No bullshit. Like my friend Kristie's grandmother. She talked straight talk. She told Kristie about the birds and the bees. Kristie's mom would never talk about sex."

"Like your mother." Something was different about Dr. Thatcher. *What could it be?*

"Ruby?"

"Huh? Oh, no, my mother would never talk about sex."

Dr. Thatcher tilted her head. I realized what was different—she had rid the gray in her hair—the deep brown was lustrous.

I continued. "The day I came home from school and washed the blood from my panties, thinking that I had accidentally hurt myself from sitting on a rough wooden bench, Mother came into the bathroom with a sanitary napkin and belt rolled up in her palm. 'You poor thing. So young,' she said. 'I was hoping this wouldn't happen for another two years,' she added. I felt shame. While my Caucasian classmates talked about going to the Emporium with their mothers to buy starter bras, my mother was ashamed of me."

"She wasn't ashamed of you, Ruby. She was afraid for you, because you were becoming a woman."

Dr. Thatcher's words made me feel guilty about how I had judged Mother.

"Mom doesn't want me or Emily to ever get married."

"Has she said this?"

"Yes, a couple of years ago. Out of the blue she said, 'Marriage can only bring you pain. I don't want my daughters to feel pain.' "

We spent the rest of the session practicing how I would talk to Mother on Mother's Day.

"Okay, Ruby. I'm your mother. Ruby, I'm very unhappy at the board-and-care home. I really want you to move out with me." Dr. Thatcher smiled.

"Oh boy. Okay. Mom, tell me again why you're not happy. Let's find a solution."

"Good, Ruby," Dr. Thatcher cheered.

We practiced a few more scenarios.

~

That evening, feeling lonesome, I called Mrs. Nussbaum to ask if she wanted some company.

"Come on up, dear. A fractured ankle doesn't stop me from cooking. I made matzo ball soup and chicken pot pies. Do you like matzo ball soup?"

"I've never had it."

"Well, come up and find out for yourself."

"Okay, I'll be there in ten minutes."

First, I went down the block to get Mrs. Nussbaum some flowers. When I walked into Mrs. Nussbaum's apartment, the heavenly smell of chicken pot pie filled the air. I took a big whiff. Rashi, with his cute little legs, came running to greet me.

"Mrs. Nussbaum, I'll put these in water for you. They're Orlando roses."

"My goodness. Thank you, Ruby. Mr. Nussbaum, bless his heart, used to bring home flowers."

Rashi was sniffing my shoes.

"Rashi, you said hello already, now go and watch television. Be a good boy."

Rashi always obeyed her orders. He waddled off to the living room.

"How could I have not noticed this decorated hallway the last time I was here? I must have been in a fog. Remember that horrible day when . . . ?"

"You were still in shock. I was so worried about you that day. That's why I had left my door cracked, to listen for the elevator."

"You're so kind." There was a picture of a man resembling Ernest Borgnine in an antique frame mounted over the hallway table. "Is this Mr. Nussbaum?"

"Yes. That's my Herman. I put him there so that he sees me coming and going." Mrs. Nussbaum stopped to touch the picture.

There was another mounted photograph, in a small hand-carved wooden frame, of a little girl. From the style of the automobile in the background, I would guess this picture had been taken a long time ago.

"Is this you, Mrs. Nussbaum? How old were you?"

"No, dear. That's our darling, Isabel. Our only baby. Rheumatic fever took her from us when she was seven. I put her here so that she can also see me coming and going."

I felt all choked up at Mrs. Nussbaum's words. I wanted to say the right thing, but didn't know what to say. Mother once said that for a parent to bury a child is the worst thing that can happen to a person.

"Come into the kitchen, Ruby. It's nice and warm there."

Over matzo ball soup and chicken pot pie, Mrs. Nussbaum told me about her life. In New York, she and Mr. Nussbaum first had a small corner store which turned into a bigger store which then turned into six stores. Ten years ago, they sold their business and moved to California to help Mr. Nussbaum's brother open up a bagel/deli shop. Mr. Nussbaum passed away five years ago and Mrs. Nussbaum adopted Rashi from the SPCA to keep her company.

"I have two very dear friends, we're like sisters. But I miss Herman so much. He was a perfect darling. So was our Isabel." Mrs.

Nussbaum ladled more soup into my bowl. "Olga and Ida. I'm the oldest, Ida the youngest. We are the three old lady musketeers. All of us widows. But they have grandchildren." Mrs. Nussbaum was silent for awhile.

"Mrs. Nussbaum, my grandmother died when my mother was only seven."

"I know, dear. The poor darling. That's why she's so lonesome and angry. Everybody needs a mother at that age."

"I know it's wrong, but I used to blame Grandmother Grace for what happened to Mother. Mom was in an orphanage for six years during the war. She wouldn't have been sent there if Grandmother had not died."

"You must not blame the dead," said Mrs. Nussbaum.

I felt horribly ashamed at myself for having said that to Mrs. Nussbaum because she could have been a grandmother too if her daughter was alive.

"Let me tell you about our little Isabel. She was a good little girl, quiet, curious, and the image of her father. Mr. Nussbaum doted on her. That year, she had the flu but recovered quickly. Around Thanksgiving, we thought she was getting chicken pox because half a dozen of her little friends in school had come down with it. She was excited about going on the train to see her *bubbe*."

"*Bubbe,* Mrs. Nussbaum?"

"Yiddish for grandmother. Herman's mother."

"Oh."

"The weekend of our big trip, Isabel ran a fever. I stayed home with her and Mr. Nussbaum went to visit his family. Isabel's temperature kept climbing so I sent for the doctor. Scarlet fever turned into rheumatic fever. My poor baby. Our little Isabel. She would have been fifty-six this year."

Mrs. Nussbaum's tears fell into her soup. I walked over to her side of the table to give her a hug. She kissed my head and stroked my hair.

"Your dinner is getting cold, darling. I'm all right."

Rashi had entered the kitchen and was by Mrs. Nussbaum's feet. She let him stay.

"Ruby, don't blame your grandmother or your mother. Life gives us and robs us. Mr. Nussbaum and I blamed ourselves when our little darling died. That first year, we spoke only a few words between us. I didn't know if he was blaming me for calling the doctor too late and he didn't know if I was blaming him for having gone to his family that week. We mourned for our little girl in silence.

"Then one day, Mr. Nussbaum came home with that picture frame. He picked out the most recent picture we had of Isabel and wrote 'We love you always' on the back and framed it. We cried that day. We cried together. He took my hand into his, and said to me, 'Mama, we'll always have each other. Isabel will watch over us.' Now Ruby, they're both watching over me."

Tears welled up in my eyes. A splitting headache usually accompanied crying, but not that night in Mrs. Nussbaum's kitchen. They were tears of sorrow and sympathy, not tears of anger.

~

Later at home, I thought about what Mrs. Nussbaum had said to me. I was full of venom as a girl. I had blamed my grandmother for dying and leaving my mother orphaned. I had blamed my mother for so many things, including the death of my goldfish when I was sixteen.

I had won a goldfish at the Chinese New Year's Festival. His name was Charlie. I had named him after Charlie Brown. Charlie's bowl, or home I should say, was on the table in the living room. I had placed his bowl next to the *TV Guide*, behind Mother's large coffee-table book of Europe. Coming home from school every day, I fed him and watched him swim.

Two months later, on a Friday afternoon as I entered our apartment, I felt something was wrong. I walked over to Charlie's bowl. He was belly-up. He was dead.

Mother was in the kitchen. In my mind I could still hear her screaming at Father the night before for cavorting with his friends and not coming home until eleven at night. She killed Charlie, I told myself. She killed him with her screeching. My only pet, and she killed him.

I sat on the sofa. I thought about how happy I was that morning in Women's Literature class. We were reading *The Little Foxes*, a play by Lillian Hellman. Mrs. Lewis had chosen me to read the part of Regina Giddens. Regina was the vicious woman who destroyed everyone around her because she wanted wealth and social position. I felt powerful reading her lines.

"Ruby," my mother was calling from the kitchen.

I ignored her.

"Ruby, I bought you some more Oscar Mayer," she said with sweetness in her voice.

I couldn't stand it anymore. Why couldn't she talk that way to Father? I stormed into the kitchen.

She was pouring a glass of milk for me. She couldn't have been pouring it for herself. She didn't drink milk.

"Don't do anything for me," I screamed at her. "I hate people waiting on me hand and foot. Go wait on your husband. Wait on yourself, but don't do it to me."

My mother stood there in silence.

"You killed my fish with your voice," I accused her.

"Your fish?"

"Yes, Charlie. You killed him." Just as Regina Giddens would have done, I picked up the glass of milk and smashed it in the sink. Glass shattered on the counter and milk splashed against the wall.

I turned around. Mother was still quiet. I wanted to shake her. "I know you work hard in school," she finally said in a soft voice. "You don't know anything! You know fuck about nothing."

Her face was white and she lowered her eyes. I stormed out of the kitchen, almost knocking her down.

Reaching my bedroom, I slammed the door with such force that the entire apartment shook. I wanted to put my fist through the wall. Almost immediately, I heard the water running from the kitchen faucet. I pictured her brushing broken glass into the trash can and wiping milk from the wall. Then I turned up the radio and drowned out the noise in my head.

CHAPTER 10

They'll Cheat You Blind

Who would have believed that I was celebrating my fourth anniversary at the St. Mark? I would never forget the day of the interview with Chad Hamilton. He greeted me at the Personnel Office which was on the second floor of the hotel. When we got off the elevator on the catering floor, he started to walk briskly down the long hallway. I picked up my step and followed. Upon reaching his office, he turned around, saw me at the doorway, gave me a big smile and asked me to sit down.

"Ruby Lin, I'm impressed. I usually lose the applicant halfway down the hall. I have this philosophy: If you can't scope out the situation and pick up your heels to meet the moment, then you're not catering material. Every client is a VIP as far as I'm concerned and I like to see my team go that extra mile."

"As the Italians would say '*Chi che non lavora, non mangia.*' He who doesn't work doesn't eat." I had my spiel. "Chad, I always give a hundred-and-ten percent on the job. I have strong work ethics. My father taught me that. He's not Italian, but the Chinese people have great fortitude."

"Well, I like a young person with confidence. Let me tell you what I want. I need someone who has the energy to handle the telephone and paperwork during office hours and still has the stamina to oversee evening events. Many fund-raisers are held during the week. You'll get Saturdays off. We have other managers to handle weddings. Sundays? It all depends. I need someone who can be flexible since the evening events are sporadic."

I leaned forward in my chair. "It sounds like a wonderful position. I'm very interested. Chad, here's my proposal. Hire me for a week. You won't regret it. What can you lose? If I don't work out, you'll have lost only one week and you can offer the job to another candidate."

Chad stood up from behind his desk and extended his hand. "One week, Ruby. Can you report to work tomorrow?"

"Yes. Thank you so much." My heart was racing and I thought I had struck gold.

~

"Dr. Thatcher, it seemed so easy landing the job four years ago. It felt like I was auditioning for a part and I got it. When I'm at work, the day goes by fast. But I'm so unhappy. I don't know when I started hating it so much."

"What's Chad like to work for, Ruby?"

"He gives me headaches. He gives everyone in the office headaches. You know the type. He asks how you are, but you know he doesn't care to hear your answer. He always has a great idea for a VIP client, but puts the pressure on us to transform idea into extra work, and always at a moment's notice. He makes himself look good with the clients, but we have to break our backs."

"Can you and the other managers ask him to communicate his ideas in a timely manner?"

"That would be like saying to him 'You're a terrible communicator.' He's the type who looks at you like *you're* the stupid one."

"Ruby. Explain to him that if he wants 'a job well done,' he must give you a reasonable amount of time. Appeal to his sense of client satisfaction."

"The problem is that I've been doing 'a job well done' all these years in spite of his last minute orders. How can I ask him to change his ways?"

"You cannot change people, Ruby. Perhaps changing the way *you* respond to him will be a good start."

Suddenly I felt tired. "I put up a facade of a confident woman, but I'm really not. I mean I'm great with coworkers and clients, but with Chad, I can never be witty enough when he's condescending."

"There are other ways to handle difficult people, Ruby. Don't forget that you're an adult who deserves respect from people at work or anywhere else for that matter; you're not the little girl afraid to speak up for herself with her father."

"I wish that little girl would go away."

"Don't send her away. I like her. Listen to her, Ruby. Get to know her."

"Father used to tell us to strive to be 'the best.' And when we were the best, whether it was head of the class or top employee, he would always name someone else who could do better. 'Your cousin is going to Stanford' or 'so and so is making eighty K a year.'

"And I can never forgive him, Dr. Thatcher. Not because of anything he has done to me personally, but because he introduced violence to the family. I can never forgive him for that. As soon as Father realized John was too big to be pushed around, he stopped beating him. Mother became his only prey. He used to beat Mother as if he were beating a rival gang member. What made it even more repulsive were the episodes when she would not let him leave the house. She would hide his shoes and slippers. Sometimes she would beg at the door, beg him not to leave. I wanted him to leave, leave for good."

"Your father had no right harming your mother, Ruby. Your mother wanted attention from him, even when the attention came in the form of violence. She didn't know how to reject abuse. Perhaps she had experienced violence long before marrying your father. She took whatever form of attention he was willing to give her."

"I used to despise her for allowing him to strike her."

"I'm sorry you had to grow up in such madness. I know at times you want to block it all out. But those are the times when you need to take care of the little girl inside, the little girl who felt helpless and scared."

I nodded.

"Do you ever see your father, Ruby?"

I shook my head. "The last time I saw him was at Emily's graduation. I have no desire of seeing him. Emily says he does ask about me and she tells him how I'm doing."

~

That afternoon after leaving Dr. Thatcher's office, my head was swimming with voices. Wasn't it enough that I would have to prepare for my reunion with Mother? Did I have to analyze my feelings for Father too? *Psychotherapy is for the birds*, I told myself. *But birds can fly*, I also told myself.

Of course it was like someone asking me not to think of a pink elephant. That evening the more I told myself not to think about Father, the more I found myself thinking about him. I thought about the many times he was late for our birthdays and other special occasions. I thought about his golden advice: "Work hard." He said,

"Work hard and you will be rewarded." I thought about his other golden advice: "Don't let anyone cheat you." Those words rang in my head.

~

I was eleven years old. It was a Saturday morning and I found out that Father had chosen me to translate for him at the auto dealer. He could have taken an older niece or nephew but he chose me to do the job. I was so proud.

Mother said Father worked harder than anyone else—that's how we were able to buy our first family car. She also said when Father was my age, he had already started working in a factory in Hong Kong.

This year will be special, I thought, as my father and I walked out the door. We'll have a station wagon like the one in *The Brady Bunch*.

The bus ride with Father to the auto shop was a quiet one. Father and I did not talk. In our family, children were not allowed to chat with adults. The adults know what is good for children and the children obey—this was a code we had lived by. During the bus ride I did not look at Father, for I imagined he was embarrassed that a child, even though his oldest child, would have to speak English for him.

We stepped off the bus at Van Ness Avenue where Chevrolet, Lincoln-Mercury, and other names lined the street. Father knew he wanted a Dodge.

"Get a Dodge; they're reliable cars," he had heard from coworkers.

I liked the sound of the word 'Dodge.' I thought of Dodge City, where Marshall Dillon lived, and fantasized that I was Miss Kitty. And now we were about to buy a car with the same name as the town under Marshall Dillon's protection. This must be an omen that we would have a good car.

We walked through the wide entrance of the Dodge dealership

and saw the shiny new cars. These cars were not just parked on the floor; they were displayed like beauty contestants.

Three salesmen were huddling in front of a desk. The one in the gray suit broke off the conversation and walked toward us.

"Good morning, folks. Nice day to buy a car," he said with a handsome smile.

It is a nice day to buy a car, I silently agreed with him. His name badge said Jim.

"Good morning, sir," Father replied in English. "I want buy Dodge."

My face felt hot when I heard the second sentence ringing in my head. *"I want to buy, to buy, Father,"* I corrected him in my mind.

"Well, you've come to the right place," said Jim. He guided us through two floors of cars. When Father saw the tan station wagon with the wooden side paneling, he slowed down. This was the one he wanted. I knew because it looked exactly like the one his friend had bought.

"Pretend we don't see anything we like," Father told me in Chinese. "He'll cheat us if he knows he has what we want." Jim showed us a dozen more cars. "The station wagon," Father said in English, not looking at the man. "How much?"

"Let's go into my office and talk," Jim said with a smile. How did he know which station wagon Father was referring to? We saw at least four of them. All that pretending, and the man knew which station wagon. Games. This must be a game for men.

"Well, you have chosen one of the best buys. We got the shipment at a great price, and we're passing the savings on to our customers." I translated this to Father.

"Saaw!" Father grunted in Chinese. The word he uttered means stupid; ridiculous. "Does he think I'm a fool?" Father asked me in Chinese, not expecting an answer.

My palms were sweaty and my face felt hot again. Jim must have sensed the meaning of Father's words for he did not wait for me to translate.

"Well, tell your father I like him. This is what I'll do." He wrote the figure on a piece of scratch paper and showed it to Father.

Father took the paper and leaned back in his chair like a poker player. "Too much," he said in clear English this time. At that moment, he reminded me of the actor Paul Newman in *The Long, Hot Summer*. He took the pen off Jim's desk, scribbled $4,700 on the other side of the paper and shoved it back across the desk.

"Oh, no! My boss would fire me," said Jim. The two men laughed. "Tell you what, folks. This is my final offer. You're getting a great car." Another piece of paper came across the desk. Father looked at it.

"Ask him to take off several hundred dollars," he said in Chinese.

I sat forward impressively and asked Jim, "Can you take off a couple hundred dollars?"

Jim tapped his pencil as he thought it over.

"Well, like I said, I like you folks, I'll do it. The car is yours." Half an hour later, Father drove the station wagon out of the showroom, with me sitting in the backseat. Children never sit in the front seat. I saw my father drive for the first time. His grip on the steering wheel was tight. I helped him watch for traffic lights and listen for fire engines and ambulances. I saw his face in the rearview mirror. He wasn't nervous; he was angry. I quickly turned my head when he checked the rearview. I didn't want him to know that I was looking at him. For a daughter to look at a father was improper. Mother had taught me that. She said a grown daughter should never look at a father and that I was grown.

There were long minutes of uncomfortable silence before he spoke.

"He cheated us. I told you he would. This car is not worth that much money. I told you to speak up. You cannot go through life not speaking up. People will cheat you blind. I wanted him to come down seven or eight hundred dollars, not two hundred."

I looked out the window, pretending his words did not hurt me, wiping the tears with my sleeve. He should have taken someone smarter for this job. I failed him. I had misused the phrase "a couple." I should have said "several." Father asked me to translate several hundred dollars, not a couple hundred. What I hadn't realized that day was that *he* should have spoken up himself. Of course even if I had thought of it, I would have been too scared to say so. A good daughter would never tell a father he was wrong.

~

To this day, I still find myself questioning the word "couple" when a client orders something. I always end up asking, "You want two?"

No matter what Dr. Thatcher says, I know I can never forgive him. For using me that day and blaming me. For everything he has done to Mother and John. No, I cannot forgive him.

CHAPTER 11

The Morning Of

picked up Mother on Mother's Day and took her to a fancy Chinese restaurant on Clement Street. This area had become a second Chinatown, with restaurants, grocery stores, vegetable stands, and fish markets.

We were both nervous, each taking turns commenting on the bustle of Clement Street. We must have drunk six cups of tea between us before the appetizer came. After eating some green onion pancakes, I felt more at ease.

"So, Mom, what did you do today?"

"I went out for a walk. I watched *Perry Mason.*"

"What a great show. I'm glad they're showing reruns."

"He's a smart lawyer," said Mother.

"Yes, he is."

"Ruby, this is an expensive place. Too expensive."

"Mother's Day only comes once a year."

"Why don't you save your money and move out with me?"

I was ready for that. *Just the way I had rehearsed it.*

"Mom, I want you to be happy. That's the most important thing. So, let's find a solution to make that happen." *That sounded good.*

"So when are we moving out?"

Oh, oh, that wasn't in the rehearsal.

"Mom, can we talk about it next week?"

"Next week? I didn't ask you to wait a week, not a day, when you came home from—"

"Mom, please. Please don't talk about that. It's not fair to bring that up," I pleaded.

"I was there for you. Your sister and I were there for you." Mother was hitting below the belt. And it was working.

"Mom, let's eat dinner. Okay? I'll think it over. I promise. Okay?" She nodded.

I had lost my appetite, but I ate anyway.

I drove her home, said good night, wished her a Happy Mother's Day and that was that.

~

A six-day wait to talk to Dr. Thatcher would have been torture. I called her on Tuesday and she gave me an appointment the following evening. Walking down Vallejo Street, I thought about how the bistros and *ristorantes* on Union Street must have been packed with tourists. It was quiet on Vallejo—so quiet I could hear birds chirping, as if to say, "The fog has rolled in. Don't catch cold tonight." Even the bougainvillea in front of Dr. Thatcher's building seemed to be hiding from the chill.

Warmth met me as soon as I opened the front door. In the waiting room I picked up a *Today's Women*. The first page was an ad for a sleep aid. Noise from the kitchen startled me. Then I heard the sound of dishes being put away. A minute later, I heard Dr. Thatcher's familiar footsteps. She peered around the doorway.

"Hello, Ruby," she said with a smile.

I smelled a soft scent of perfume. *Hmm, I wonder if she has a date later.*

The heater in her office was on.

"Dr. Thatcher, you won't believe what I've done."

"What is it, Ruby?"

"I told Mom I would think it over, moving out with her."

"Were you being honest with her? About thinking it over?"

"Yes, I'm afraid."

"Why are you afraid?"

"There's something I haven't told you, Dr. Thatcher. Something that happened when I was in the sixth grade."

"Do you want to tell me now?"

"Yes. It might take up the whole session. It's a biggie."

Dr. Thatcher nodded and smiled at me.

I looked at the tiny digital clock: 7:02. "Dr. Thatcher, this happened seventeen years ago. One morning while running across the street to get doughnuts for me, my mother was hit by a car. She had lost so much blood, we almost lost her. Her back was broken in six different places. . . . If I had seen her lying there . . . then she wouldn't have lost so much. . . ."

I told Dr. Thatcher the whole story—how my carelessness cost my mother dearly—how Ben, the parking attendant, had saved her.

Dr. Thatcher leaned forward in her chair. "Ruby, why haven't you told me about this before? This was a major trauma in your life."

"I don't know. Lately, with Mother wanting to move out with me again, I'm getting these flashbacks about that day, about that summer."

"Ruby, I think you know what I'm going to say. I'll say it anyway. The little girl cannot be blamed for what had happened to your mother. No one should be blamed. It was an accident. A horrible accident. You'll need to say it to yourself. The little girl is not to be blamed." Dr. Thatcher's earrings jingled as she shook her head to emphasize "not to be."

I looked down at my hands.

"What are you thinking of, Ruby?"

I looked up at her gentle smile. "All these years, the sight of doughnuts makes me sick."

"We know why. The little girl was blaming herself. It's okay to let go of the guilt, Ruby. It's up to you to tell her that."

I took a deep breath. Feeling like a prisoner released after seventeen years, I wanted to jump out of my chair and hug Dr. Thatcher. But I didn't. I showed my respect and admiration for her by smiling as the tears rolled down my face.

CHAPTER 12

Joan of the Black-and-White Movies

Mother had grown tired of waiting for me to give her a response. She had asked Molly's daughter to help her find a studio. I felt relieved that I didn't have to tell her 'no,' but also guilty that someone else's daughter had to help her look through want ads.

And so I thought my sins were forgiven when Mrs. McKenzie invited me to her ball to raise money for Children's Hospital. She was my favorite client, the one who called me "Tall Blonde."

The ball was held at the McKenzie mansion in St. Francis Wood, the neighborhood that did not have apartment buildings, only multimillion-dollar homes. There was just one word to describe the evening. Opulent. I wore my deep red crushed-velvet bustier gown and the Swarovski earrings that Emily sent me for my last birthday. I felt like Eliza Doolittle, timid without her escort. I watched couples dance. I felt awkward standing by myself. Then a man appeared. A middle-aged distinguished-looking man who could have passed as

Robert Conrad's double. Robert Conrad was Federal Agent James West in the television show *Wild Wild West* in the 70s. No one else looked as good as he did in tight pants and a bolero jacket.

"Good evening, I'm Gil Taylor. Mrs. McKenzie asked me to introduce myself."

"Hello, I'm Ruby Lin."

"I know. Are you having a good time, 'Tall Blonde'?"

"Oh. Mrs. McKenzie told you about that?" I felt the blush coming on.

"She tells me everything. I'm her accountant."

"Oh." *You already said that,* I scolded myself in silence. Shyness took over. "It's a lovely party. But I do have to go to work in the morning. I think I'll call it an evening."

"You can't do that. You've just arrived. I have strict orders from Mrs. McKenzie to persuade you to stay."

"Did she really?"

"Of course. And I want you to stay. One dance, Ruby Lin, and I'll let you go."

"All right, but don't get upset if I step on your toes. I haven't danced in years." I had heard that in a movie.

After three dances, I found myself mesmerized by his voice, his looks, his charm.

"Look at the time, Gil. I need my sleep. Thank you for a wonderful time."

"May I call you, Ruby?"

I would have been disappointed if you hadn't asked.

"Yes, I'd like that. The St. Mark is in the phone book."

"I know. Good night."

"Good night, Gil." *I'm glad I wore this dress after all.*

~

It took me eight weeks and five days to wake up to the fact that he was a liar.

That first week of courtship conversations, both of us dreaded saying goodbye every time we parted. My heart beat a little faster when he took my hand into his and said, "I want to spend more time with you." I felt excited over the idea. I was more excited over the fact that he would see me in my many glories. Surely he would fall deeper in love when he saw my strong points: how I fit in at any intellectual gathering, and how I earned admiration from peers. That enchanted evening was two months ago.

Why isn't he here, spending a whole day with me? Saturday dinner and a roll between the sheets is his idea of spending more time with me? He couldn't seem to say 'yes' to any of my ideas of spending more time with each other. "I can ask a coworker to fill in for me on Sunday and we can go away somewhere," I had proposed.

"No, honey. Let's not plan so far ahead. I'll call you during the week, okay?" he said on my answering machine.

Joan Crawford, my heroine from black-and-white movies, would not find that agreeable. I know how she would have handled the situation. If this were a black-and-white movie, the scene would open with a close-up of the clock on the mantel chiming six times. A second later the doorbell rings. Joan puts down her cigarette, gets up from the sofa and slowly walks to the door. As the man reaches for the doorbell again, the door swings open. He is tall, broad shouldered, and handsome. He looks dapper in the sports jacket that she has given him. When he enters, he smiles, as if to say that he is pleased to see her. She has chosen "The Dress"—a tailored, long-sleeved black dress—the kind of dress a woman would wear to a funeral in the morning and then to a cocktail party that night. Instead of greeting him with the expected lingering kiss, she gives him a peck on the lower lip that leaves him still puckering as she resumes her place on the sofa. He awaits her invitation to sit beside her, but she does not grant him the courtesy. She takes a long drag from the cigarette, tilts her head back to blow out the smoke ring and extinguishes the cigarette by slowly grinding it in the ashtray. He should have known that this is the cue for the kiss-off scene.

"You're afraid," she starts. "You're afraid of me, aren't you? You were scared to approach me but you did. And now you're afraid. You ask yourself, 'What did I do to deserve her? I wasn't expecting to run into a woman like her. Yet here she is. If she is a great woman, then I'll have to be a great man. Am I a great man?' "

As she delivers this well-rehearsed speech, he is still standing. Feeling unprepared for this conversation, he slips his hand into his pocket and composes himself against the mantel.

"Oh yes, you're afraid," she continues. "So afraid you can't even think about it. It's too frightening to think that maybe you got lucky. To be loved by a woman like me is the kind of luck that a man can only dream of." As she delivers that last line, she walks toward the front door and signals him to leave. All this time, he is speechless. As he steps outside onto the doormat, she slams the door shut before he can collect his wits. So there he stands for a minute, looking bewildered and feeling foolish.

What a triumphant scene for Joan! He got off easy. She could have been drinking when he arrived. If she had been, he would have received a glass of scotch flung in his face before slinking out.

I played that scene in my head all that afternoon. Dr. Thatcher was on vacation for two weeks and my Saturdays were free. Six o'clock finally came, but I didn't have the advantage of playing out the scene in my living room. The man had asked me to meet him at a restaurant. I was punctual. Joan was always on time for a performance. Not only was the man late, he didn't even dress appropriately for the part. He wore a drab shirt without a jacket. I managed to restrain myself through the greeting and ordering of our meal.

The scene began. I had the first line. "So, let me ask you something. Is a tumble once a week your idea of a relationship?" Joan was always direct.

He took a sip of water from his glass. He smiled nervously and reached across the table for my hand. I kept both hands in my lap. Sensing that the conversation required his sharper skills, he withdrew his hand. "I just don't like to be rushed into anything," he explained. "But you must know by now that I save Saturday nights for you. I save the best for you. And I'll be able to free up more time in a few months. So, why don't we plan a mini-vacation. Where would you like to go, somewhere where there's a lot of beach?"

I looked at him as I would at something disgusting. He nervously took another sip of water. It was my turn to speak (I could hear Joan's voice in my head). "I'm so sorry that you feel rushed. I had no idea we moved at different speeds. Forgive me."

He raised an eyebrow at my response, and he was about to interject, but I didn't give him a chance to steal my lines.

"We move at different speeds and in different directions and we are obviously not compatible. I would love to slow down for you, but I can't. Life's too short. Why waste any more time? As a matter of fact, why waste time having dinner together? You won't mind canceling my meal, will you?"

I reached across the table to give him a fake kiss in the air, grabbed my purse and walked out. He did exactly what I thought he would do. He followed me.

"Can't we have a quiet dinner and talk about this?" he said while squeezing my arm.

I shook myself free.

"Don't let this upset you. Go back before your dinner gets cold," I replied.

"But I didn't plan on spending the night by myself," he muttered. As he stepped toward me, Joan possessed me and I dug my high heel into his right shoe. He bit his lip and I saw his eyes water.

"Oh, I'm so sorry. That must have hurt. I'd better go before I step on something else. I can be so clumsy," I apologized. I was really apologizing to myself. How could I have given my heart so easily?

I went home, unplugged the phone and threw away the black skimpy idea of a gift he had given me a month earlier. Joan would have had a couple of scotches, and she would not have cried. But this was not the movies. I wept like a teenage girl who has found out that the boy she loves doesn't love her. How did I become such a gullible person? Deceitfulness was not a quality which I sought in a man. How could my choices be so wrong? I drank two bottles of Pepsi on the rocks and made a folder for all the cards he had sent. I then filed him in the bottom drawer in the closet along with the other losers.

That was the last time I let some man choose me. *I will do the choosing from now on—good or bad—at least they'll be my choices.*

CHAPTER 13

Tired of Remembering

The lyrics to the Earth, Wind & Fire song *September* were in my head that Saturday morning. *Somewhere out there is a man who is sensitive enough to understand me and strong enough to let me be me.*

"Dr. Thatcher, I've been thinking about placing a personal ad."

"For?"

"To meet guys. I don't have time to join clubs and I don't feel comfortable in sports bars."

"Are you going to use *The Bay Guardian?*"

"No. I like the ads in *Savvy*—the trendy magazine for young professionals."

"What would you say in the ad, Ruby?"

"I know what I'm *not* going to say. I'm not going to put down that I'm Asian. I don't want men answering my ad because they have stereotypes about the submissive Asian woman."

"What about men who don't have stereotypes but prefer to date Asians? Wouldn't you be disqualifying yourself by not stating you're Asian?"

"That's just it. I don't want to date any man who would dismiss me or prefer me because of my skin color. It's all so ridiculous. Before I became an American citizen, I was a British subject because I was born in Hong Kong. I wasn't an English citizen, but a subject. What does it matter where we're born or what we look like on the outside?" I caught myself getting irritable. "Of course, if I like their letters, I'll tell them I'm Chinese-American."

"Do you know anyone who's had success with personal ads?"

"Yes. I have a girlfriend who met a great guy that way. They've been together for three years. I wouldn't be surprised if they get married sometime soon. You might not believe this, but my mom almost went that route. Well, it was really her grandmother who sent Mom's photo to these men in America. My mom and her grandmother were living in Hong Kong. Mom said she got marriage proposals in the mail! But she didn't want to go to America and leave her grandmother. She was only eighteen. She told her grandmother she wanted to marry for love. The irony. She wanted love, and look what she got instead."

"Going off to a foreign land and marrying a complete stranger . . ." Dr. Thatcher sighed. "That would have been very risky."

"Yes. Who knows if those men were lying in their letters? Who knows if they were decent at all? I'm glad she didn't listen to her grandmother."

"How is your mom, Ruby?"

"She seems content in her studio apartment. And she's really going to her doctor's appointments even though she still won't take advantage of psychotherapy. She's also going to the pharmacy to get her prescriptions refilled."

"I'm glad it's working out, Ruby."

"One thing that's not working out is her constant criticism and overwhelming negativity. I don't enjoy being around her. I think she's angry with me that I didn't choose to move out with her."

"Are you practicing your new communication skills?"

"Yes. But she doesn't know how hard I'm trying."

"*You* know, Ruby. That's what counts."

"The other day at lunch, she complained about the buses, the neighbor across her backyard, the landlord, and the bank teller. And that was before the appetizers came."

"Perhaps she's frustrated with her new life. If she doesn't have any friends, then she depends on you and Emily to be good listeners, and I know that can be a tall order."

"I'm confused, Dr. Thatcher. All this looking at the past makes me confused. I never know whether I'm irritated by what she's doing at the present or it's my unwillingness to forgive her for something she did a long time ago."

"Try to separate the hurt of the past from those of the present. I know it's hard to do. But you can do it. I know you can."

"I'm not making much progress with these sessions, am I?"

"Don't say that, Ruby. Remember, two steps forward and sometimes one step back."

We spent the rest of the session talking about how old pains get buried in our psyche and new pains trigger the old ones to surface.

~

The following Monday at work, I met a new client. Marcus Robinson was the coordinator for the Mayors' Conference.

"Mr. Robinson, please have a seat."

"Please call me Marcus," he said in a firm, yet friendly voice.

"Marcus, you can be sure that the Catering Department will do a top-notch job for you. We have a wall full of letters from appreciative clients. Even the Queen raved about our services."

"Ruby, you don't have to sell me. I'm just here to acquaint myself with the layout of all the meeting rooms. I have to know where everything is before I brief my staff."

"Well, Marcus, here are some floor plans that you can give to your staff. See how detailed they are? They even show where the electric outlets are located."

"Thank you."

"Why don't we look at some of the meeting rooms and the grand ballroom. The ante-ballroom—or the baby ballroom, as we call it—is occupied right now."

While watching Marcus go in and out of each room, I couldn't take my eyes off him. I knew that face—a brown face with warm gentle eyes. I recalled that posture—a heavyweight in his forties but light on his feet if he had to run. In the grand ballroom, he stood in front of the stage, as if to imagine a politician delivering a speech. Then he turned around, and said, "Ruby, these facilities are beautiful. This is going to be one hell of a conference."

I walked him out to the main lobby, and mustered the courage to ask, "Marcus, is your father's name Ben?" I felt the goose bumps when the words came out.

"No. Marcus Senior." He saw the disappointment on my face. "An old teacher, someone like that?"

"No. Someone who saved my mother's life." My heart was beating fast.

"Not my dad, Ruby. If he had saved anyone's life, we would have heard about it. Believe me."

"Well, Marcus. Thank you for coming by. I'll see you in four months?"

"Yes. Ruby, I'm joking of course, but would you have given us a break in the bill if my father had been Ben?"

"You bet. It would have come out of my paycheck and I would have been honored."

"Take care. Thanks for the floor plans."

"You're welcome, Marcus."

~

That night at my Ethnic History class, Mr. Carpenter was lectur-ing on Afro-Americans in California. "Ever since 1919 Black Republican leader Frederick M. Roberts had . . . in Los Angeles. In 1934 he was challenged by . . . Hawkins . . . campaign and defeated him. . . ."

My mind was elsewhere. I was thinking about Ben, running across the street to call 911 for my mother. He was my Black American hero.

~

That summer, I had rehearsed a thank-you speech:

Ben, you saved my mother's life. I was on the front steps that morning and I saw you running across heavy traffic. You're my hero, Ben. Someday, when I'm old enough, I will send you a big gift to say thank you. Thank you, Ben.

But because I didn't leave the apartment all summer, except on Sundays when it was Father's day off, I did not see Ben for three months. When September came and I walked by Ben's parking booth on my way home from school, I was afraid to talk to him. All I could do was smile nervously at him. "Don't talk to men," Mother had warned time and time again. I was also afraid to ask Father if I could talk to the man who saved Mother's life.

So every day, I smiled shyly at him. Every day he winked at me as if to say, "You're welcome, little girl."

CHAPTER 14

I Can't Go On

Ifelt I had served enough time in grueling psychotherapy. My six-month project had turned into a year-and-a-half and I was exhausted. This was no laughing matter for a former straight-A student.

"Dr. Thatcher, I desperately need a break."

"A break from therapy?"

"Yes. Is it okay with you?"

"Ruby, you don't need permission from me to take a break. How long a break were you thinking of?"

"A couple of months, and I really mean a couple, not five or six."

"I'm going to miss you."

"I'll miss you too. I need to try out life on my own for awhile, that's all."

"I understand. I'll be here when you return. If you should change your mind and want to come back sooner, I'll be here too."

I nodded.

"Did you send out your personal ad?"

"No. I decided I'm really not in the mood to go through with that."

"But you were so excited, Ruby, when you first told me."

"I know. I chickened out. Besides, what are the odds that I'll find Mr. Right from an ad?"

~

I had mixed feelings when I walked out of her office that day. Part of me wanted to "graduate" from hard work. And part of me had become so fond of Dr. Thatcher that I drove myself into a frenzy thinking about the day when we would say "goodbye" for the last time. Taking a two month hiatus seemed a reasonable test for the ultimate separation. I had grown to respect and admire Dr. Thatcher, even though I knew almost nothing about her personal life.

The first Saturday without my appointment felt awkward. Typically I'd spend at least an hour writing down topics for the session as I would for a staff meeting at work. So, not wanting to waste precious time sitting at home, even though I could have studied, I called up a girlfriend whom I had not seen in many months and asked her to meet me for lunch.

"Lauren, let's have a leisurely lunch so we can catch up."

"Sounds great, Ruby. You want to pick a place?"

"How about Chavelle's, one o'clock?"

"See you there."

Chavelle's is three blocks from Dr. Thatcher's office on Union Street. I was definitely not ready to cut the umbilical cord even though I had suggested the temporary separation.

~

I had met Lauren at another hotel job. It was during the first year after I came home from San Diego. She was a "very together" twenty-year-old while I was a lost lamb. Lauren left the organization two months after I started the job, but we kept in touch and over the years we had become dear friends. Seeing her was always like being with a real Mary Richards from the *Mary Tyler Moore Show*.

Lauren was the epitome of a working girl with a positive attitude. If it hadn't been for Lauren, I would still be working at The Cresmont Hotel where my boss had his entire family working there and I was subjected to their constant gossiping and arguing.

"Ruby, if you're unhappy, quit. There are other jobs," Lauren had advised.

"But he hired me when I really needed the work, and he's really generous at Christmastime," I offered in his defense.

"It's an unprofessional environment, Ruby. Don't forget. I was there. You deserve better," Lauren added.

Her reassuring voice gave me the courage to hand in my resignation letter the next day.

Lauren was also there for me whenever I made a bad choice in men and she would always calm me by saying, "The good ones are out there. We can't let the rotten apples discourage us from finding the good ones."

She also influenced me in cleaning up my vocabulary. "Asshole," "fucker," and "bitch" came out of my mouth often when I couldn't find other words to describe an unreasonable boss, a cheating boyfriend or a conniving female. One day I saw the annoyance on Lauren's face and realized I was offending her with the swearing. So I stopped using those words.

Seeing her today will be a treat. I sat by the window at Chavelle's and watched for her.

"Lauren! Over here."

"Ruby!" She gave me a warm hug.

"Lauren, you look great."

The silvery-blue in her sweater accentuated the golden shine in her hair. She had gained a few pounds in all the right places.

"You look great yourself. How's work?"

"Don't ask," I said. "I'll talk about anything but work."

"Okay, how's your mom and your sister?"

I brought her up to date. The waiter delivered the wine and poured two glasses.

"Your turn, Lauren. What's new?"

She sat forward and moved her glass aside. "Ruby, I'm getting married." She was beaming as she stretched out her left hand to show me her engagement ring.

"Wow. How many carats?"

"Almost two. It'll take us five years to pay it off."

"David is the lucky man, right?" I had to make sure. So many men would want to marry her. Damn, if I were a man, I would have proposed long ago.

"Yes, Ruby. Who else would put up with my habits?" She smiled, showing off her slightly crooked teeth.

"I can think of a few. Well? When and where?"

"Eight long weeks away. Nothing complicated or overwhelming. We're just driving up the coast with my folks and his. Then the two of us will continue north and spend a week in British Columbia."

"I didn't name names, but I was telling Dr. Thatcher that you two met through a personal ad and you're a perfect match."

"I lucked out, didn't I? Ruby, I'm really getting married!"

"This is the best news I've heard in I don't know how long. Now, tell me. What can I get you as a wedding gift? And I'm not buying you anything that's practical, no matter what you say."

"There's just one thing I want from you, dear friend, and that's for you to help me find my dress and shoes. I've decided to wear white.

I couldn't believe it when you called this morning. I told David you must be psychic. Wanna go shopping with me?"

"Are you kidding? Of course. I'm going to remember this afternoon until I'm a hundred years old." I left my seat to give Lauren a hug of congratulations. Hugging Lauren made me think of my sister. I felt teary-eyed but also happy at the same time. "I like David. He's a good man. If I am psychic, then I see a wonderful life for the two of you. This is a celebration."

Our food arrived.

"Let's order dessert too, Ruby. Sweets for the sweets."

I raised my glass to Lauren. "May you always have sweet moments and cry only happy tears."

"Thank you, Ruby. The same wish for you, always."

~

The intoxication of Lauren's wonderful news lingered through the day, but I couldn't help feeling sad for myself. As busy as I thought I was, I found myself feeling desperately lonesome at times. *I wonder what it's like to be so comfortable with a man that I would not care about what I look like without makeup or to be so loved that I would wake up every morning knowing he adores only me.* The next morning I wrote a check for the personal ad I had written weeks ago, and walked to the mail box even though it was a Sunday.

~

Feeling sentimental the following Saturday afternoon, I pulled out a family photo album from the closet and made myself a cup of cocoa. It didn't make sense that I would want to look at family photos when I told Dr. Thatcher I needed a break, but that was my frame of mind. Melancholy one day, giddy the next. One thing was certain.

I would not have to talk about my feelings for the next two months. I was on psychotherapy vacation.

On the living room floor, I opened the vinyl-covered album. This album contained pictures taken in Hong Kong. Father used to borrow a camera for special occasions because owning a camera was a luxury that most families could not afford.

The first page of the album held two enlarged photographs of my parents on their wedding day. They were young and beautiful. Mother looked like a Chinese Doris Day and Father a Chinese Marlon Brando, but not as muscular. Mother said her wedding dress was a rental. So was Father's suit.

The second page was a studio shot of me and John. I was five, he was two. We sat on a miniature wooden bench, and John's legs dangled in the air. I had my arm around my little brother. This was before Emily came along. How strange that I do not remember posing for this picture. However, I do remember Mother coming home from the hospital with John, and how I begged to hold him. "All right, but be very careful," my mother had said.

I took a sip of my cocoa and closed my eyes to picture our home in Hong Kong. We had shared a flat with two other families. The kitchen was communal and each family lived in one room.

There was little space for furniture. I remember my brother and I slept on bunk beds. John was afraid of heights so I had the top bunk. When Emily came along, she slept on the floor with our parents. The other pieces of furniture in the room were a four-drawer dresser and Mother's vanity table. Mother's vanity table was the most beautiful thing I'd ever seen or touched. The mirror was shaped like a king's crown and the delicate drawer handles were painted gold.

I remembered how I loved to play teacher by myself. My brother was interested only in his Matchbox cars and my sister was a baby. What made playing teacher fun was climbing up on Mother's vanity table and imagining that the huge mirror was my blackboard and Mother's lipstick was my chalk.

"Aah!" my mother gasped when she saw her mirror covered with writing and her lipstick ruined. "Do you know what you're doing?" she'd yelled. "This is an expensive piece of furniture. Your father bought it for me on our wedding day. I hope I won't scratch the glass taking lipstick off. Look at this! Go wash your hands!"

I obeyed Mother's orders. I even stayed in the communal kitchen a long time to avoid a scolding. When I returned to the room, Mother was still wiping her mirror. Calculating that I best keep quiet, I took out the multiplication table and pretended to study. I was only seven, but Mother said I was ready for the multiplications. Three times one equals three; three times two equals six.

A month later I was already on the sevens of the multiplication table. "Seven times one equals seven. Seven times two equals fourteen." Mother was in the kitchen. My brother and sister were napping. I took the opportunity to play teacher again. After quietly taking out Mother's lipstick, and this time her handkerchief as well, from the little drawer, I climbed onto her table and wrote $7 \times 1 = 7$. I was about to write 7×2 when I saw my mother's reflection in the mirror. I knew I was in trouble by the color of her face. It was red like her lipstick. She yanked me off the table, ran into the kitchen, and came back with a towel. She did all this without saying a word to me.

My arm was sore from Mother's pull but I kept quiet. I picked up my multiplication table which had been flung across the floor, and I climbed to my top bunk. Father came home, and immediately Mother yelled at him for lending money to his friend.

"We can't afford necessities and you show off as a big man. Well, let me tell you, you are not a big man. You're a fool."

My brother and sister were stirring from their naps. "Seven times eight equal fifty-six. Seven times nine equals . . ."

"You think that money will buy you friends? They're using you. They're not—"

From the reflection of Mother's mirror, I saw my father pick up a flashlight to strike my mother. I buried my face in my times table until I heard my father march out of the room and my mother following him.

~

To this day, I cannot remember any more. To this day, I cannot remember the answer to seven times nine.

Mother doesn't have the vanity table anymore. It was too costly to have the table shipped to America. The piece of furniture that once held so much promise was left behind. Mother had let go. I must also let go.

I drank the rest of my cocoa, closed the album, and put it back in the closet. I didn't want to look at any more photos. A feeling of great regret swept over my body like a wave of chills. *You can't call Dr. Thatcher. These two months will be a journey you'll have to take alone.*

~

Working and going to school finally took a toll on the body. The mind had been taxed as well. I dreamed that I was walking in the woods.

> *The blue sky suddenly turns dark and it's cold. I turn around, heading for home but there's a fork in the road which wasn't there before. Left or right. Right or left. I choose left. Feeling cold and scared, I begin to run. The faster I run the more terrified I am that someone is chasing me in the dark. Afraid to lose distance, I keep on running without looking back. My chest is tight and my legs are tired. Tears distort my vision and I stumble on a rock. As I fall, I let out an agonizing "NO."*

~

At work, I looked at my reflection in the locker room mirror and saw a haggard face. I knew I had to conquer these dreams or they would destroy me. The more I told myself at nighttime to go to sleep and think only pleasant thoughts, the more likely I was to have nightmares.

Deficient in sleep and exposed to people's sneezing and coughing on the bus, I came down with a cold. I'd usually pump myself with over-the-counter medicine and go to work, but this time I thought I was going to die. I called in sick and stayed home. After taking three Motrin tablets every two hours, my aching head still felt like it was squeezed between a metal clamp. I was certain that aliens had taken over my brain, torturing me so that I would be rendered helpless before they'd take me away to their planet. Couldn't they have waited for me to take my exam for Fundamental Physics? I had enrolled in only one class over the summer and was sure I would ace the course. "Aliens find their victims in people who live alone," Marilyn had told me after she had watched a television show about Unidentified Flying Objects.

By day three at home, I was blowing out green mucous. That's when I called the Acute Drop-In Clinic at the medical center. The taxicab driver did a double take when I crawled into the passenger seat. I must have looked hideous.

The doctor asked me, "Why didn't you come in sooner?"

"I thought it was a bad cold."

"It's a bad sinus infection, young lady. I suggest you not wait so long next time."

"I'll know not to next time."

"You'll feel a lot better after a day or two of antibiotics. Folks used to die from infections, before the discovery of antibiotics."

"Well, Doctor, that's what it felt like. I thought I was dying. I was kicking myself for not having any life insurance."

"You won't need any. You'll be fine, Ruby. Go home and take care of yourself."

"Thank you, Doctor."

~

That afternoon, Mrs. Nussbaum called to say she was coming down to see me and that she had soup for me. How she knew I was home sick is a mystery that I didn't spoil by asking her. *She's like a guardian angel who talks to everybody*. Perhaps one of the cab drivers told her he'd seen a ratty-haired ghost from this building.

"Mrs. Nussbaum, you're always doing things for me. How can I repay your kindness?"

"You don't think about repaying anybody right now. You think about getting well."

"I felt better already just sitting at the clinic's waiting room, knowing that if I were dying, I would be in good hands."

"Don't talk like that."

"My parents used to stop fighting whenever one of us got sick. As a little girl, I used to get these excruciating headaches and would throw up. Mother would put warm towels on my forehead. Father would gently rub Tiger Balm on my temples. They never fought when one of us got sick. But we couldn't be sick every day."

Mrs. Nussbaum shook her head sympathetically.

"I don't want you to catch my germs."

"Don't worry about that. Be a good girl and drink that soup. I'm not leaving until you're finished."

"You know what, Mrs. Nussbaum? I used to hate soup. But because of you, I like soup now. Mother used to make winter melon soup, black mushroom soup, soups with Chinese herbs. She made them especially for Father, but he would come home late and she would toss the whole pot down the drain."

"Your mother was showing her sadness. I understand your mother. Mr. Nussbaum had a sister who married a man who did not appreciate her. She became a bitter woman. When her husband died, she became even more bitter because she didn't know how to appreciate herself."

"How sad. Is she still alive?"

"Yes. All alone in New York while her children and grandchildren are here in California. Ruby, I made turkey soup too, so you won't be bored tomorrow with drinking the vegetable soup. I'll put it in the refrigerator. Just warm it up in the microwave for two minutes. I brought you a loaf of sesame challah. I know you like it."

"Mrs. Nussbaum, thanks for taking such good care of me. Your soups are delicious medicine. Whenever I'm sick, I get into this altruistic mode. I think about doing something worthwhile, like opening up a restaurant. You know, the kind that serves hearty foods, soups, comfort food to nurse people back to health."

"Why don't you, dear? You're young and ambitious. It does take a great deal of energy. I can tell you. On your feet all day. I used to have dainty feet. Look at them now. But being my own boss was worth it."

"I want to be my own boss too. Someday."

"There's no tougher boss than yourself. Long hours. No vacation pay. No sick pay."

"I won't mind. I know I can handle the long hours. It must have been rewarding to have something to call your own. What about Mr. Nussbaum? Was it difficult having a husband as a business partner?"

"No. We were a good team. I was the brains of the operation. He was the customer relations man, I used to call him. He loved people and pastrami. My Herman. The only time we argued over a business matter was naming a new store. So we named them all 'Nussbaum Delights.' "

"I'm only talking, Mrs. Nussbaum. I don't have the guts to quit my job. It's just talk."

"Talk is good. All important decisions start with talk. But I better stop talking and let you rest. Sleep well, dear. I'll see you tomorrow."

"Good night, Mrs. Nussbaum. Thank you for everything."

~

The antibiotics had begun to work their magic the next day. I called Chad to let him know I would return to work soon. He told me all about his experiences with sinus infections.

"All the time, Ruby. I used to get sick all the time. Then I had sinus surgery and it changed my life. I'll give you my doctor's name. Great guy. Rest up, Ruby. I'll need all my lieutenants next week. If you want to come in sooner and work shorter days, that's okay with me too. I'm counting on you."

What a jerk. Someday I will have enough courage to leave. Today I have enough strength to wash my hair.

Marilyn called to tell me to stay home as long as I needed to. "Are you sure you don't need anything?"

"Yes, Marilyn. Thanks for offering. My neighbor is taking really good care of me. She's like a 'cool' grandmother."

"Well, you take it easy. We miss you, but we don't want you in here."

"Okay."

That afternoon, with clean hair, I decided to reorganize the closet. There were still boxes that I had not unpacked since I moved into this apartment. In one box, I found shoes from high school days. Platform shoes that were two inches high in the front and five inches in the heel, and sandals. How many pairs of sandals did I have?

Underneath the boxes of shoes was Mother's gray tin box where she kept her documents. After all the moving, from home to home, somehow I had inherited the tin box.

I remember the first time I saw the box. I had found the yellowed photograph of my Grandmother Grace. This time her photograph was nowhere in sight. Instead I found plane tickets and boarding passes from our voyage to America, the lapsed life insurance policies on my parents, and even immunization documents. Mother must have taken Grandmother's picture out.

There was a piece of paper at the bottom of the box. It was folded over twice. I unfolded what appeared to be an important document with a seal stamped across the top. I read it out loud: "California State Board of Health. Bureau of Vital Statistics. County of Monterey. Sex of child: Female. Father's full name: Lee Ming. Mother's full maiden name: Yee Shee. Color or Race of Father: Yellow. Color or Race of Mother: Yellow."

My hands were shaking when I realized what I was reading. A few teardrops fell onto this precious piece of paper. My heart felt as if someone had placed a warm compress over it. In my hands was my grandmother's birth certificate. She was born on August 27, 1912, in the city of Salinas. Her real name is Lee Yun Kwai. I read it over and over again. Then I sandwiched it between two pieces of cardboard and placed it in my fireproof filing cabinet.

One sheet of paper had solved the mystery of my grandmother. I never knew what her name was because Mother said children did not need to know names of their elders. "Addressing them by their appropriate title is all you need to know," she once scolded. Also, Mother never told me that Grandmother was born in America. I wondered why. How I wanted to call Mother to tell her about my excitement, but I remembered what Dr. Leu said to me. "She keeps the past in her mind. She will not talk about the pain because she would not know where to begin."

~

That evening, Mrs. Nussbaum came over with a box of food. I showed her the treasure I had found. Reading the certificate out loud to Mrs. Nussbaum made me tremble with joy once more.

"Mrs. Nussbaum, what I can't understand is why my grandmother went to China. She was an American. Why would anyone leave America?"

"This is a good country, but there have been times when this country did not love its people. It did not love any group of people who looked or behaved differently from those who made the rules. The Chinese people, like all the other groups, were not treated well by ignorant and angry men."

"You're right. I take history for granted. I wonder if my grandmother worked in a factory or on a farm. Mother never told me that her mother was born here. I know she wants to forget about her childhood, but why would she forget about something important like this?"

"Maybe it's not important to her. The poor darling lost her mama at so young an age, nothing else is important."

"I'm really angry, Mrs. Nussbaum. Not at Mother, but at Grandmother. If she hadn't left California, then Mother would have been born here and her life would have been so different. She would have been second generation Chinese-American, making me third generation. Instead, I'm an immigrant."

"What's wrong with being an immigrant?" Mrs. Nussbaum went into the kitchen. I followed her. "This great country is made up of immigrants. My parents were immigrants. They faced hostilities when they got off the boat. The Jews were accused of stealing jobs. Every 'in group' used that excuse to intimidate the newcomers. The atrocities human beings commit on other human beings, I get very nervous thinking about it." Mrs. Nussbaum lined the counter with Corning Ware, and turned on the oven.

"I'm sorry to bring up the subject. I didn't mean to open up wounds, Mrs. Nussbaum."

"I'm not upset with you, dear. We have no control over what happened in the past. We can only learn from the mistakes."

"That's what my history teacher said. We can only learn from the mistakes."

"Yes. We cannot regret decisions made by others. I don't regret that your grandmother went back to China. If she had not, perhaps your mother would not have been born, and then you, Ruby, would not have been born either. I would not like that."

"And I wouldn't like that either. You're so wise, Mrs. Nussbaum."

"It takes many years of practice. You'll be just as wise when you're old, but you have many years of youth left."

"I hope so. Be a wise woman, I mean."

"Did you take your antibiotics today?"

"Yes. They worked almost immediately. I felt so good this morning I actually opened the window and looked out. I watched people, cars. It's great to be alive. Just two days ago, I was lying here feeling sorry for myself, that I've never been to Europe even though I've studied languages. And now my head doesn't hurt and I'm no longer blowing out green stuff."

"If you feel strong tomorrow, we'll go to the park." Mrs. Nussbaum said, as she slid the big dish into the oven. "Fresh air is what you need," she added.

I set the table in the kitchen, and opened the living room windows. Those words came back to me as if I was reliving that day.

~

"Fresh air is what you need," Father said to Mother the day she finally came home after six months in the hospital. She brought home a walker. I had heard a neighbor say, "It's a miracle that she's able to walk again."

The following weekend my brother, sister and I got into our Sunday best and took along a plastic bouncing ball. Emily and I wore our matching powder blue dresses with the sewn-in petticoats, and my brother wore his white shirt and brown corduroy pants with suspenders. We were the best-dressed children at the park that morning. We looked like we had just come out of church, even though we never went to church.

After helping Mother out of the car and finding a bench that did not have residues of pigeon droppings, Mother ordered us, including Father, to play ball. Father made the first toss. "Here, Little One," he said to my sister. She caught the ball that was the size of her body and bounced the ball, by using both hands, to my brother. My brother tossed the ball to me and I to Father.

After a few rounds I started to think of how other kids would dress at playtime. They would not wear their Sunday best. They would wear old clothes or clothes made to play in. And their bouncing ball would be dirty—not clean like ours. Mother insisted we wash the ball after every outing. She did not want the filthy ball in the car until it was washed and wiped dry. Mother always had a stack of napkins in her bag, enough napkins to wipe the entire station wagon dry. The last time we were at the park, we had to wash our ball in the drinking fountain since there were no restrooms. An old woman yelled at us, "You people are crazy! The fountain is for drinking. You dirty it. You clean it!"

As my attention turned back toward the present ball tossing exercise, I looked over to where Mother was sitting. She seemed happy that we were having fun. Every two minutes, she called out, "Be careful!" to one of us. She did not want us running after the ball and slipping in our patent leather shoes.

I thought to myself, yes, my parents had stopped fighting, but they also had stopped talking to each other. Mother's clumsy walker became a convenient way for my parents to be apart, even at the dinner table.

I looked at Mother, now propping herself up with her left hand on the walker and her right hand on the bench. Her face told me her thoughts: *How can he love an invalid? I don't blame him for being distant. He works so hard, six days a week. And I can't even take the dirty clothes to the Laundromat.*

Why couldn't my parents love each other like the couple in *An Affair to Remember*? In the last scene of the movie, Cary Grant cried and held Deborah Kerr in his arms when he found out she had become an invalid. "If it had to happen to one of us, why did it have to be you?" he tells her.

"Don't worry, darling. Oh, darling, . . . then I can walk," she murmurs. A wheelchair did not keep those two people apart.

On the way home from the park, I looked out the window from the backseat of the car. As the car came to a stop at a red light, I saw my father's face in the rearview mirror. He looked unhappy. He drove into Chinatown, passing the many vegetable stands. Chinese movie posters covered the front wall of one store. *Love Star* was the name of the movie. The Chinese word for 'love' is made up of many brush strokes. In the center of the word 'love' is the word 'heart.' How clever. Love is made of heart. I had always liked the American phrase 'I love you with all my heart.' The strokes that make up the Chinese word for 'love' are soft, not rigid and angular. 'Love' was almost never used at our home. I never heard my father say 'I love you' to my mother. Once, while scolding us, he did say, "I work hard because I love my family."

Men and women in movies had no qualms saying those three little words. I wondered if Father had said them to Mother when he proposed to her. I wondered if those words could have made them gentler people.

~

"Ruby. Ruby?" Mrs Nussbaum was calling me back to the present. "Ruby, dinner is ready. Come eat, dear."

"It smells so wonderful. I'm hungry."

"Don't forget to take your antibiotics. One with each meal."

"Yes, Mrs. N. I'm being a good girl."

On the kitchen table were a tureen of chicken soup, a basket of warm rolls, and a dish of steamed asparagus. *This is what it's like to have a loving grandmother*, I told myself.

"Has Rashi eaten?" I asked.

"Yes. He's watching *Wheel of Fortune* now."

"He's a funny dog. Do you know why he likes that show?"

"It's because of the spinning wheel and that opening tune. I don't know what I'll do if that show ever goes off the air."

I popped an antibiotic pill into my mouth and washed it down with a gulp of water. "*Yuk.* Why can't they make them smaller? I can see why my mother hates to take her pills."

"How's your mother, Ruby?"

"She's okay, I suppose. We haven't talked in weeks." I felt comfortable telling Mrs. Nussbaum. "I can't stop myself from wishing that one day she'll call to tell me she's happy with her life."

"Perhaps your mother is as happy as she'll ever be. She has two healthy and beautiful daughters."

The chicken soup was seasoned with onions and garlic. I inhaled

LOVE MADE OF HEART

the aroma. "Sometimes I think that if Emily and I lived perfect lives, then Mother would be happy because she lives vicariously through us. This will sound silly, but when I'm with Mother, I have to be careful not to tell her too much about my job or she'll find out that I'm unhappy. If she knows I'm depressed, then she gets depressed for me."

"Be yourself, dear. Mothers have a way of seeing the truth. She might be more unhappy if she knew you were pretending for her benefit."

"Mrs. Nussbaum, you should offer workshops to confused adult daughters."

"No. Daughters find answers for themselves. They don't need an old woman telling them what to do."

"I'll call Mother tomorrow. I was waiting for her to call me first, but I'll call her."

"That would make any mother happy."

"Mrs. Nussbaum, when are you going to make matzo ball soup again?"

"I can make it for you anytime."

"No, don't fuss, please. Just whenever. I really liked it."

"It's comfort food, isn't it?"

"Yeah. Just like Chinese rice porridge. I always crave it when I think I'm getting sick."

"Well, one day when you're not so busy, you show me how to make rice porridge and I'll show you how to make matzo balls."

"Ooh. Matzo ball porridge. We could be on to something. Hey. How about The Matzo Ball Porridge as a name for a restaurant?"

Mrs. Nussbaum had a thoughtful expression on her face.

"No?" I asked. "Too nutty?"

"I didn't say that, dear."

"What was Mr. Nussbaum's favorite soup?" I asked.

"Oh, Herman liked everything."

"Was it love at first sight, for you and him?"

"No, darling. I don't believe in that. He was a plain man, a little on the chubby side. He had bad teeth. He had to go to the dentist all the time. I was a skinny girl. He'd say, 'Eat, dear, eat.' I fell in love after we married." Mrs. Nussbaum had a thoughtful look. "I love him so much." *She used the present tense.*

~

After dinner, I cleared off the table. "Mrs. Nussbaum, you make yourself comfortable in the living room."

"I made apple pie for dessert."

"Ooh, my favorite."

I thought of Dr. Thatcher. *If she were here, she would see that I'm not wasting my time. I miss seeing her smile. I'll have so much to tell her when I see her in another month.* She was constantly on my mind.

While the pie was warming in the oven, I joined Mrs. Nussbaum in the living room.

"Ruby, what are these?" She was pointing to the wall. "They're beautiful."

"I painted them. Well, I wrote them with a Chinese brush."

"They are so beautiful, Ruby."

"Thanks. Each character is a Chinese word. The two words in the same frame, on the right, is my Chinese name. My name means jade flower. All Chinese first names are made up of two words."

"How do you say it?"

"*Yook Faah.* Thank God Mother gave us English names, because can you imagine the ridicule I would have received going to school as *Yook Faah?*"

"I went to school with a Rosie Pupik."

"What's funny about that?" I asked.

"Pupick is 'navel' in Yiddish. If you had that for a last name, believe me, you'd change it."

I laughed. Mrs. Nussbaum laughed too.

"Then there was Harold Shmuckler. Poor kid. Every time the teacher called on him, the whole class would collapse." Mrs. Nussbaum broke into laughter again.

It was contagious. I giggled. "*Yook Faah*, Harold, and Rosie," I said in an authoritative voice, "go stand in line."

After we settled down, Mrs. Nussbaum asked me about the middle frame.

"That's 'grace.' That's what I named my grandmother. You see, most Chinese children don't know their grandparents' names because kids are supposed to address their elders by appropriate titles. There was never a need to know their names. Anyway, see how the word 'grace' is made up of two parts? The top is the pictogram of a person resting on a square mat and the bottom pictogram is the heart. See how the brush strokes curve like the shape of a heart?"

Mrs. Nussbaum nodded. "How do you say 'grace' in Cantonese, darling?"

"I don't know. I wanted her English name to be Grace, so I looked up 'grace' in the Chinese-English dictionary and copied the character."

"It's like a painting." Mrs. Nussbaum walked over for a closer look.

"I've always been fascinated with the written Chinese language even though I only know a few words. It's just incredible that the language consists of over forty thousand characters and there's no alphabet. Each character is made up of combinations of strokes. There is the radical part which will give a clue to the word's meaning and then there's the phonetics part which gives a clue to the sound of the character."

"It must be a very difficult language to learn," said Mrs. Nussbaum.

"I suppose . . . for people whose first language has an alphabet system. Many people cannot grasp the concept of constructing words using an art form that is thousands of years old. But I think it's equally hard for Chinese people to learn English because not only do they have to learn the ABCs, they also have to learn verb tenses. There are no tenses in the Chinese language. I think that's why my father failed to master the language. He couldn't grasp the concept of verb conjugation. He knew how to make money, but he couldn't read forms."

"Darling, there are native speakers who cannot read forms."

"I know, but they're not treated as ignorant foreigners who 'ought to go back to where they came from.'"

"You can't fight bigotry, Ruby." Mrs. Nussbaum had a faraway look. I wondered if she was thinking about her parents who were immigrants.

"The only people who has any ground to say 'Go back to wherever' are the Indians, don't you think?"

"I don't have the answers, darling." She was standing in front of the last frame.

"Mrs. Nussbaum, that's the word for 'love.' Because there aren't verb tenses, the Chinese people use other words to denote time. I love him ten years ago. She love him now. Why have different forms of a verb to confuse matters? Life would be simpler if we didn't have to conjugate verbs."

"I see what you mean, Ruby. Languages are so complex. This word 'love,' it has so many strokes. It looks like a family crest."

"It does! See the radical that has the horizontal line and two side strokes? That's the radical for 'cover.' Below that is the radical for 'heart' as in the word 'grace.' In the center of love is heart. Isn't it beautiful? Love, made of heart."

"Very beautiful. How do you say 'love' in Chinese?"

"Well, in Cantonese, it's pronounced *'oy'*."

"Like *'Oy'* in *'Oy vay'?'* Mrs. Nussbaum smiled.

"Yes!"

"I like it. Love is made of heart," said Mrs. Nussbaum. "I learned something today. About the Chinese language and about my Ruby being so talented."

A funny feeling came over me when Mrs. Nussbaum said those words. I felt warm inside and it wasn't from the apple pie.

After Mrs. Nussbaum left that evening, I went back to the living room to look at my brush paintings. *The written Chinese language is truly beautiful. I'll paint a few more characters and give one to Mrs. Nussbaum.*

~

I called in sick the next day to let the body rest. The sinus infection had wiped me out. I did go out for a bit of fresh air when Mrs. Nussbaum walked Rashi in the morning. In the afternoon, I curled up on the living room sofa with my pillow and blanket to watch a movie on television. It was a poignant story, *Since You Went Away*, with Claudette Colbert as the mother, Jennifer Jones as the older sister, and Shirley Temple as the younger sister. The setting was wartime. The father had gone away to serve his country and the family had to take in a boarder in order to help pay the bills. The older sister fell in love but her sweetheart died. It was a tearjerker. The ordeal had brought the family even closer than before, because family love and support held them together. At the end, the father came home. I used a stack of tissue to dry my tears.

Since you went away; the words echoed in my mind like a sad song as I turned off the television set and put my head down on the pillow. I thought about that summer—the summer when Mother was in the hospital.

~

Emily was only six years old. Father said she needed an adult's care, and she'd be sent off to our aunt who lived in San Bruno and had four children of her own. Emily took her doll, Pebble, with her. That day, when we dropped her off, she hung on to Father's legs and sobbed so hard she let Pebble fall to the ground. I picked up Pebble and brushed the pavement dust from her face. Then I squatted in front of Emily, and told her a lie: "Pebble is sick, Emily, and this is the only place where they have medicine for her. She'll get better if she stays here. But she'll be scared, so you need to take care of her so that she won't be scared."

Father held Emily tight, kissed her on the cheeks, and said in Chinese, "Take care of your baby like your sister says. You are the doctor, Little One." My father scored points with me that day.

Our aunt came out of the house carrying a toy monkey and coaxed in Chinese, "Come in, Emily. Your baby will like it here." Emily and Pebble went in.

I was allowed to see my sister on Sundays, Father's day off. Even with other kids to play with, we always found her by herself whenever we visited her. She was even distant with me. She carried Pebble with her everywhere. She couldn't let her go.

"Emily, Mimi is here to play with Pebble." I sneaked Mimi in one day, but I didn't want the adults to know *I* was still playing with dolls.

"Pebble doesn't want to play. She's very sick," Emily said, her face thin and pale.

"Should we give her some medicine?" I knelt in front of my little sister.

"No. I gave her some already. She doesn't want to play." Emily turned away from me.

"Okay," I said. "We won't play, Emily. We'll just sit here quietly and let Pebble sleep."

Emily rocked her baby.

Many Sundays she and I just sat quietly and cried. I couldn't have told Emily the truth—that Pebble wasn't sick. Watching my little sister cry tore me up.

Our brother never cried. That summer, John stopped talking to us. He grunted yes or no when it was necessary. So many times I wanted to tell John I was scared too. I had a speech in my head:

John, you should eat more and drink lots of milk and grow big. Bigger than Father. He won't dare touch you if you're his size. Or maybe the two of us can push him to the ground and punch him out the next time he hits you. But I have a feeling he'll change from now on. With Mother in the hospital, he'll take care of us because God will punish him if he doesn't.

But John spent the days going out with his equally glum friends; I saw little of him. And when I did see him, I couldn't muster the courage to speak.

I had prayed every night that Father wouldn't come home in a foul mood. Since Emily was at our aunt's house, who would comfort John, if Father took his frustrations out on our brother? My prayers were answered—Father came home late every night to cook dinner, shower, and sleep. *Peace at last!*

Each day started out with a bowl of cereal with chocolate milk. Then I would comb my doll Mimi's hair. I thought of Mother lying in a hospital bed. Who was combing her hair? One morning, I decided that there was no need to brush my hair anymore. So I stopped, and began watching television.

It was during that summer that I learned impeccable manners from black-and-white movies. I watched how Gene Tierney greeted her guests, how Susan Hayward excused herself from the table, and how Katharine Hepburn said, "Thank you." I found my heroines in characters portrayed by Bette Davis and Joan Crawford. These women were sophisticated, smart and strong. They were always able to take care of themselves. I wanted to be just like them.

But peace turned into war that same summer. My brother, who could have been my friend, became my enemy.

One evening Father brought home a live frog. "I'm going to cook frog soup for you kids on Sunday," he announced in Chinese. "It's in this tank and I'll put it under the kitchen sink. John, you stay out of here."

Father didn't have to warn me. Everyone knew I was afraid of slimy creatures and frogs were the slimiest. Frog soup! Why did he even bother? Guilt, maybe. Mother used to cook soup all the time, but he was never home to eat it.

The next day when I woke up, I saw that Mimi was not under her blanket. Could it be that I left her in the living room where we had watched television last night? She wasn't there. She was nowhere in the apartment. I was frantic. Father was at work. My brother was out. Who could have taken her? John. Who else would have?

I waited all day to confront him. At four o'clock he walked through the front door. "I know you did it," I shouted. "TELL ME WHERE SHE IS!"

John pretended he didn't hear me, turned on the television, and sat down on the sofa.

This time, using my Bette Davis voice, I asked him again. "I'm going to give you thirty seconds to tell me where she is. If you don't tell me, I'm going to throw your precious airplanes out the window and watch them crash on the sidewalk."

"You're crazy," he muttered.

My face was hot, and my hands were shaking. I turned around and headed toward John's room. I would have to carry out my threat.

"She's sleeping with the frog," he said, as I was halfway down the hall.

Oh, God, the one place I didn't think of looking. I ran into the kitchen, pulled open the cabinet door under the sink. The tall narrow plastic tank was transparent, and I saw Mimi and the frog. Father had poked holes in the lid. At least Mimi had oxygen. If I open the lid the frog would escape. I sat on the floor in despair and watched Mimi float.

My head began to throb. Then I heard the front door slam shut. John had gone out again. I couldn't wait for Father to come home. It would be hours. Besides, if Father knew what John had done, he would have taken the belt to him. *If John gets a beating because of my squealing, then he'll kill Mimi for sure.* I had to rescue her myself.

Slowly I loosened the lid to the tank. Then I watched the frog's movements. When the frog was near the bottom of the tank, I quickly peeled the lid off, grabbed Mimi by her hair and slammed the lid back down. The frog came to the surface of the tank, but it was too late. The lid was now clamped tight.

My Mimi was cold and wet. Her dress felt slimy and her hair was tangled looking like seaweed. I took off her dress, bathed her in warm water, shampooed her hair, and wrapped her in a towel. Then I tucked her into my bed, putting pillows all around her. I told her no one would ever harm her again. I would not let them. She forgave me.

That evening when Father came home, I did not rat on John. On Sunday Father brought out the frog soup in a big bowl, and served each of us a big helping. "Eat! It's very tasty," he said, with a proud smile because he had cooked something. "More tender than chicken," he added.

I took my bowl to the living room. I scooped out the frog meat from the broth, and wrapped it up in a paper towel. How could I eat that slime? I drank the liquid so that Father would not get angry. When Father came out to ask if I wanted more, I shook my head.

"Good?" he asked me.

I nodded. I was nauseated.

John and I never spoke of that incident, but it created a deep hatred in the two of us. If he had only taken something else of mine, perhaps I could have forgiven him. But he took an innocent doll and tried to drown her. That I could never forgive.

So it was. My sister was far away, and my brother became my enemy. But I began to hate myself as well. Father had been visiting Mother every day, but one day he told us that Mother didn't want him to visit her anymore. Every night when Father came home, I wanted to say, "Mother is lying. She does want you there. She's just saying that so you won't have to rush from work. Go be with her, please!" I never had the courage to say it out loud, and my excuse was that children must never tell adults what to do. I hated myself for being a coward.

In movies, lovers always confessed their true feelings when they were about to become separated. In those daily visits that did not occur, my parents could have forgiven each other for past insults and injuries and pledged to start a new life. It was a turning point they let slip by.

Then September came. My uncombed hair had become a gross knot. Father tried to comb out the ratty mess, but he had to cut ten inches off my hair. So on the first day of junior high school, I had short hair. No one knew that just before summer I had long beautiful hair. And no one knew I had a little sister who was far away, and no one knew my mother was in a hospital room, all by herself.

CHAPTER 15

New Attitude

Walking down Buchanan Street the first Saturday after my two-month break, I felt revitalized. From the hill, I could see sailboats dotting the Bay. Leaves were beginning to fall and there was a crispness in the air. I turned onto Vallejo Street.

Dr. Thatcher greeted me at the waiting room. Following her down the hall, I watched her long flowing skirt sway from side to side. It felt good to sit in my wing chair.

"How are you, Ruby?"

"Dr. Thatcher, I've missed you so much."

"I've missed you too, Ruby. How were the two months?"

"I have so much to tell you. I don't know where to begin. I didn't make a list and so much has happened."

"You're excited."

I took a deep breath. "First, I saw Mom two weeks ago. We had lunch. I told her about my girlfriend getting married. She didn't want to listen, she changed the subject. She's that way about people and marriage. We talked about Emily. All in all, I had a good time with her. I felt like saying 'Let's do it again next week, Mom' when we said goodbye, but I stopped myself. You know how I always go overboard when things are good."

"Take it one step at a time. If it feels good this time, then perhaps extend the visit a little longer next time."

"I found out something amazing about my Grandmother Grace. Look at my hands. I'm shaking just thinking about it."

"What is it, Ruby?"

"She was born in California. Isn't that incredible? She was an American."

"Did you find that out from your mother?"

"No. I found her birth certificate in Mother's gray tin box when I was cleaning out my closet. But I didn't bring up the subject with Mom because I want to keep it as my private treasure, for the time being. I'm sure Mother had put it there for safekeeping, so I'm not hiding anything from her. I just want to have it all to myself for a while longer. Plus, I didn't want to risk upsetting her if it is something that would make her sad."

"It must have been a startling find for you. When was your grandmother born?"

"August 27, 1912. That would have made her twenty-one when my mother was born. And her name was Lee Yun Kwai. So that means her father's surname was Lee. She was born in Salinas, right here in California."

"You look so happy, Ruby. I've never seen you like this."

"I feel good. So good, I'm not fretting about taking Fundamental Physics again. I had a sinus infection and missed a big exam."

"I'm sorry to hear you were sick."

"Everything happens for a reason. That's what I learned in the last two months, Doctor Thatcher. If I hadn't been sick, then I wouldn't have been home cleaning my closet, and I wouldn't have found the birth certificate."

"You have a new outlook, Ruby." Dr. Thatcher looked radiant. Her hair was two inches shorter. "How's work?" she asked me.

"Work is fine. But Chad's the same. I have something to tell you and it's not work-related. If you weren't already sitting down, Dr. Thatcher, I would be asking you to."

"You do have a lot to tell me, don't you?"

I took another deep breath. "After getting the news from my girl-friend that she was getting married, I thought, why not send in that personal ad? So the next day, I wrote a check and sent it off."

"When does the ad come out?"

"It came out already. And I've gotten responses. I'm dying to read this one to you. It came two weeks ago."

Dr. Thatcher was smiling at me as a girlfriend would at delicious news.

Dear Intelligent . . . One:

I must be honest and let you know that I did not read your ad. Someone else had read it and gave it to me. I told him that answering ads was not my idea of meeting people, but after reading yours, I decided it would be foolish not to write to you. Then I had to sit down and think about what to write since I am not much for letter writing. I'm the type of fellow who picks up the phone to talk to a friend no matter what the distance is between us.

In describing myself, I can only repeat what friends say about me. They say I am loyal, kind, generous, hard-working, and down-to-earth. I tend to agree with them. There are other qualities perhaps you will find out for yourself. Enclosed is a picture of me taken last year in Alaska. I try to visit a state each year—not alphabetically.

I'm looking forward to hearing from you and perhaps we can go out for coffee or tea.

> Sincerely,
> Vincent Yao

"His telephone number is at the bottom. Looking at the prefix, he doesn't live far from me."

"That's a very nice letter. Are you going to call him?"

"That's the big question. Am I going to call him? Here's his picture. He's kind of handsome, don't you think? And I like the way he stands. But he's Chinese and you know how I feel about dating Chinese men."

"You've never dated them, Ruby."

"You're right. I've never given them a chance. I'm wondering if I should start now. The ad also offered an answering center where I leave an outgoing message and the respondents can call to listen to it, and then leave me a one minute message. Vincent's voice gave me goose bumps. What a great voice. I asked for letters and photos as well because I didn't want to meet anyone illiterate and I also wanted to see what they looked like before calling them back. I know looks aren't everything but they're important to me."

"Did you get other nice letters?" Dr. Thatcher handed back the photo.

"Several, but this is the one I read over and over again."

"What did your ad say, Ruby? I'm curious."

"I have it with me. Here it is. I had a big head when I wrote it. Here goes . . .

Intelligent, warm-hearted, responsible, no-nonsense beauty looking for her counterpart (age 35 to 40). Please send reply and photo to Box 269.

"The letters came faster than I could read them. I should have deleted the word 'beauty' in the ad because some men obviously could not read past it. I received letters and photos from men who were under thirty-five and over forty. Some men assumed they would qualify as my 'counterpart' just because they have a you-know-what."

Dr. Thatcher laughed. "Why that age range?"

"I'm twenty-nine and I would prefer someone older, but not someone twenty years older."

"Ruby, a lot *has* happened since we last saw each other. I hope you won't rush into anything. But do enjoy yourself and have some fun for a change."

"I am having fun, Dr. Thatcher."

"I'm glad your two months have been rewarding. See you next Saturday?"

"Yes. See you Saturday."

"Ruby, one more thing."

"Yes?"

"Be careful."

"I will. Thanks."

I was so happy that day I practically bounced out of Dr. Thatcher's office.

~

On my way home, I stopped by the flower stand to buy snapdragons for Mrs. Nussbaum and myself. She and I had developed an easygoing but caring relationship where she didn't expect me to stop by every day and I didn't feel invaded whenever she called me to say she had food for me.

Mrs. Nussbaum wasn't home so I left her flowers in a carafe of water in front of her door with a note that said,

Dear Mrs. N.,
Thank you for being in my life.
Love, Ruby.
P.S. I've got exciting news.

My mailbox was stuffed. I spent the afternoon reading replies and looking at the accompanying photos. There were a few more nice letters, but nothing like Vincent Yao's. I called up the ad's answering center. None of the others had his deep voice either.

After reading his letter one more time and calling in my message box to hear his voice again, I decided to call him. His answering machine picked up the call and I found myself stumbling with the message even though I had rehearsed it a dozen times.

Hello, this is Ruby Lin. You answered my ad number two six nine. I enjoyed reading your letter and I would like to meet you over coffee next week. I look forward to hearing from you. Bye.

After I hung up, I realized I had forgotten to leave my home telephone number and so I had to leave a second message. How embarrassing.

To be coy, I let my answering machine pick up calls that evening. I didn't want him to think I was sitting around waiting for him. He called. I played back his message over and over again.

Hello Ruby, this is Vincent Yao. Nice to hear from you. If you're not busy after work on Monday, how about meeting somewhere near your workplace or mine. You choose. I'm in and out tomorrow. Talk to you soon.

Oh, what a voice.

The arrangement was to meet at five-thirty inside the Seasons Cafe which was three blocks from the St. Mark. It was close enough for me to walk there and far enough so that my coworkers would not see me going on a date.

Having timed my entrance for five thirty-three, I was quite taken by the three-dimensional Vincent Yao. He looked even better than his photo. I suppose a man always looks better in a well-cut suit. He reminded me of Michael Landon who played the part of Little Joe in *Bonanza*. I was pleased with his good manners when I walked up to the table. He stood, we said hello, and he waited for me to sit down first.

The coffee date began.

"Ruby, I'm a little nervous. I've never answered a personal ad before."

"Well, that makes us even, because I've never written a personal ad before."

"Would you like something to eat?" he asked.

"Just a *latte* for now."

"I didn't have time for lunch today so I hope you won't mind if I eat in front of you."

"Well, in that case, I'll order something too."

After we politely discussed the weather and our jobs, I steered the conversation.

"I really enjoyed your letter, Vincent."

"I'm glad," he said in that marvelous voice. "I almost didn't mail it, but I'm . . . I'm really glad I did." He looked into my eyes.

An hour later, I asked one of my test questions.

"Tell me, Vincent. If you could do one thing over in this lifetime, what would it be?"

"Wow. Just one thing?" He chuckled.

"Just one." I raised my index finger.

He filled his cheeks with air, reclined in his chair, and exhaled. "I'll have to say . . ." He paused before continuing. "Going away to college. I always wanted to go back East and experience college life away from home like my oldest brother did."

"What stopped you?"

"I really don't know. It was all right, going to Cal State. But if I were to do it over again, that would be it. What about you?"

"Travel. My sister constantly reminds me that if I hadn't been so carefree with my paychecks all those years I could have seen Europe. That's a dream of mine—to see Europe and I don't mean fourteen cities in twelve days. I want to really see it."

"I would too. See Europe, I mean."

The tune *I Could Have Danced All Night* was in my head all evening. Another hour later I wanted to say "let's do this again tomorrow," but I didn't. I knew the etiquette of the first date.

"Ruby, I really enjoyed meeting you. I hope we can do this again."

"I'd like that. I don't have to work Friday night. Perhaps dinner?"

"That's great. That's really great." He said it with sincerity in his voice. "It's dark. Let me walk you to your car."

"I don't drive to work. The bus stop is right outside."

"Okay, I'll watch you get on the bus safely and then I'll scoot." So he did. He watched me get on the bus and waved goodbye. Be still my heart. I slept like a happy child that night.

~

The next four days felt like four weeks. After our Friday dinner date at Paradiso, I couldn't sleep a wink. I tried to remember everything we said to one another. I called up Emily the next morning. Thank God she was there. I was about to burst.

"Emily. Sit down for this. Are you sitting?"

"I'm sitting."

"Your sister's in love, and before you say anything, let your sister talk."

"Okay, Sis. Talk."

"I'll give you details later, but here's the news flash. I met a handsome, intelligent, considerate Chinese guy through a personal ad and I think he's the one."

"The one?"

"You promised. I'm still talking. He's thirty-five, a civil engineer at PG&E, youngest of four brothers, no sisters, has had long-term relationships, never married, no children, is a baseball coach, generous when we go out, has a deep sexy voice, looks like Michael Landon, ready to settle down, hasn't kissed me yet, and he's so nice, Emily. Whew. How's that?"

"*You* better sit down, Ruby. He sounds too good. What's his name?"

"Vincent. Vincent Yao. And he likes to travel. He's been to twelve states already. That's ten more than I've seen."

"I'm happy for you, Sis. But if this gets serious, I'm flying out to grill him."

"You do that, Emily. Because this is serious. I'm serious. I've never felt this way before. He's a male version of me! Perhaps it's fate— I belong with my own kind. He's Americanized and I'm . . . American-televisionized."

Emily laughed. "You're kooky."

"But I'm a lovable kook."

"Yes you are, Big Sis. When's your next date?"

"Today. After my appointment with Dr. Thatcher. We're going to Tiburon."

"Have fun. Send me a picture of this guy. I'll pass it around, in case he's 'wanted' by the police."

"You make me laugh, Em. Love you. I'll call you soon."

"Love you, Sis. Have fun. And be careful."

"I will. First, I must get some sleep. Falling in love is exhausting."

~

Spending so much time choosing the outfit to wear for the afternoon, I ran out of time to prepare for my two o'clock session. I was downright silly.

"Dr. Thatcher, life is wonderful. I wish we could skip this session and go out for coffee."

"Does the letter you read to me last week have anything to do with your delightful attitude?" Dr. Thatcher smiled at me.

"I've seen Vincent twice already and we're going to Tiburon this afternoon. He's wonderful and so down-to-earth. No pretentiousness."

"Are you answering the other letters?"

"No. I don't see why. None of the other letters sparked my interest. Plus, I didn't like any of the other photos. One picture was so blurry, it made me wonder if the guy was trying to hide something."

"Tell me about Vincent, Ruby."

Telling Dr. Thatcher about my first two dates felt like chatting with a girlfriend.

"Dr. Thatcher, all these years coming here and talking about my childhood and analyzing dreams and learning new ways to communicate, I've never really set a goal for myself. I have one now. Maybe meeting Vincent gave me this insight. I want to walk out of here one day, knowing I've become a great woman, not just a good woman, but a great woman."

"What is your definition of a great woman?"

"Someone who is not judgmental, controlling and impatient.

Someone who is forgiving of others. Someone who can say 'no' without feeling guilty."

"First, Ruby, are you giving yourself credit for having done a lot of work in the past two years and that you are a good human being?"

"Yes, I do. I want to take the work to a higher plane."

"You have, Ruby. Practice is the only way we can change our behavior. You've been working very hard."

"If Vincent only knew how hard I've been working in these sessions. And I'm going to work twice as hard, now that he's in my life." As soon as the words came out of my mouth, I knew I was talking like a lovesick teenager. How could I have said it, after two dates. *You must be nuts.* An overwhelming sadness swept over me.

"Ruby, is something wrong?"

My look gave me away. "Silly, isn't it? I just met the guy. What's the matter with me, Dr. Thatcher? One minute happy, next minute sad. I was full of zest when I walked in, now I'm depressed."

"Why, Ruby?"

"I don't know."

"Perhaps it's the thrill, and fear, of falling in love."

"Yeah. Maybe all this talk about being a great woman and hard work and changing behaviors is too much for me. What if I'm not up to the task?" I felt suffocated.

Dr. Thatcher must have sensed my discomfort. "Take a deep breath, Ruby. And another. Remember we talked about the importance of exercise, diet and sleep? Are you exercising, eating properly and getting enough sleep?"

"I've been slacking off in the exercise department. You're right. I always feel so much better when I exercise."

"Don't forget that even walking does so much good. Moving about does something to the chemistry in the brain."

The tiny digital clock on the table between Dr. Thatcher's wing chair and mine said 2:50.

"Thank you, Dr. Thatcher. Do you mind if I use the phone in the other office before I leave?"

"No. Go right ahead. Have a good week, Ruby."

"You too. Bye."

I was glad I had written down Vincent's telephone number and wouldn't have to wait until I got home to call him. "Hi, Vincent, I'm so glad I caught you. I'm feeling a bit under the weather. Can we postpone Tiburon?"

"Of course. Can I do anything? Bring you anything?"

"No. You're very thoughtful. I'm going to take it easy and I'll call you soon. Bye."

"Bye, Ruby. Take care of yourself. I'm here if you need anything."

Instead of going home, I walked to Fort Mason. I had to rid the cobwebs from my head. There was a psychic fair; the place was packed. So I continued on to Marina Green. Kites in the shapes of animals and airplanes painted the sky. To my right, a German shepherd was catching a Frisbee, to my left a soccer game; I wanted to disappear in the crowd. I couldn't believe I had told Dr. Thatcher that "I would work twice as hard, now that Vincent was in my life." What was I thinking? I walked towards Crissy Field, but my feet were sore. So I hailed a taxi, went home, and gave myself a good long cry. They were neither sad nor happy tears. I was scared of my feelings for a man whom I had just met. I was scared that Vincent would change my life.

Then I erased the first message he had left on the machine. *You're not a teenager,* I scolded myself. I put his letter away in the desk drawer and distracted myself with schoolwork.

On Monday, Vincent called me to ask how I was feeling, and invited me to dinner. I declined his invitation, telling him I was expecting a hectic week. But I thought about him all week long. *What's the matter with you, Ruby Lin? If you like him, call him. Be brave. You have nothing to lose*, I told myself. Several times I picked up the telephone, but each time I hung up before pressing the last digit.

He called Saturday morning. I had hoped he would.

"Ruby, you can be frank with me. Do you not want me to call you anymore?"

"No. I mean . . . I don't want you to stop calling. I'm just in a funk, that's all. I hope I'm not being rude."

"You're not rude. I thought I had said something to offend you."

"No, you haven't."

"I'm glad to hear it. I thought I blew it." That wonderful voice of his melted me.

"I'm working tomorrow, but I get off at five-fifteen. So, if you're not busy—"

"I'd like that, Ruby. Same place as our first date?"

"Same place. Same time. See you then. And, Vincent, thanks for calling."

"I'm glad I did. See you tomorrow."

~

I wore what I had worn that Saturday of the canceled date—the taupe rayon dress for such an occasion. It had long sleeves to accommodate either outdoor weather or air-conditioning, a flared skirt to make me feel feminine, and a wide neckline to show off the curves of my collarbone.

Vincent was already there, just as on our first date. He was in casual attire. The broad shoulders were his, not padding from a suit. After catching up with each other's week and dispensing with polite conversation, I felt an irresistible urge to tell him what was on my mind.

"Vincent, I need to tell you something about me."

"I'm all ears."

"I'd rather you not lean forward like that. Because I'm nervous already."

"Okay," he said, and he relaxed his shoulders. "I'm still all ears." He flashed a Michael Landon smile.

"Don't laugh, but you are the first Chinese guy I've dated. I'm not sure how to explain this . . . but I think it's because of my father and other elders while I was growing up. They weren't good role models and I've never been attracted to Chinese men. Well, that's not true. I was attracted to this neighbor of my best friend. I was in high school. He had this awful view of women, and I'm embarrassed to repeat it."

Vincent gave me another Landon smile.

"He said there are three kinds of women: the kind you can talk to and be friends with; the kind you screw, excuse me for repeating his vulgarity; and the third kind—the kind you married. I think a lot of Chinese men feel that way."

Vincent was waiting for me to continue, and when he saw my uneasiness, he leaned forward. "Ruby, are you asking me what I think of women?"

"Yes. Yes."

"I don't have any sisters, so I didn't know much about girls when I was growing up. You know, mothers are not girls. You know what I mean. I liked girls in school. They liked me. I have women friends. They're mostly wives of my buddies. But if you're asking if I have the same views as the guy you're talking about, then no, I don't share those views."

I was delighted with his answer and so relieved I brought up the subject.

"I'm very happy you answered my ad."

He reached across the table for my hand. We sat there, hands clasped, until the waiter delivered our food.

Saying goodbye that evening was just like a movie. I accepted his offer to drive me home. There was parking near the building, which was a miracle in itself. He walked me to the front door, but did not ask to see my apartment. The good-night kiss was short, but the embrace that followed told me I had found the arms I had longed for. *I Could Have Danced All Night* was in my head again. I played out our good-night scene over and over before falling asleep.

~

Over the next month, I met two of the three brothers and their girlfriends.

"Who's older, Frank or Bill?" I asked.

"Bill is. He's Number Two. Frank's Number Three. Bill's the one who saw your ad in the magazine, so please, honey, don't mention it because Dee will kill him for looking at personal ads."

"But he looked for you, not for himself."

"I know, but you know how women are." We both laughed.

"When do I get to meet Big Brother Robert?"

Vincent took me in his arms. "Brother Number One and his wife are coming out to visit in a few months."

"I know you told me, but I forgot. Where do they live?"

"In D.C." Vincent wrapped his arms tighter around me. "They'll love you. They'll all love you."

~

I met his parents a few weeks later at a fund-raiser for the San Leandro Grammar School that Vincent attended and where he now coached Little League baseball. The following week the Yaos invited me to dinner.

"They seem like nice people," I told Emily over the telephone.

"What do they look like? If you say Vincent looks like Michael Landon, then does his father look like Lorne Greene?"

"Very funny, Little Sister."

"Hey, I'm serious."

"No. Mr. Yao is tall and slender; he's got gray hair. Mrs. Yao looks like our aunt in San Bruno. Square face, average height, a little thick around the waist. She doesn't smile. Like it's a strain for her to smile at people."

"Are they controlling people? Is she a nag?"

"I don't think so. But they're extremely superstitious about numbers. They invited me over for dinner last Saturday and I brought them this gorgeous bouquet of flowers. Vincent's father took one look at the bouquet, saw that it had four red roses, and immediately divided the bouquet in two. He reminded me that the number four is bad luck. 'We did not buy the house across the street because the address is three one four Cypress. Our address is three one seven.' Then he told me about his brother having four daughters and not one of them is in business or has married into money. 'Bad luck,' he said."

Emily was annoyed with the double standards. "Does he know that he has four sons and according to his belief, that would be bad luck? But I suppose sons can never be bad luck. Four sons can counteract any bad luck, but four daughters cannot."

"It's silly, isn't it? Just because the Chinese word 'four' sounds like the word for 'death'?"

"What's important is that you like Vincent."

"It's beyond *like*, Em."

~

Lauren and David, the newlyweds, liked him. "He seems like a solid kind of guy—sure of himself, but doesn't brag," said David. Lauren said, "He has honest eyes. I can always spot honesty." I watched the interaction between Lauren and David with envy. There was no pretense in how they loved each other. *Maybe. Just maybe someday, I'll be the envy of my friends too.*

Mrs. Nussbaum liked him. Vincent had a way with old people. From opening doors to helping them carry heavy packages, he would have impressed the grumpiest of old folks. After introducing him to Mrs. Nussbaum, she began giving me twice the number of care packages. "He's a perfect darling," she said.

I saw Mom many times in those months. Each time, I wanted to tell her about Vincent and each time I envisioned her shaking her head, saying, "You'll regret it. Just like me, you'll regret it." So I didn't tell her.

His friends treated me like a sister. "Ruby, we've known Vincent a long time, and we've never seen him happier. It's all because of you."

We were inseparable. If he wasn't at my place, I was at his.

~

How ironic that a Chinese descendant opened my heart like no other man. Saturdays were extra special. We'd buy the early edition of the Sunday paper and eat breakfast on the coffee table.

"Vincent, how many Chinese girlfriends have you had?"

He didn't answer right away. "What does that matter, honey?"

"Tell me," I insisted.

"Two."

"Tell me more. Why do men give only shortcut answers?"

"Wait a minute," he said. "You asked how many and I answered."

"What were they like? Why didn't it work out?"

"Ruby, Ruby, Ruby. They weren't the right one. They're history."

"Were they traditional?"

"Can we talk about us instead?"

"Good answer." I snuggled up and rested my head on his shoulder. "You're right."

"I'm always right."

"You know what's funny? You're something that came out of my dreams. We're both Americanized, but we come from the same culture. I don't have to explain being Chinese to you."

Vincent kissed me on the head. "You're a dream yourself."

"I'm glad it didn't work out with the other women. I'm the winner."

He kissed me again. "You're the winner and keeper of my heart."

~

That afternoon, I ran the last block to Dr. Thatcher's office. I felt as if I were talking to a mother who was also a friend.

"Dr. Thatcher, I really love him. It's time for me to settle down with someone."

"I'm happy for you, Ruby. Have you considered all the changes this will bring about?"

"Yes. Vincent and I have talked about everything. He's wonderful."

"Wonderful people belong together."

"I just can't believe that I met him. And he's real."

I spent the rest of the session going down the lists of traits that Vincent and I shared. "We're both intelligent. Kind. Generous. Hard-working . . ."

~

Six months after our first date, Vincent picked me up from work on a Friday night. Marilyn and Clyde both came out of their offices. They had met Vincent before, so they were shooting the breeze with him.

"Where are you two going this evening?" asked Marilyn.

"That's none of your business," interrupted Clyde.

"It's an innocent question," Marilyn defended herself.

"To dinner," I answered. "I hope anyway, because I'm starving. I didn't have lunch."

"Starving employees at a fancy hotel?" Vincent jested.

Chad came out of his office to play the "boss" bit.

"So, you're Vincent. You're the guy who's turning our little Ruby into a clock watcher, leaving at five on the dot."

"And I'm going to make sure she does that whenever possible."

My hero.

After saying goodbye to everyone, we walked over to the Seasons Cafe. The waitress showed us to a table in a corner and removed the RESERVED sign.

"Why do they need to put out 'reserved' signs?" I questioned. "It's not even five-thirty."

"They do if a customer calls ahead and asks them to."

"Oh?" I was intrigued.

"I wanted to make sure we got our table," Vincent explained.

We ordered dinner. After our waitress left the table, Vincent reached into his pocket. He took out a tiny velvet box and handed it to me.

"What's this?" My hands were shaking.

I opened the box and was dazzled by the brilliance of a diamond engagement ring. It sparkled like Lauren's. I couldn't have picked out a lovelier design. It was a princess-cut stone on a gold band. The diamond must have been at least two carats. Vincent reached over to take the ring out of its box and slipped the precious gem onto my finger. It was a little loose.

"Ruby, hear me out, okay? Some people will say we're rushing into this, and perhaps we are. But what's wrong with rushing into a good thing? My parents have a great marriage. So does my brother and all my friends." He squeezed my hand and gazed into my eyes. "You're my heart and soul, honey. Will you marry me?"

My head was in a fog. I was speechless. I looked at his Landon smile. So many times in my teenage years I had fantasized that Little Joe from *Bonanza* would propose to me. I thought about our first date; it seemed like yesterday.

"Ruby?" Vincent squeezed my hand again.

"I'm . . . I really want to say yes, Vincent, and this makes me very happy, but I wasn't expecting it to really happen so soon. Half of me was ready on our third date; the other half is in shock."

He rubbed my hand with his fingers and adjusted the ring. "My brother gets credit for the timing. He and Esther are coming out in a month. They won't get a chance to come out again for another two years. Her folks live in Louisiana and they alternate visiting parents. I want him to be there when I get married. I know you'll want Emily out here. I'm ready to send your sister a round-trip plane ticket."

The song, *I Could Have Danced All Night*, that filled my head on our first date came back then. I pictured us saying "I do" and walking off hand in hand. *I'm not daydreaming—Little Joe is asking me to be his wife. He's everything I want. But I really should discuss this with Dr. Thatcher first. No! You're not a little girl. You're a woman. This is your life. This is your moment.* After deciding that this answer deserved an Audrey Hepburn voice, I said, "Yes, Vincent, I will marry you."

CHAPTER 16

A Dream Come True

Emily and Vincent spoke on the telephone many times after I announced the big news. They became long-distance buddies. Hearing him refer to Emily as "Future Sis-in-Law" made me love him even more.

Emily called me at work one day. "Sis, in case you're wondering what I really think of Vincent, I think he's a very caring person. I can't wait to party on your special day."

"Thanks, Em. You know how much it'll mean to me—to have you here. You can give me away."

"Have you talked to Mother yet?"

"Yes. She didn't even react. I asked if she wanted to meet him. She said 'no.' She said, 'I'll meet him after you're married. I'll take the two of you out to dinner.' Is that weird or what?"

"Well, that's Mom's way of giving approval. She doesn't take just anyone to dinner."

"I suppose. Maybe she thinks I'll call off the wedding, then she won't have to meet him at all. Em, you think she thinks I'm making a big mistake?"

"Ruby, you're thinking too much. Parents wonder if their child is marrying the right person. What mother wouldn't?"

"What about you? Do you think I'm rushing into marriage?"

"Well. You guys are taking the big step rather soon in most people's opinion. But so what. Mom and Dad went steady for four long years and look what happened? A long courtship didn't make them any happier."

"But why won't she meet Vincent? I know she'd like him. How can anyone not like him? Mrs. Nussbaum says he's a perfect darling."

"Ruby, I think I know why. It's not exactly the same comparing Vincent, a fiancé, to my friend from high school, but I remember when I was a junior in high school . . . I wanted my friend, Letitia, to come over because she was my partner in dance class and we had to learn this routine. Anyway, her stereo wasn't working. We had to use ours. Letitia is black. You know how racist our parents are. Ben saved Mom's life, but you know, they said he was different. I knew if I had asked Mother if I could bring Letitia home, then the answer might have been 'no.' So, I didn't ask. Letitia and I strolled into the house one day. Mother was speechless at first. But after she saw that it was 'a done deal' and that Letitia was my friend, she was okay with it. She even invited Letitia to stay for dinner. That's how Mom is. Maybe she thinks that if she meets Vincent before the wedding and doesn't like him, that would upset you. So why not wait until it's 'a done deal'?"

"Oh, Em. I should listen to you more often. And I'm not being sarcastic."

"Ruby, even if Mom didn't like him, you would go through with it, wouldn't you?"

"Yes. There's no turning back now. He's it. Thanks for the pep talk, Em. This is costing you a fortune, daytime rates. Talk to you later. Love you."

"Love you too. Bye. Ruby, one more thing. Enjoy this. You're supposed to be having fun."

"That's what Dr. Thatcher says too. She's always reminding me to enjoy the moment. Thanks, Em. I will."

~

There's nothing like being in love. Saturday morning I found myself at a Little League baseball game. The last time I sat on bleachers was in high school. From twenty feet away, I watched Vincent talk to his team of six- to eight-year-olds. Each player received a high five from him before going into positions on the field. The four kids on the bench fidgeted in their seats; two of them turned their heads as if searching for their proud parents in the crowd. *I wonder if these kids will call me Mrs. Coach after we're married.*

Vincent walked over to shake hands with some people seated in the first row. Then he looked up. When he found me, he tipped his cap and flashed his smile. I waved. The woman sitting next to me looked at me.

"The coach is my fiancé," I told her. I blushed hearing my own words.

That day I learned something about Little League baseball. A pitching machine provided a certain amount of fairness for everyone at bat. Every kid on the team got a chance to play at least two innings. I also learned something about my husband-to-be. He had a way with children and they adored him.

Wearing my pager was a mistake; it went off three times. The last call made me miss the ninth inning. Vincent's team won. I wished I had been there. After all, this was the first game of the season. By the time I returned to the bleachers, two other teams were about to start a new game.

~

Vincent and I celebrated his victory that evening. I borrowed Mrs. Nussbaum's secret recipe for chicken pot pie. From the stationery store on Chestnut Street, I bought him a photo album with a baseball motif on the cover.

"I promise I won't answer non-emergency pages in the ninth inning from now on."

"You gotta do better than that. No more beepers at my games from now on, period. I wanted you to see the parents go hog-wild. I thought they were going to lift me onto their shoulders!"

"And I missed it? To show you how serious I am about being there cheering you on from now on"—I presented him with the album—"I'll be the photographer at every game and I'll fill this book."

"Thanks, honey. You're the greatest."

Mrs. Nussbaum's recipe was simple to follow. She had underlined "peas" and written over it "a must." While the pies were in the oven, we pored over travel brochures.

"It's too bad we only have a week for our honeymoon," I sighed.

"Pagers aren't allowed there either. We're going to a place where the St. Mark can't find you."

"Don't get embarrassed when I tell everyone, at hotels, at restaurants, that we're newlyweds. They give freebies, discounts, to newlyweds."

"You're a Chinese woman through and through."

"It's called being smart. Besides, Mrs. Nussbaum taught me that. She's not Chinese."

Vincent sorted the brochures into piles and gave them names.

Pile 1 for "beachcombing." Pile 2 for "culture and nightlife." Pile 3 for "undiscovered getaways." Our destination was secondary to me; my primary thought was to start my life as a married woman with the man I had chosen.

"I watched you with those kids today. You're a natural." I removed the brochures of Europe from the "culture and nightlife" pile. When we go to Europe, it won't be for a week.

"They're a great bunch of half-pints," said Vincent. "I can't wait until my kid is out there."

"Your kid?"

"You know what I mean, honey. Our kid. Our little kid."

"Since we're on the subject, I've been meaning to ask you, we don't have to rush with having kids, do we, Vincent?" My heart was beating fast.

He took me into his arms. "There's no need to rush. I know how much work it is to start a family. I've seen couples turn into enemies over how to raise their kids. That won't happen to us. We're both planners."

"I'm glad you're a coach to those kids. It'll be like easing into parenthood. In a few years we'll have our own."

"Two, Ruby, I'd like to have two."

"Well, let's see if you'll still want two after we have one. Men! You guys talk as if you're ordering pizza."

"You'll see, Ruby. I'm going to put you on a pedestal. You'll be my queen. I'll be a great husband and a great dad."

"I know you will."

~

Sitting in the wing chair the following Saturday, my mind was occupied with visions of wedding cake, champagne glasses, and a room full of friends toasting my happiness.

"Dr. Thatcher, it would make me very happy if you would come to the banquet that Vincent's parents are giving us."

"Ruby, thank you very much for the invitation, but I cannot accept social invitations from my patients. Meeting your loved ones and friends might interfere with the work we do in this room and I cannot jeopardize that. I hope you'll understand. I will be thinking of you that night, Ruby. I'm very happy for you."

"Thank you, Dr. Thatcher. May I at least bring in pictures of the party?"

"Yes, of course."

We spent the entire session talking about how happy I was.

~

The engagement period for many couples is a succession of trying times. Since ours was only a month long, there were few opportunities to test ourselves. We passed the few we had with flying colors.

The night Vincent announced our engagement to his parents, Mr. and Mrs. Yao asked us to stay after dinner for a little talk. Even though Vincent and I both felt we were ready to take this step in life without getting anyone's permission, I still felt trepidation that his parents would tell us not to rush into marriage.

"Ruby, I would like for you to know that Vincent's mother and I are very happy that you have come into our son's life. He has never been happier. We've been thinking it over, and . . ."

Oh, here it comes, I told myself.

"Well, kids, look around. This is a big house—too big for just the two of us. We raised four boys in this house and now there are just us two. We have five bedrooms, six if you count the room in the basement. What Vincent's mother and I are trying to say is that we would like to see you two save money the first couple years of your marriage. You're welcome to live here."

Vincent's mother nodded as her husband recapped his generous offer. And I thought they were going to tell us to postpone the wedding. I looked at Vincent's face as he gave me a quick smile that meant he was just as surprised as I was.

"You're so generous and so wonderful! This is a beautiful home. It's the home you've built together. That's what I want for Vincent and me—a home of our very own, something we can be proud of."

"That's all commendable, Ruby," his father continued. "Vincent's mother and I want to help you two get started on the right foot. Live here for a few years, save your money and get the house of your dreams." *The offer of a couple of years had turned into that of a few years.* "I hate to see young people pay all that interest on a loan when they can put down a larger down payment right off the bat."

"We'll be fine, Mr. and Mrs. Yao. It'll be our first joint project as a married couple—making compromises and coming to some agreements. We won't leave the Bay Area, if you're worried about that."

"As a woman, Ruby, I know about your feelings." Vincent's mother finally spoke. "I know what it's like to have your home the way you want it. You can have the same freedom here. Remodel the kitchen if you like. I don't cook much anymore. You make any changes you want if it will make you happy. Daddy is right. Save your money. We want to see you get ahead."

"Really, I think your offer is extremely generous and I'm so happy you've welcomed me into your family. I'm sure you understand why we want our own home. I would feel awkward living with my husband's parents even though I think they're wonderful people. I've been on my own so long and I'm set in my ways, but I look forward to sharing a home with my new husband."

"No need to feel awkward, Ruby. Mommy and I are quiet people. You two won't even know we're home half the time. Isn't that right, Mommy? We can divide the house into your rooms and ours. We won't take 'no' for an answer, kids. You'll save a lot of money in just two years. We'll move the living room furniture into the den. You can buy new furniture, even paint the rooms if you like. You'd be foolish not to accept."

I couldn't stand it anymore. If I had taken some deep breaths, I probably would not have said it, but I did say it. "It all sounds very nice, but there is still one matter. I won't feel comfortable running around naked in front of my in-laws."

Mrs. Yao's mouth dropped. Mr. Yao looked agitated, as if someone had called him a poor man. Vincent was suppressing a laugh. I imagine he was thrilled at the idea that his bride would be prancing around in her birthday suit.

Mrs. Yao had started pouring a second cup of coffee for her husband, but she dropped the cup while handing it to him. All three of them jumped to their feet to wipe up the mess.

Vincent said, "It's getting late, Mom, Dad, and we have a long drive."

Mr. Yao nodded.

"You kids must be tired. Drive safely," Mrs. Yao said nervously.

I apologized to Vincent on the way home. "I wasn't trying to be disrespectful, Vincent. I didn't mean to shock your parents that way. But I felt pressured and they were dismissing my decision, our decision, so I blurted out the business about running around naked."

"That's all right, babe. But I expect you to live up to your promises."

"Actually I'm glad your folks brought up the subject. We do need to start looking for a bigger apartment or think about buying a house."

"Let's plan the wedding first, go on our honeymoon, then worry about that. Okay?" He turned his head and stole a kiss.

"Hey, keep both hands on the steering wheel," I scolded. I reached over to run my fingers through his hair. "Okay, but will you give up your apartment and move in with me? I don't want to pack and unpack twice."

"Anything you say."

We were on the Bay Bridge approaching San Francisco. Looking out the window and seeing Coit Tower, the Pyramid Building, and the entire Financial District all lit up made my heart sing. I looked down at my engagement ring. The diamond couldn't have been more beautiful.

~

Vincent's parents insisted on picking out the wedding invitations. They didn't like my choice; they said it wasn't festive looking. I had wanted crimson ink on cream-colored paper; they wanted gold foil borders with gold ink on red glossy paper.

"Ruby, it'll make my parents happy. They've been planning this party since I was twenty-one."

"But how the invitation looks is important to me."

"I know, honey. But weddings are for parents, not for the bride and groom. You know that. It's a time for parents to show off."

"It's also a day for the bride. I want everything to be lovely, including the invitations."

"I like what you picked out, sweetheart. We'll find a solution." He kissed me.

"How about if two versions of the invitation are sent out?" I proposed. "I'll use my choice for your friends and mine, and the one your parents chose for their friends and relations."

"I think that's a great idea, honey. See how easy it is to turn a conflict into agreement?"

~

After we had solved the problem of the invitations, we sat down to draft the guest list.

"Ruby, my parents want to meet your parents before the wedding."

"I can't see that happening, Vincent. You know I don't see my father and my mother doesn't like people. I told you that, remember? I can't put her through an evening of social pressures. She's very delicate. It'll make her sad to see how close your parents are. I don't want to make her sad."

"But your parents will be at the wedding, won't they?"

"How can they, Vincent? They hate each other, and I can't invite one and not the other. It's already a great effort to make the day a happy and proud event for your parents. Why don't we focus on your parents and make it a beautiful day for them?"

"I feel bad that your parents won't be included."

"Don't feel bad. That's the way it is with my family. That's the way it has been for years. I told you how miserable they were as a couple. I'm not going to ask them to pretend, not even for a minute. Please don't ask me."

"I won't, honey. I'm sorry." He kissed me on the forehead and wrapped his arms around me.

"Mom said she'll take us out to dinner when we come back from our honeymoon."

"Honeymoon. I can't wait."

His breathing made me feel safe and secure. He didn't know that any fantasies my parents had about me being a "good girl" were destroyed long ago. A good girl would live with her parents and take care of them. A good girl would never make decisions on her own. I decided that being a good woman was more important to me than being a good girl. In my opinion I was a good daughter to my mother and I would be a good wife to Vincent.

~

Vincent's brother Robert and his wife, Esther, flew out a week before the wedding. They both worked at the same pharmaceutical company. That's how they had met. He was in Research and Development; she was in Marketing. I got to know them a little better at the big family dinner and later over brunch, when just the four of us met at The Decadent Eatery. Watching the interaction between Robert and Vincent made me proud of the man I was about to marry.

"Honey, Robert was the big brother of all big brothers. He was always there for us. He never pulled that 'you're cramping my style' bit with us," Vincent reminisced.

"I didn't have to. You guys were well trained," Robert laughed. "Ruby, welcome to the family," he said to me.

"Thank you. And thank you for making time for us."

"We wanted to get to know the woman who has passed the Yao Test, and the one who's getting baby brother," said Esther.

"The Yao Test?" I asked, afraid to hear the details.

"Oh yes, the test that's administered ever so gently, the patient doesn't even know she's getting it," Esther continued.

"Esther, don't do that to Ruby. You passed, didn't you?" Vincent nudged a little closer to me.

"All I'm saying is that a woman has to be extra special to be welcomed into the family. Join the club, Ruby. It's a very exclusive club."

"It'll be a big club as soon as Bill and Frank are married," I said. "I've met their girlfriends. They're both very sweet."

"Yeah, but will they pass the test?" Esther raised her eyebrows. "What am I saying? They won't even be invited to take the entrance exam; they're not Chinese."

"Now, honey. Vince and Ruby are probably nervous already. We're not going to scare them with in-law stuff. Every couple has in-law stuff. C'mon, folks, let's order some food."

The conversation after that intro was less mysterious and quite enjoyable. They invited us to visit them anytime we wanted to. Esther said she would take time from work to show us around.

Later, I asked Vincent about the "Yao Test." He grabbed me from behind, nuzzled and tickled me until I begged for mercy. "That's the Yao Test," he teased with a ghoulish voice.

That night while snuggling under the blanket, we watched Clark Gable and Claudette Colbert in *It Happened One Night*. Gable's character was a journalist and Colbert's an heiress. Their worlds were so different, but they fell in love. Falling asleep in Vincent's arms, I couldn't give a hoot about the Yao Test.

~

Emily's arrival was better than Christmas. Vincent picked her up from the airport and brought her back to my apartment. I had wanted the two of them to spend some time together face-to-face. When Vincent dropped her off, they looked like the best of friends. I cried happy tears when I saw her walking in.

"Em, I don't like this. You having to fly out on Sunday."

"I don't like it either. But nothing in the world would have stopped me from being your witness tomorrow. Besides, you guys are flying out to your honeymoon. I have to go back to school."

"I'm so happy to see you, Sis. Yippee!" I jumped up in the air.

Emily gave me a kiss on each cheek. "You silly goose," she said with affection.

Vincent put one hand on each of our shoulders. "You two have a lot of catching up to do. I know when I'm in the way. I'll say good-night, sisters."

"I'll make myself at home while you two smooch." Emily started for the hallway. "Bye, Vincent, see you tomorrow."

"Bye, Emily. I mean, bye, Sis," Vincent said playfully.

Vincent and I said good night. He gave me a long kiss and a tight embrace to remind me how much he loved me. "Good night, soon-to-be Mrs. Yao. Sleep tight."

"I will, Mr. Yao. Sweet dreams."

~

Emily and I were two giggly sisters in my apartment. Knowing that Father was not told about the wedding and that Mother would not be there, Emily had to be the diplomat that weekend. She reserved Friday evening for me, Saturday morning for Mom, Saturday afternoon for the wedding, and Sunday for Father.

"Ruby, instead of sleeping in the living room, why don't I sleep on the floor in your room and we can yak all night."

"A slumber party?"

"Yeah. Let's take Pebble and Mimi off the shelf."

"The four of us. Just like old times, Em. But no sleeping on the floor. The bed is big enough, for all of us."

I showed Emily where everything was. In the bedroom, in front of the full-length mirror, we stood side by side.

Emily had her arm around my waist. "We're beginning to look more and more alike."

"Hmm. But why are you taller, Little Sister?"

"Why do you have bigger boobs?"

"I give up." I kissed her on the cheek. "I love your hair. So shiny. So bouncy. I wouldn't look good with hair that short."

"Sure you would." Emily walked behind me and showed me by bundling my hair.

"Sure. The front would look good. But the back. I have a flat head back there."

"You do not, Ruby."

"Yes. Feel it. Mother must have let me sleep on my back when I was an infant, never turning me over. How else would I get such a flat head?"

Emily patted the back of my head. "Poor baby."

~

I couldn't fall asleep if I had wanted to. Getting married the next day, having my sister near me, it was all too much to absorb. But I remembered Dr. Thatcher's advice, "Enjoy the moment."

It was eleven when we climbed into bed.

"Em, what did you tell Father? He must have asked why you're here for the weekend."

"I said a very dear friend is getting married. It's the truth. You're a dear friend who happens to be a sister."

"I'm sorry you had to do that. I couldn't have invited him, Em. What if he had accepted? We haven't seen each other in years. It would be a travesty to make him Father of the Bride. It's my special day and I don't want anything or anyone to spoil it."

"I know, Ruby."

"How is he, Em?"

"Same old Dad. Still bragging about how much money he's got. It's really sad. The one person he trusted most turned out to be the one who screwed him. I never did like that woman."

"Maybe she feels that sponsoring someone to America gives her the right to take his hard-earned fortune. A relative! I predict she'll get her just desserts. They always do."

"It all makes sense now, Ruby. Mother's breakdown. Imagine?

Your husband giving away your life savings to the woman you hate. I would have killed him."

"I think Mom has always been mentally frail. What he did finally pushed her off the cliff. Let's talk about something more cheerful, Em."

"When I get married, I'm going to elope."

"While we're on the subject, how many admirers are there?"

"Well, I'll say one, even though there are these two other guys who are awfully cute. The special one is still Marshall."

"Have you two . . . ?"

"No. No, no, no."

"Why don't you make the move?"

"I don't want to muck up a great friendship with sex. We can talk about everything, and we have fun together."

"But isn't it tricky to have fun with a man and not have the intimacy?"

"It's easy. I avoid going over to his place and I don't invite him over to mine. Roller blading, tennis, movies, lots of brunch dates, street fairs. It works, for now."

"Em, I'm scared. Tomorrow will be here when I wake up and I'll be saying words like 'for better or worse . . . till death do us part.'"

"Is 'obey' in the vows?"

"No. I don't think that word is used anymore."

"How do you feel, Ruby? Truthfully."

"I'm in love, Em, and I know my love will grow. He's so lovable. He's not afraid to show his affections. He's firm on his positions, whether it's political or moral. He's generous, but not in a flaunting way. He's warm to people, but not gushing. I feel safe and protected when he's around. I don't have nightmares anymore. And of course there are superficial reasons why I love him. Don't you think we look good together?"

"You look great together. As a matter of fact, you two look very natural, like you've been around each other for a long time."

"I'm glad you like him, Em. He's very fond of you. He knows how close we are. So don't be surprised if he calls you when we have our first disagreement."

"If and when that happens, I'll tell him to give in, if he knows what's good for him."

"I'm drifting off, Em. Sweet dreams."

"Good night, Sis. Good night, Pebble and Mimi."

"Good night, girls."

~

On the morning of our wedding day, Vincent came by to have coffee with Emily and me. Then Emily took my car to see Mom.

"Vincent, please don't let the barber cut your hair too short. You know how I like it kept a little long. The photos taken today will be in our wedding album and I want us to look natural."

"Anything you say, soon-to-be Mrs. Yao." He kissed me. "I'm having lunch with my brothers afterward."

"Bye, darling. Say hello to the boys for me. Remember, not too short."

"I promise, honey."

~

I poured myself another cup of coffee. It was a beautiful morning in my glorious city. The breeze from the living room windows made me feel giddy. But also contemplative. *Marriage is a joint project. It's the most important partnership that anyone could commit to. I know nothing in life is perfect. No perfect man or woman. No perfect marriages. But I know ours will be a good one, because it will be just the two of us making joint decisions.*

My thoughts were interrupted by a gust of wind slamming one of the windows shut. *If I were superstitious, that would be a bad sign. Good thing I'm not.*

I had a long day ahead of me. Lauren and Marilyn were coming over to construct "the bride." Marilyn had offered to highlight my hair, but I wouldn't let her. She was a brunette that week.

~

That afternoon at five, our minister performed the six-minute ceremony. It was a compromise. I wanted a short and sweet ceremony; the Yaos wanted an extravagant evening to show off their son and his bride.

That evening, twenty of the thirty round tables were for the Yao relatives, friends and business associates. After the ten-course banquet, the clinking of glasses from each table to toast us, and the cake cutting, Vincent and I finally had a moment to ourselves.

"You look very handsome in your tuxedo. I think the women are swooning."

"And you look gorgeous, the most beautiful woman in the room."

"What happened, darling? Did the barber ignore your instructions?"

"Is it really that short?"

"It's so short here above the ears, looks like he shaved it."

"Mom wanted it short. She says it looks sloppy when it's long."

She says? "Our wedding photos will look like you have a crew cut."

"It's not that bad, honey! It was important to Mom. You understand, don't you, honey?"

I counted to five in my head. "You promised this morning."

Vincent held me tight and whispered in my ear, "I'm sorry, honey. Don't be angry with me. I wasn't thinking."

I couldn't stay angry, not with Earth, Wind & Fire on the DJ's turntable. It was their rendition of Lennon and McCartney's *Got to Get You Into My Life*. Vincent sang into my ear. I forgave him.

That night I understood the fascination of being a bride because I was certainly the center of attention. On what other occasion would a woman get to see all her friends in one room dancing, eating cake, and drinking toasts to her new life.

All evening I heard, "Isn't she beautiful? Doesn't she look lovely?" Emily said I was 'drop-dead gorgeous.' I felt radiant in my champagne silk off-the-shoulder long-sleeved sheath. Lauren had styled my hair into a French twist. Marilyn did my makeup; she had given me a face massage. She said a bride must look soft in her wedding photos. And the three-inch drop earrings by Swarovski were the *pièce de résistance*. I danced the night away. It was just like a movie.

Many hours later, after most of the guests had left and I was in bare feet, I overheard Mrs. Nussbaum and Emily chatting with Vincent and Mrs. Yao.

"Well, Sis-in-law, what advice do you have for me?" asked Vincent.

"Give Ruby her space, Vincent. And I don't mean extra rooms in the house," Emily responded without hesitation.

"You're getting a wonderful daughter-in-law, Mrs. Yao," Mrs. Nussbaum added. "She's a kind-hearted—"

"I know. Ruby's a good girl," Mrs. Yao interrupted.

I talked myself into believing that as soon as the wedding day was over, everything would work out and that I would have my way from then on. It seemed like a fair trade—one day of compromises and concessions for a lifetime of happiness.

~

After a glorious week of lying on beaches in Maui, we came home from our honeymoon. Saturdays continued to be our special day together, starting with the early edition of the Sunday paper and home-cooked breakfast, ending with snuggling in bed at night.

Being the organizer that I was, I started collecting information on first-time home loans and clipping open-house announcements in the newspaper. Vincent didn't share my enthusiasm and, at first, I thought it was just first-time-home-buying jitters. One evening while I was showing him some open-house ads, I saw a gloom over his face.

"There's no need to find a house when there's already a house we could live in," he said with a cold voice. "There's this duplex."

"What duplex?"

"Brother Frank's duplex, and he's offering to sell me, us, half the interest."

"That's very nice of him, but I really don't feel comfortable doing business with family members. Remember on one of our dates, we talked about not mixing business with family?" I reminded him of this, but I could see from his reddened face that my response was irrelevant at that point.

Putting my arms around his neck, I reminded him of our appreciation for privacy. "To have relatives as neighbors is too close for comfort."

He walked away from me and snapped on the television with the remote control.

My head began to throb. I took three deep breaths. "Did you know about this offer all along? Why wasn't I told about it sooner?"

"It was supposed to be a surprise."

"A surprise? Where we'll live as a married couple can't be a surprise. I don't understand, Vincent."

"That's just the point. We're a married couple now. You're a wife now."

CHAPTER 17

Two Strangers

Vincent's behavior towards me had changed. Even his tone of voice had changed. The playfulness in his "good morning" and "good night" had disappeared.

In response to our friends' inquiries about where our next home would be, we took turns making up excuses that we had not settled on a neighborhood. As for the wedding gifts, we left them in their boxes, stacked in the hall closet. I had lost interest in taking weekly inventory of "our treasures."

~

"Dr. Thatcher, it's like living with a stranger. We're both avoiding an argument, but one of us is going to blow. It'll be me. I just know it."

Dr. Thatcher advised me to talk to Vincent calmly. "All newlyweds face these kinds of problems. You love each other, Ruby, and the two of you will solve this together. We can practice how you'll talk to him without attacking his views. Sometimes the best move is to give yourself time to think things over. You're still getting to know each other. Don't think in terms of winning or losing. He's not your enemy."

~

Taking Dr. Thatcher's words to heart, I asked Marilyn to work Sunday for me so that I could go to a homecoming party for the Yaos and their closest friends, the Chans. The foursome had returned from their monthlong trip to China. This jointly hosted party was a festive affair. Vincent's brothers and their girlfriends were there. Mr. and Mrs. Chan's two daughters with their husbands and their combined six children filled the house with abundant energy. Big boxes of dim sum were delivered for lunch. There were enough shrimp dumplings and barbeque pork buns to feed a village.

"C'mon, Ruby," coaxed Loni, one of the little girls. "Hide with me." Her brother, Alex, was the seeker. "Forty-eight, forty-seven, forty-six . . ."

"Okay," I said. "But this is a pretty big house. We might get lost."

"No, we won't. I've been here before. Hurry, Ruby, hurry."

Loni pulled me by the hand into the den. We heard Alex down the hall yelling, "Twenty-eight, twenty-seven, twenty-six. . . ." There were two sofas in the room. One was against the corner. I pulled out the couch and motioned for Loni to get behind it. After squeezing myself into the space, I pulled the couch back to its original position. We huddled in the corner, and listened for Alex's footsteps.

From down the hall, Alex had already found one of the hiders. Seeker and hider now joined forces to find the others. I heard Mrs. Yao's and Mrs. Chan's voices.

"Let's spread it out on the floor." Mrs. Chan was talking. "I think I bought three yards." They had brought back all kinds of souvenirs for relatives and friends.

My legs were beginning to feel numb from squatting behind the couch. Loni put her index finger to her lips to tell me to "shush" as Alex yelled from the hall, "I'm going to find you."

"I really should have bought more of this one. So beautiful," Mrs. Chan was speaking again.

"Take some of mine. I don't have time to sew," Mrs. Yao offered.

"No. Save it. That one, the red one, give that to Ruby. Looks like something she'd like."

"No. She's the fussy type. Don't like anything," Mrs. Yao snapped.

"A very nice girl."

"A very rude girl," Mrs. Yao interrupted. "On her wedding day, she rejected the necklace I offered her. Said she did not wear jewelry. Very rude, that girl. It was not for her to wear. Would be crazy to wear something that valuable. I wanted my son to keep it in the bank."

Little Loni was fidgeting and I was scared that the two women would discover us hiding in the room. I put my index finger to my lips and Loni mimicked me in silence. Alex and two other children were now in the room. "They're here somewhere," said Alex.

"Don't step on the fabric," yelled Mrs. Chan. "Go play somewhere else."

I heard the sound of a cardboard carton being opened.

"That Ruby is a hard-working girl," Mrs. Chan praised.

"She has to. Her father did not send her to college so she has to work in a hotel."

I couldn't believe my ears.

"How about the bracelet?" Mrs. Chan asked Mrs. Yao. "Did she like the bracelet?"

"Ha! I told her that I had four bracelets, one for each daughter-in-law. Robert's wife picked hers out when she joined the family. Ruby had three to choose from but she said she don't like to wear jade. For heaven sakes, her Chinese name is jade. People must have thought we didn't give her anything on her wedding day. Very embarrassing for the Yaos."

"She's a modern girl," Mrs. Chan offered in my defense. "Modern girls don't like old-fashion Chinese jewelry."

No, it wasn't that. My mother told me to be careful about accepting jewelry from a mother-in-law. And she was right.

"Well, I'll have to be careful with this one. Modern girls know how to manipulate good boys."

Manipulate? I can't even manipulate won ton skin.

Mrs. Chan did not offer any opinion that time.

"Robert and that Americanize wife stay in D.C. because she has him wrapped around her finger. If I don't be careful, this one will take Vincent away too."

"That won't happen. Vincent is a good boy," Mrs. Chan comforted.

"He is a good boy," said Mrs. Yao in a soft voice. "My youngest and the most responsible. He knows how much I have sacrifice. Nothing changes. Married or not, he knows that his duty as our son comes first. I never worry about my Vincent, not the way I had to with his brothers. He's the only one who understands that first comes one's parents, then one's children, then one's wife. His father and I have taught him well."

"Vincent is a good boy," Mrs. Chan agreed.

I felt sick to my stomach, squatting in a corner with a seven-year-old little girl while listening to my mother-in-law talk about me as if I were her enemy.

Alex and his brother Larry came back into the room. I heard them opening and closing cabinet doors. "We can't find them," Larry whined.

"I told you to go play somewhere else," Mrs. Chan yelled again.

"Are you hungry? Let's eat," Mrs. Yao said to her friend. They left their treasures in the room and walked out.

"Loni, my leg hurts. Let's hide somewhere else," I told the innocent little girl.

"Okay," she said without arguing.

Sneaking down the hallway, we were both caught by Alex and his brother. Loni let out a big scream. My head was pounding.

~

That night in our apartment, Vincent was his old self again. I had scored points by taking the day off to go see his parents with him. He had rented a Marx Brothers movie. With his arm around me, we watched Groucho's character, Otis P. Driftwood, make love to Mrs. Claypool, played by Margaret Dumont. I kept my frustrations to myself; after all, this was the first relaxing moment we'd had together since our argument.

At work the next day, I couldn't get out of my head what Mrs. Yao said about me. Perhaps I should have waited for my Saturday session with Dr. Thatcher, but I couldn't contain myself. That night all through dinner, I rehearsed in my head what I would say to Vincent.

After dinner, while I was washing dishes and Vincent was putting away the dry ones, I clumsily blurted out my question. "Vincent, remember our first date? Remember when I asked you what your one regret in life was, and you said it was not going away to college? Was it because your mother didn't want you to go?"

"Mom? What does she have to do with it?"

"I overheard her telling Mrs. Chan that she's worried you'll move far away like Robert."

"Ruby, are you dragging my mom into our troubles?"

"I didn't know we were having troubles. We just need to agree on where we'll live. We can work it out."

"Then why are you talking about my mom? If you're blaming her for our failure to communicate, then you're out of line, Ruby. You have no right accusing my mom of anything."

"Can't you see that your parents might have planted subliminal messages so that you wouldn't go away to college?"

"I didn't want to go that bad. It was no big deal."

"Don't you see that your parents have held you back? You said you wanted to be like your brother Robert. He broke free—"

"Stop it, Ruby. You're talking about the most wonderful woman in the world. This is a woman who does everything the old-fashioned way—she even cleans the kitchen floor on her hands and knees. You have no right to talk about her or my dad that way."

"I have every right. I'm not a little girl and you're not a little boy. All those things you told me when we were dating? Don't you remember them?"

"Don't analyze me. We shouldn't be having this conversation. I'm surprised at you, Ruby." He went back to the living room, turned up the volume of the television and slept there that night.

~

Timing is everything and this was the worst. A certain piece of mail arrived the next day. It was an envelope from Franklin Funds addressed to Vincent and his mom. Instead of putting it with his stack of mail on the dining room table, I placed the unopened envelope on the kitchen counter.

Vincent deduced my annoyance when he saw the single piece of mail pulled out from the rest. "Honey, this is a quarterly statement for an account that Mom started for me. She started one for each of us. She puts money in twice a year and we're supposed to add to it on our own. She says every dollar deposited will be worth triple its value in ten years."

I took a deep breath. "How would you feel if I had an account with my daddy?"

"Why are you talking like that? I wouldn't think anything of it if you did. Honey, are you angry because Mom's name's on it? It doesn't mean anything. Everything I own is yours. You know that. She's a practical woman. She says she knows we'll be married forever, but you never know, just in case, she says. I know we don't have to worry about that kind of stuff like other couples."

"You're contradicting yourself, Vincent."

"Don't be like that. I can add your name if you want. Let me ask Mom. Please try to understand."

"I can't deal with this right now. I have to study for an exam."

"Deal with what? Why are you treating me this way?"

I wanted to cry. I wanted to put away my books and talk to him. But instead, I was cold and distant. Had he forgotten our marriage vows? He'd said, in front of the minister, "I promise to love and cherish . . ." I took my books to the dining room and stayed there until he fell asleep. I couldn't have handled it any other way. Pretending that I wasn't upset was no better solution. I told myself that the morning would bring about a fresh outlook.

I was wrong. I woke up with a headache. The next few days we were back to being strangers again.

~

After a week of thinking it over and reasoning with myself, I decided to visit the woman who had so much power over my husband. Fight fire with fire. No. I would fight with kindness.

That Saturday I announced, "I'm going to visit your mom, Vincent. And I'll bring her a present."

"That would make her very happy," Vincent said approvingly. "It's about time you two got to know each other. She loves you. My whole family loves you."

~

I had told Dr. Thatcher about my imminent visit to Mrs. Yao, but not about my plan to challenge her. From Orchard Supply Hardware, I bought Mrs. Yao a high-tech mop system, the kind that requires no bending and wringing. It was my Trojan Horse.

"Mrs. Yao, this is for you. Look! The height of the handle is adjustable. No more bending, kneeling, and getting your hands all chapped."

"Ruby, you shouldn't have spent your money."

"My pleasure. You work too hard."

I picked up the newfangled gadget and opened the broom closet to put it away for her. I was not in the least surprised to see that she already had a high-tech mop system tucked in the back of the closet.

"Mrs. Yao, you have one already!" I said aloud. *Now I've got you,* I said in my head.

"Yes, Ruby. But you won't give my little secret away, will you, Ruby? Men like to think that their women love them enough to wash the floors by hand. We wouldn't want them to think we don't love them, would we, Ruby?"

"But I'm sure they would love you even if you didn't do any cleaning."

"Ruby, you're still young. You'll learn how to get respect from men. Didn't your mother teach you?" She said that in a condescending tone.

How dare she suggest that my mother is like her.

"Why don't I take this back to the store, Mrs. Yao."

"Yes, Ruby. You do that."

Should I tell this woman I can see right through her, that I know she is the manipulator?

As two opposing generals would meet face-to-face on the battlefield, Mrs. Yao broke the silence. "Ruby, come into the sitting room. I want to show you something."

She motioned for me to go before her—a diplomatic move on her part. Once inside the room, she gestured for me to sit down on the Chinese silk brocade sofa. I sat on one end; she sat on the other.

"Look around, Ruby. What you see is just a small sample of my hard work as a good wife. Do you think that I didn't have to sacrifice?"

I wanted to answer, but she held up her hand to stop me.

"Do you think that all this came to me easily? No. Every woman has a plan. You'll have yours. A good wife is one who takes care of her husband and children so that they are free of worries. I worry for them. Now that you're part of the family, I'll worry for you."

I opened my mouth to interrupt, but she continued speaking.

"You have married into a loving family, Ruby. We love you." She pointed to the monstrous *cloisonné* vase at the corner of the room. "See that vase, Ruby? My husband gave that to me when I gave him our first son. There have been many other beautiful gifts since then, of course. I was spoiled by not only a husband but also by four sons. They spoil me because they know there isn't anything I wouldn't do for them. All I ask is that they share their troubles with me. I know what's good for them. Always have. Always will. Young people these days live such hurried lives. They forget to reap the benefits from listening to the wisdom of their elders. I would hate to see you and Vincent turn into one of those couples who forget that family comes first. Family decisions always weigh more than individual ones."

From wanting to interrupt, to wanting to shut her up, I now wanted to tape this monologue so that I could take it to Dr. Thatcher.

Bette Davis and Joan Crawford both stepped into my head. "Mrs. Yao, I'm going to do everything in my power to make our marriage work. Just as you and Mr. Yao are a tight team, Vincent and I will be one too. You're an inspiration to us."

She squinted as if to view me through a rifle sight.

We said goodbye to each other. I picked up my high-tech Trojan Horse and left her home.

Driving away, feeling like a soldier who had survived a battle without sustaining great injuries, I knew I would not have changed anything if I told Vincent about my conversation with his mother. The establishment she had built and fortified was not about to crumble because of me. I would have to find a way to win my husband's loyalty. It would take time and I would make time. After all, I was becoming a patient woman. That was part of the definition of a great woman.

~

The next day, I put my plan into action.

"Darling, let's take a look at this duplex," I said with sweetness in my voice.

"You mean it?" Vincent jumped to his feet.

"Yes. You should look at it too, really look at it and ask yourself, 'If this weren't my brother's, would I still like to live here? Is this Vincent Yao's idea of a home sweet home?' " I proposed.

"I'll do that, honey. You do the same. Who knows? It might be something you'll like."

"We'll find out together." I emphasized *together*.

~

Mr. and Mrs. Yao invited us to dinner Friday night. Mr. Yao cooked crab and Mrs. Yao served capellini with asparagus. Vincent had told her that this was one of my favorite meals. Dinner was pleasant. Father and son chatted about baseball coaching; Mrs. Yao talked about Vincent's brothers.

After dinner, she brought in coffee and cheesecake. "It's decaf," she announced. "I don't give my boys caffeine so late in the day. Ruby, you remember that, now."

"We drink Sleepy Time tea at night, Mom," Vincent answered for me.

"Good, you listen to your wife," Mrs. Yao advised.

"Ruby, Mommy made this cheesecake," praised Mr. Yao.

"It's delicious. Everything was delicious." I smiled at Mrs. Yao.

"Mommy makes the best won ton. When you have time, Ruby, Mommy will show you how to wrap won ton," Mr. Yao offered.

"It's not easy," Mrs. Yao declared.

"Ruby is a magician. She can do anything," my husband exaggerated.

Mr. Yao put down his coffee cup and pushed his plate aside. "Kids, we have something important to talk to you about."

Mrs. Yao and Vincent also put down their cups. I was getting nervous.

"We heard from Frank that you're buying half of the duplex," Mr. Yao began.

"We're just looking," I interjected.

"You'll like it, Ruby," Mrs. Yao chimed in. "It's very nice."

"I don't even know what neighborhood it's in," I mumbled.

"It's on Cherrywood," Mr. Yao answered.

"Cherry Street? How lovely." I was impressed.

"No. Cherrywood," Mr. Yao corrected.

"That's funny. I thought I knew all the street names in the City."

"No, Ruby. It's not in San Francisco. It's two miles down the road," Mr. Yao clarified.

"Here? But we both work in the City," I asserted.

"You can't find such a good deal in San Francisco," said Mr. Yao.
My face felt hot. I can never hide embarrassment or anger.

"You two can take BART into the City. The BART station is just
two minutes away," Mrs. Yao announced.

"Kids, it's better that you live close by," Mr. Yao said in a soft voice.
He leaned forward. "Mommy and I are getting old. We're both retiring this year. Robert and Esther just gave us the most disappointing
news. They said they're not going to give us any grandchildren."

"Bill and Frank," Mrs. Yao added, "are still dating those girls."

"They're both very nice women," I injected.

"They're not Chinese," Mrs. Yao snapped.

Mr. Yao's turn again. "We're not asking you kids to do it for us.
You're still honeymooners. But we wanted the two of you to know
that as of next year, we'll both be available to be full-time baby-
sitters. We are so excited. It's been a long time since we've had babies in the house. Mommy loves babies."

I studied Vincent's face, but he wasn't looking at me. He didn't
have any expression on his face, which made me curious as to
whether he and his parents had planned this conversation.

"Everything in due time," I started. "First, Vincent and I are going
to enjoy our first year of marriage. Then we're going to set up house-
keeping. Then we'll plan a family. We have time. I'm only twenty-
nine."

"Ruby, twenty-nine is not so young. I had my first when I was
twenty. If you wait too long, you'll run the risk of jeopardizing the
baby's health."

Vincent was not defending me the way he did at the beginning of
the evening.

"Ruby, Mommy is not saying you are old. We are concerned that if
you wait too much, we'll all be too old to enjoy little ones. Babies

are a lot of work. We have the energy now. We are useful now. Think
it over."

Mrs. Yao smiled at me. "You can have a second honeymoon anytime. Go to Europe after the baby is born. Most couples would never
be able to. Who would watch the children? You two will have us to
watch the baby."

"Mommy, what a wonderful idea. Let's send the kids to Europe
for giving us our first grandchild."

My head was hurting as I swallowed the bitter aftertaste of the
coffee. Vincent had kept quiet all that time. When we said goodnight
to the Yaos, they were arm in arm, looking like a couple who had just
found out they're expecting their first child. I felt as if my head
would explode.

Neither Vincent nor I talked on the way home. I avoided looking
in his direction during the entire ride. I felt betrayed. His lack of par-
ticipation in the conversation about us and children made me suspect
he was forewarned or prepped for the delightful evening.

Back at our apartment after I had taken three extra-strength Ex-
cedrin tablets and was getting undressed, the built-up pressure
cooker in my head finally let go. "Tell me, Vincent, did you and your
parents sit around and plan all this? Let's find a fool who thinks she's
going to get married and live out her dream life. Why didn't you
bring your mommy and daddy to our first date?"

"Ruby, you're upset and you'll say things you don't mean."

"Did they read my ad and did they draft the letter for you? Or did
they get you a subscription to Mail Order Brides Unlimited, but it
would have taken too damned long?"

"They were going to send me to Hong Kong to find a wife, but I told them 'no,' that I wanted to find her on my own. Are you satis-fied?"

"I'm in disbelief. This is a bad dream, Vincent. I know it is. It's bad enough that we can't agree on where to live and your mother thinks I'm her enemy."

Vincent opened his mouth to interrupt me, but I raised my voice to stop him.

"Now your parents are telling me to give them a grandchild, not in a few years, not in a couple of years, but NOW! This is like one of those crappy movies on television that makes me sick."

"You call our life a crappy movie? You call my parents' generous offer crappy? They're saying that they're ready-and-willing baby-sitters because they love us, and they'll love our baby. It's not my mom who sees you as an enemy. It's you who sees her that way."

"I'm very tired, Vincent. Please. I'm going to sleep in the living room because my head is pounding. I'm very tired."

"Look at me, Ruby. Listen to me. I love you. I want a wife and children." He gritted his teeth. "I'm human." He was almost in tears.

Perhaps if he had held me in his arms to say those words, I might have been more tender with him. But instead I took my pillow and slammed the bedroom door behind me. I tried to remember every conversation we'd had before our wedding day. Had I misunderstood everything he told me? *What have I done?*

~

The next morning I pretended to be asleep when Vincent walked across the living room. Then I heard his footsteps in the kitchen. A minute later I heard the closing of the front door. My throat felt scratchy and every muscle was aching. I rolled over to go back to sleep. When I got up and glanced at the clock on the mantel, I was shocked to see what time it was: 1:50. *Shit*.

~

Not only was I late for my appointment, I looked like a woman who had not slept at all. Dr. Thatcher poured me a glass of water.

"I'm not ready to have a child. Is it my fault, Dr. Thatcher? What have I done?"

"Ruby, will you and Vincent be willing to talk to a marriage counselor?"

"What's the use? Isn't a marriage counselor for couples who have problems that could be solved through compromises? Do you see any room for compromises here?"

"Only you and Vincent can answer that, Ruby. Remember what we talked about? Talk to him calmly. He's not your enemy. He might be just as tormented as you are with his parents' expectations."

"He didn't say anything. He agrees with them."

"Do you really know that, Ruby, or is it your conclusion because you are hurting?"

"I don't know, Dr. Thatcher. I really don't know anything right now."

~

After the session, instead of going home to face Vincent, I called Mother. She was home and agreed to go out with me. I took her to Mel's Diner. Mel's was the place I used to go to whenever I felt sad. As soon as I walked through its door and saw the jukebox, the old-fashioned counter seating, and the black-and-white checkered floor, all my troubles temporarily disappeared.

Mom and I sat in a booth, with its own jukebox selecting station.

After ordering a chicken burger, to be split between us, I inserted a quarter and selected three tunes.

"Mom, how are you?"

"Fine. You're not looking well. What's wrong?"

"Nothing is wrong, Mom. I'm just tired."

Sensing that Mother would not believe me, I flipped the panels of the selection box, not intending to choose more tunes.

"How's Vincent?"

"He's fine. We're both fine, Mom."

I felt her eyes studying me.

"Marriage is not easy, Ruby. I didn't know anything about being a wife when I married your father. No one told me that everything would change. Are you pregnant, Ruby?"

"No, Mom. No."

"Perhaps if your father and I were together, then we could be your protector—"

"Mom, I don't need any protecting. Protecting from what?"

"From in-laws, Ruby. You think I don't know. I do know. A new wife should have strong protectors and I am not strong for you."

Looking at Mom's face, I saw sadness and pity. The tables had turned. My own mother was pitying me. I wanted her to be angry with me. Or for her to tell me to fight for the man I love. Or to tell me to be calm and reasonable. I wanted her to say the words that Dr. Thatcher said.

"Did you accept jewelry from them, Ruby?"

"No, Mom."

"Well, you're damned either way. If you accept, they call you a gold digger. If you don't accept, they call you disrespectful."

The first tune I had selected from the jukebox came on. A light went on in my head—I realized that moment I was expecting my

217

mother to be someone she wasn't. I was not Samantha Stephens, the good witch on television, and my mother was not Endora, the spiteful witch. I looked at Mom's eyes and wished I had not shared my unhappiness with her.

"Mom, it's Johnny Mathis. Remember? You used to play his record, and when I became a starry-eyed teenager, I played it over and over again until it sounded like oil popping in a skillet?"

"I remember. *The Twelfth of Never* and *Chances Are*. I remember."

"Mom, please don't worry about me. I'm a big girl. I can take care of myself." I regretted having dragged my mother into my mess.

When I dropped her off at her place, she looked like she wanted to say something, but she didn't.

I hugged her.

"Be strong, Ruby," she said to me as she waved goodbye.

"Don't worry about me, Mom," I answered with confidence.

I sat in my car to think. I should have known that she would see the truth on my face. Just like the time I came home with a bloody knee.

~

I was in the fourth grade. I had lied to her about helping the teacher after school, but instead I was at a classmate's backyard jumping rope. I fell that afternoon while playing. I was not supposed to play. "Proper young ladies do not play like that, with their legs in the air," she said many times. My right knee was cut and I couldn't hide the wound when I came home. Mother saw my knee and immediately took out the first aid kit.

"I tripped and scraped it on the concrete steps in front of school," I said nervously.

"Then why didn't your teacher put a bandage on it instead of letting you come home like this?" she asked in Chinese.

"She was already gone when this happened." Another lie came out of my mouth.

The next morning as I was walking out the door to go to school, she called out to me, "Don't play today. Let the wound heal." I felt so guilty about having lied to her that I never followed that classmate home again.

~

Vincent was not home when I arrived. The telephone rang. It was Emily.

"Sis, Vincent told me about everything. He sounded very sad. Are you okay? What's going on?" Emily's gentle voice made me cry.

"It's a mess, Em. I'm up against a team of bulldogs."

"Can't you guys talk it out, just one-on-one?"

"If only it were that simple."

Emily listened to my version of what had been going on since we came home from our honeymoon.

"Sis, I love you," said Emily. "I don't like hearing you cry like this. You two have to sit down and talk."

"Em, I hear Vincent at the door. Love you too. I'll be all right. Really. Talk to you later."

Vincent sat on the living room sofa and stared into space. He looked like he had just received gut-wrenching news.

"Emily?" he asked.

"Yes. She cares for both of us," I said with a smug tone.

"So do my folks," he mumbled.

I sat beside him.

"Vincent, please tell your parents we'll work it all out. You and me. Tell them we'll decide where we want to live, when we'll start a family, and how we'll raise our child."

He didn't respond.

"Vincent?"

"Do you or do you not love me?" The sleeping tiger had awakened.

"That's not the question," I corrected. "Do you or do you not understand the meaning of marriage and partnership?"

"I understand, Ruby. You obviously don't. You don't understand the meaning of family support, family ties, and family love," he yelled.

"Why didn't you tell me about any of this before we were married?" I yelled back. "The duplex, the plan to have a child immediately, the amount of involvement from your parents."

"Because it was inappropriate then. You were a girlfriend. You are family now. You have people who want to take care of you."

"I thought you wanted the lifestyle we talked about. Do you remember telling me that you wanted the freedom of living life the way you want to, not how family thinks you ought to?"

"That's nonsense. You always remember things I never said. We are married now and you better get it through your thick head that the only chance, the only chance in life for success, is to depend on family support."

"But how about our marriage vows? What happened to love, honor, and cherish?"

"I don't understand you, Ruby. I do love, honor, and cherish you. That's not the problem. You're throwing away a chance of a lifetime. That's the problem. It's like winning the lottery and saying you don't want it. A chance to buy our own home without giving a bank the interest. My folks are offering us the world and you spit in their faces."

I felt as if someone had punched me in the stomach. We didn't eat dinner that night and we slept in separate rooms.

We avoided each other for three long days. *Everything will work out. Just give it time. Time for the two of us to cool our heads.*

I called him up at work to arrange a date at the Seasons Cafe. He was agreeable. *How could we not bring our hearts and minds together at the place where so many intimate conversations took place?*

A client kept me on the telephone so I was late. Vincent looked agitated. He didn't even get up to greet me. The waitress came over.

"Just coffee," he said.

"*Cioccolata* for me, thanks." After the waitress left, I turned to him. "I'm sorry for being late. I couldn't get off the phone."

He nodded.

"How are you, Vincent?"

He didn't answer. Instead he took out a piece of paper from his breast pocket. "I made a list of things we need to talk about."

"You made a list?"

"I made a list after you called."

All of a sudden, I felt a sourness in my stomach. *I didn't know heart-to-heart talks could be done with a list.*

"I've talked it over with my folks and—"

"You've talked what over with your folks?" I interrupted.

"Ruby, my mom's heart is breaking. She's all torn up about us."

My chest tightened. "What about me? You don't think my heart is breaking?"

"Don't you see it's our duty to make our parents happy? We have no right to cause them misery."

I was so shocked I couldn't come up with any words. My head hurt.

Vincent continued. "I never said this before, but there's something wrong, something really wrong with the way you see family ties. You don't talk to your dad. I haven't even met your parents."

"What's your point, Vincent?"

The waitress delivered our drinks and hurried away.

"That's not the way family should—"

"I don't—"

"Let me finish, Ruby. Please. Mom says you're just nervous. You're worried that she'll turn into a nosy, meddling mother-in-law. She wants you to know that she understands about your rotten childhood. Give her a chance, Ruby. She wants what's best for us. She knows what's best. We're her kids."

My hot chocolate wasn't nearly as hot as my face was. "Will you go to marriage counseling with me?"

"What?"

"Couples counseling."

He looked surprised. "You're already seeing a shrink."

"It won't be Dr. Thatcher. It'll be someone who doesn't know our history."

"I can't, Ruby."

"Why not?"

"It's not about me. I don't abuse you. I don't sleep around. It's about you."

I reached into my purse to get two Motrin tablets and I washed them down with the now lukewarm cocoa.

"What does Thatcher say about all this?"

"Of course Dr. Thatcher is on my side. She's my therapist. I'm asking you to go to marriage counseling—where we can tell an unbiased person our troubles. I want you to see my side."

"And I want you to see my side. I've been beating my head against the wall. Here. See this list?" He smoothed out the paper. "Everything on this list makes sense. Home. Children. Parents. Saving money."

"Where's wife or partner on that list?"

"It's—"

"It's not there because it's not important to you." Tears welled up in my eyes. *Don't cry,* I said to myself.

"Honey." He handed me a napkin. "You are important. You're my wife. You're a part of me."

I heard his words, but they sounded hollow.

"You haven't answered my question about going to see a counselor."

"No one can help us, Ruby, except ourselves. Not that I'm telling you what to work on with Thatcher, but can you ask her about selfishness, disrespecting elders, and plain old stubbornness?"

I looked at his hardened face. There was a coldness I had not seen before. He folded the piece of paper and tucked it into his pocket. We sat there in silence.

My headache was dulled, but I had a knot in my stomach. My pager went off. The number was Marilyn's extension. "Looks like I have to get back to work." My voice was that of a defeated woman.

He stood as I grabbed my purse, and he gave me a quick obligatory kiss. I was out the door before the tears flowed.

That night I didn't get home until eleven. Vincent wasn't there. The closet door stood open. He had taken all his clothes.

CHAPTER 18

The Bird

My eyes were puffy when I walked into Dr. Thatcher's office two days later. I had to see her before my Saturday appointment.

"He didn't even leave a note. He cleared out. Just like that."

"Where did he go, Ruby?"

"To Mommy and Daddy. Emily told me. He called her. He was hoping to get her 'to talk some sense into me.' Now she's pissed at him."

"What happened, Ruby?"

I told Dr. Thatcher about our conversation at the cafe. She reminded me to take care of myself and we practiced what I would say to him and how I would say it at our next conversation.

~

I avoided calling him at his parents' home. We met several times over the next two weeks for coffee. Neither one of us brought up any meaningful topics. "How's work?" "How's Emily?" I think we were both wishing the other person would surrender first. The thought of having another coffee date with my estranged husband made me sick to my stomach. So I invited him over Saturday morning. Surely he would remember how special it was to eat breakfast together and share sections of the Sunday paper while we planned our life.

He arrived with a dozen pink roses. I almost cried. Over French toast, his favorite breakfast, and freshly ground coffee, we tried to recapture married life. I felt awkward, conscious of my every word and gesture. We separated the paper; he took the sports section.

We ate in silence. I couldn't focus on what I was reading. He looked at his watch before finishing his food. I told myself not to get angry.

If someone had been watching us, then they would have been able to tell me what triggered the argument that ensued. I only remember his leaving with the rest of his belongings and my calling Dr. Thatcher to cancel our appointment.

I couldn't bear to talk about it that day. I couldn't even cry. The sun came out around eleven so I got into my car and drove to Stinson beach. After staring at the ocean for two hours and still no tears and no relief, I went home. There was a message from Dr. Thatcher telling me she hoped to see me the following Saturday.

By late afternoon I realized I had not eaten any lunch. Sitting down to a cold meat loaf sandwich, I remembered the harsh words from the morning.

Vincent had reminded me that my problem was that I never wanted to be a part of the family; that I didn't know what love was; and that I would grow old and die alone.

"That independence crap was all right when you were single. But you're part of a family now. You don't have to be independent anymore!"

I reminded him that I would rather be old and alone than be suffocated by people who use the word "love" to justify their selfishness.

He reminded me that blood is thicker than water and that I was not blood-related to him.

After all the years of undoing what my parents had taught me, how to keep quiet and docile, how to be selfless and not think for myself, I found myself married to a man who wanted me to regress to those helpless years.

"The problem with you, Ruby, is that you do not take the role of a wife seriously. Because you were unable to talk to me rationally, I had to go to my parents to get help. They are the ones who truly love me. Did you think that marriage is buying a home and going off to do whatever you please? Don't you have any sense of duty? Just because your parents didn't give a damn about family, you don't have to be that way! You better wake up! Have you looked into the mirror lately? You're still Chinese, no matter how independent you think you are. I'm willing to let bygones be bygones if you're willing to shape up and be realistic."

"What a noble speech! I know what my problem is! My problem is that I was blind and you've helped me take the blinders off. I look into the mirror every day; I see a woman who has self-value. You're right about my sense of duty. I choose my duties. I do not let others choose them for me. I have undone most of the damaging brainwashing from my childhood, but you are oblivious to the fact that you're an adult now, no longer a child who must mind your parents. Don't you see how people can misuse traditional ideas to stifle free thinking?"

"Ruby, this is not sociology class. You don't have to tell me about free thinking. I chose you. You were my choice. My folks approved the marriage because I told them how much I loved you, that you

were the only one for me. I was stupid to think you would honor tradition."

"Approve? You had to have their approval? I'm the stupid one. I
didn't see through your disguises."

His last words were, "My family says it's time to cut our losses."

~

I was a mess at work. One morning while juggling two telephone
calls, I had forgotten that I had put one client on HOLD for five minutes. Luckily the caller was Mrs. McKenzie. "That's quite all right,
Tall Blonde. I had you on the speaker phone," she said casually.

All week long I made mistakes—spilling coffee on purchase orders, forgetting to give the chef final head-counts for my clients, and
neglecting to check my tickler file. I tensed up every time the telephone rang. Perhaps Vincent would call to say he was wrong, that he
would move back home, and that we would live happily ever after.
He never called.

Friday, Marilyn and Clyde dragged me out to lunch in an attempt
to cheer me up. They took me to the burger place across the street.

"I do appreciate your concern, guys, but I'll be all right," I told
them.

"Of course you'll be all right. Vincent will come begging soon
enough," Clyde said with surety in his voice.

"I'm sorry," interrupted Marilyn, "but I think we should change
the subject because Ruby needs cheering up, not our predictions of
what Vincent will do."

"Sorry, Ruby," Clyde apologized as he patted my hand.

"I think you're both wonderful. What would I do without you?"

Marilyn moved her chair closer to me. "I've got something very
funny to tell you." She took a sip of water. "My cat was hysterical this

morning. I was brushing my teeth when I heard her scratching at the door. When I opened it, she had one paw up in the air, her head was tilted, and she was meowing as if to say, 'Mom. I've got something to show you. Come on. Let's go, Mom.' I laughed so hard I thought I was going to die. But, when I followed her into the kitchen, I found out what it was. A bird! A dead bird! I screamed. It was awful. Eeew. My cat didn't know why I wasn't pleased with her gift. She had this adorable look on her face. 'Mom, I got it just for you.' And I was about to lose my breakfast."

Clyde made a funny face. "Well, if we're going to talk about animals, I have a story too. But it's not that sickening. I was at my folks' house last weekend, reading in their living room, when I heard this strange sound from the chimney. What could it be? From the chimney? Too early for Santa Claus. It was a . . . He had . . . in the chute. I hurried over . . . couldn't figure out . . . didn't want to. . . ."

I watched Clyde's lips move and heard clips of his story as I started to remember the day when Emily and I both followed Mother to the Laundromat.

~

Emily must have been four years old. School was out for summer break and on a beautiful Wednesday, the three of us walked to Suds Laundromat.

Emily wanted to be helpful. "Mama, let me hold the Tide," she begged.

"No," Mother snapped. She reached into her pocket and took out her little bag of napkins. "If you want to hold something, why don't you hold this?" She always carried napkins; she believed in wiping everything before touching it or sitting on it.

We had the place to ourselves and Mother loaded three washers. We were seated on the long bench when we heard wings flapping. A bird had flown into the room and was trying to find its way out. It flew into the big glass window and was stunned. It then recovered itself and flew aimlessly about the room. Emily grabbed Mother's pant leg with one hand and covered her eyes with the other hand.

"Poor, poor bird," Mother sighed. "Found a way in, but not a way out." She grabbed and rolled up a *Chronicle* that someone had left on the bench. Mother looked like a ground-crew member at the airport runway waving a flashlight to give clearance to a departing plane. She waved the rolled-up newspaper to direct the bird towards the door, but it did not work.

The bird flew into the window again and again. Mother and I watched its futile flight end on the bench where we had sat. The little bird was dead. Emily was sobbing. Mother put down the newspaper the way a doctor puts down a stethoscope when the patient's heart has stopped beating. I kept my eyes on the bird and used all my power to imagine it coming back to life, but it didn't work. I couldn't save it either; it would never fly or sing again.

Mother grabbed me by the wrist. "Don't tell your father. He'll say it's a bad luck sign for us. Do you hear me, Ruby?"

"Yes, Mother."

Father had told us that when an animal dies in front of you, it means a bad thing will happen to you.

Emily cried all the way home and did not want to go to "the launjery place" anymore. I felt sorry for the bird, but more sorry for Mother. She had wanted so much to save the bird but its fate was out of her control. Poor little bird—found a way in, but not a way out.

~

". . . thank God . . . looked a little . . . but wasn't injured . . . ," Clyde was still talking. "He was chirping on the tree when I last saw him."

"Ruby, are you okay?" Marilyn was tugging at my sleeve.

"I'm fine. Just a little tired, that's all." I took a sip of water.

The waiter brought our food.

I'm not going to be that bird. I thought I was thinking in my head, but the words had come out.

"What, Ruby?" Marilyn had a puzzled look on her face.

"Nothing. Nothing. I'm glad Clyde saved the bird."

CHAPTER 19

Not My Cup of Tea

"Dr. Thatcher, it's over. We're getting a divorce."

"Is this what you really want, Ruby?"

"What I really want is to be married to one person, not to his domineering family. I'm not a quitter, Dr. Thatcher."

"I know you're not."

"But if I don't quit, then I'll have to go to the Yaos and announce defeat."

"It's not defeat, Ruby. Do they know how much you and Vincent are hurting?"

As tears streamed down my face, Dr. Thatcher looked at me with tenderness.

I blew my nose and sat up in my chair. "For the first time, I can see their point of view. 'Why is our son's new wife rejecting us,' they must be asking themselves. 'Why doesn't she see that we love her and want to give her everything that would make her life easier. A home, family support, guidance, everything a girl would want.' Maybe that's the problem, Dr. Thatcher. They were hoping that I would be a good girl. Just because I told them Vincent and I had no intention of moving far away, it didn't mean I would be obedient too. They read too much into me. Or maybe Vincent's stubbornness about choosing me already cost them a concession, a big one."

"That's no way to see a daughter-in-law. You're a person, not a concession."

"I wonder if Chinese parents ever see their grown children as adults. And if they do, I'm not sure if they could ever respect their children. I was brought up to respect elders, only elders. You can admire someone younger than you, but it wouldn't be respect." I blew my nose again. "It would all be so simple, Dr. Thatcher, if this were another time in history. I know about the 'obedience pyramid.' Respect your elders and in turn, those younger than you will respect you. Everyone knows the rules. It works like a well-oiled machine."

"Would it be possible for you and Vincent to get away for awhile? Away from relatives, just the two of you?"

"No, Dr. Thatcher. That would be like offering a prisoner a smaller cell."

"I'm sorry, Ruby."

"Mom and Vincent never did meet each other. It's as if she knew I would fail."

"Why do you say that?"

"I didn't try hard enough to arrange for them to meet. First, Mom didn't care to, then I chickened out. Arguments about where to live. I couldn't have let Mom . . . She would have hated him, blaming him for everything."

~

In the mailbox that afternoon, there was a card from Emily. Sitting on the lobby bench, I opened it. It was a Boynton card with the big round cat gritting its teeth. Inside, Emily had written, "Sis, there are plenty of us who love you for who you are." While reading her tender message again, the words 'you are' had smudged from my teardrops.

Mrs. Nussbaum was coming through the front door, so I hurriedly wiped my face with my sleeve. I helped her close the door.

"Thank you, Ruby. I bought two pounds of turkey meat. I'm making turkey loaf tonight and I'll bring you some tomorrow. For you and Vincent."

"That's great, Mrs. Nussbaum. Are you expecting company tonight?"

"No. Just cooking by my lonesome self. Rashi has an ear infection. The poor thing, he's been sleeping."

"Then would you mind if I invited myself to have dinner with you tonight. Vincent's not here."

"I would love it, dear. Come up about six."

"Okay."

∼

Before going upstairs to Mrs. Nussbaum's that evening, I went out to get her some flowers, and wrapping paper for the present I had intended to give her, before I was distracted with dating Vincent, and the wedding. Then there wasn't a day when we weren't arguing or being cold with each other.

Mrs. Nussbaum answered the doorbell while holding a potato masher in her hands. "We're having garlic mashed potatoes with our turkey loaf," she greeted me.

"Ooh, an early Thanksgiving dinner."

"Ruby, what's all this?"

"Do you like Stargazers? They'll open up in a couple of days."

"I like all kinds of flowers. Thank you, dear. They're beautiful. Dinner will be ready in fifteen minutes."

I followed Mrs. Nussbaum into the kitchen. "Can I help?"

"No. You sit."

While she arranged the flowers in a vase, I pulled out the gift from under my arm.

"Mrs. Nussbaum, this is for you." I set it on the counter in front of her. "If my sister were here, she would say, 'Please open it now. So I can see your reaction.' "

"More gifts? The flowers were gifts already."

"Open it."

Mrs. Nussbaum gently pulled the tape off the wrapping paper. Then she pulled back the half-inch-thick bubble wrap and revealed my home-made gift to her.

"Do you like it? It's the Chinese word for 'love.' Remember? *'Oy.'* I thought you might like it near Mr. Nussbaum's and Isabel's portraits."

She hugged my modest gift to her bosom. I gave her a quick kiss on the cheek.

"I hope you like it. I purposely made the heart stand out. Do you like it?"

"It's beautiful. It's beautiful, Ruby. I'll hang it up right now. You can tell me where to put the nail."

We hung the print above the two portraits—like an umbrella over Mrs. Nussbaum's loved ones.

"Love, made of heart," Mrs. Nussbaum said in a soft voice.

With her arm around my waist, we walked back to the kitchen. The world is a wonderful place when there's turkey loaf with mashed potatoes on the table and a loving grandmother telling you to eat.

"Will you let me borrow your turkey loaf recipe, Mrs. N?"

"Of course. You look through the box and copy any recipe you want."

"I think I've mastered your chicken pot pie. But it always tastes better when you make it."

"I don't measure, dear. It's a surprise every time."

"Ah, that's the secret."

Mrs. Nussbaum got up from the table to silence the whistling teakettle.

"I haven't been inviting you and Vincent over because I know how honeymooners like their privacy."

My fork slipped from my hand and it fell to the floor.

"Dear, is Vincent away on a business trip?"

I couldn't lie to her. "No. He's not away on business. I was going to tell you when. . . ."

"What's wrong, dear?" She walked over to the counter to get me another fork.

"Please don't let what I'm about to tell you upset you. It's all for the best. Vincent has moved out. It was a mistake, our marriage. It was a big mistake."

"*Vay ist mir!*" Mrs. Nussbaum had her hand on her face. She said something else in Yiddish and shook her head. Then she stood beside me, and handed me a clean fork. "The first year is the hardest, dear." She kissed my head before sitting down again.

"The last few weeks felt like years. We couldn't even make it through six months. It's over. He's filing for divorce."

"No, Ruby. Vincent can't do that."

"He's doing it. I'm relieved he's doing it. The faster he does it, the faster he'll be free to marry someone who will make his parents happy."

"Ruby, why are you saying these things?" Mrs. Nussbaum was agitated.

"Because they're true, Mrs. Nussbaum. You see, I didn't pour them tea and by not doing so, I showed them disrespect."

"Pour tea?"

"In old China, when a girl marries a boy, she says goodbye to her parents, knowing she will never see them again. The girl then goes to her in-laws' house and becomes their property. On her wedding day she pours tea for her husband's family which symbolizes the acceptance of her place in their home. From that day, the girl must obey her husband and her husband's family. She's wrapped in security, knowing that her life has been laid out for her; and all her decisions have been and will be made by others. If she's lucky enough to be the wife of the oldest son, she'd have a chance to be the woman of the house when her husband's mother passes away."

"Vincent's parents are like that?"

"Not exactly. They didn't expect me to serve them, but they did want me to obey them. It's my fault, Mrs. Nussbaum. You see, these days the tea ceremony is performed for fun, so that the bride would get a piece of jewelry for every cup of tea she pours. With the Yao clan, I could have easily gotten a dozen pieces of gold or jade. But I told Vincent early on that I didn't like jewelry and I didn't like outdated ceremonies, even if it was for fun. He was so smitten with me, he went along. But I can imagine his parents' disappointment when he told them of my defiance. I should have told them what kind of girl I was, am. I'm not a girl anymore. I'm a woman with a strong will and I don't want to be bought. I'm not Yao material. They don't want me. I don't want them."

"Darling, have you told your mother?"

"Not exactly. But I think she knew it wasn't going to work. Maybe that's why she didn't want to invest too much time getting to know Vincent. I'm very confused, Mrs. Nussbaum. I think all the answers were there from the beginning, but I ignored them because I fell in love. And Vincent assumed I would want everything his family wanted to give us."

Mrs. Nussbaum walked over, kissed me on the head again. "We'll warm up our dinner and start all over. I made apple pie for you."

CHAPTER 20

I Wanted to Be Just Like Her

It was one-forty when I arrived at Dr. Thatcher's. In the waiting
room that served several therapists, there was a young woman
reading a *Time* magazine. She didn't look up when I entered, so I sat
down at the other end of the room to give her privacy.

I was there twenty minutes early because the waiting room had
become my place for meditation. Since Dr. Thatcher's appointments
started on the hour and the other therapists started their sessions ten
minutes after the hour, normally there would be no one else in the
waiting room. So, having someone *invade* my space annoyed me at
first. Then I grew intrigued.

I picked up a *Psychology Today* and found an article about Eye
Movement Desensitization and Reprocessing (EMDR), but I kept
sneaking glances at the young woman. She was impeccably dressed: a
white wool suit and a Fendi handbag over her shoulder. I had noticed
the handbag when I first walked in.

I couldn't see her face. Even though she sat erect, her head was
down. The room was quiet—I could hear myself breathing. I won-

dered what she was doing because she had not turned the page in twenty minutes.

Then Dr. Thatcher peered around the doorway and the young woman jumped to her feet, causing the strap of her purse to slip from her shoulder. She tossed the opened magazine on the chair next to the one where she was sitting. "I'm Daphne," the woman stammered. I saw her face then—she had soft eyes, big ones, thin lips, and sunken cheeks. She repositioned the strap of her purse.

Dr. Thatcher escorted her down the hallway. *Wait a minute! What about me?* I heard myself crying. Then I heard Dr. Thatcher's voice explaining: "Daphne, you're an hour early for our appointment." Daphne responded meekly, "Oh! I thought it was for two." "No, it's for three," Dr. Thatcher said in a sympathetic voice. "Would you like to walk around, window shop? But you're welcome to stay and read. There's coffee and tea in the kitchen." "I'll come back in an hour," replied Daphne.

I heard both sets of footsteps going towards the front door. The magazine on the chair was opened to the page Daphne was reading. I walked over to look. It was a full-page ad for floor tile. I felt an emptiness in my stomach—I remembered my first session. *Poor Daphne.* Dr. Thatcher returned and greeted me with a smile. I followed her down the hallway. Her soft rayon skirt swayed from side to side.

~

"Dr. Thatcher, my mother is in the hospital again. Third time in three years."

"What happened, Ruby?"

"Wednesday afternoon, at work, I got a call from Mt. Zion Crisis Center, telling me they were holding Mother for twenty-four hours. I rushed over there. When I arrived, the case worker told me the police had brought her in. What the police told them was that Mother had gone into a restaurant and ordered noodle soup. When the soup was delivered to her table, she took a sip and told the waiter to take it away because it was not hot. The owner of the place said it was hot. He also claimed that Mother shouted profanity at him and then started to walk out. He yelled out, 'You haven't paid your bill!' Apparently, this upset my mother and she started screaming more profanities. It was then that the owner of the restaurant called the police. The officer who answered the call took one look at my mother and knew she was no vagrant, just someone who should be on medication. I'm sure police officers see it all the time. He took her to Mt. Zion."

"How is your mother now, Ruby?"

"She looked fine today, compared to the way she did on Wednesday. Since Mt. Zion only holds people for the first twenty-four hours, they've moved her to San Francisco General. Here's the miracle: Do you remember Dr. Leu from three years ago? He's still there! I went to visit Mom this morning. It's Day Three already, that is, day three of medication working in her system. She's been a naughty girl—probably stopped taking her meds months ago."

"What's going to happen now?" asked Dr. Thatcher.

"Her social worker will find her a place to live. Another board-and-care home. Mom was refilling her meds, but she wasn't taking them. It was a mistake to have her leave the first board-and-care situation. But she wanted so much to be independent. If only there was an elf who would watch her take her pills every night."

"Is she receptive to the idea, about giving up her studio?"

"She is now. Now that she's calm and reasonable. She thinks Dr. Leu is a saint. So do I. She'll do whatever he recommends."

"And how are you doing?"

"My heart sank when I saw her at Mt. Zion. She looked so angry;

she didn't even want to talk to me. There are so many kind and caring people in this world. Dr. Leu, the nurses and the social workers all remember my mother. She had made an impression on them."

"It's been quite a month, Ruby."

"In a way, we're lucky that this happened outside the home because Dr. Leu told me that home assessments no longer exist. State budget cuts have eliminated agencies like OMI. Dr. Leu said if Mom had been at home starving herself again, it would have been extremely difficult for me to get immediate help because the police will not take someone in as a Fifty-One-Fifty just because that person won't go to the hospital."

"It's sad that our tax dollars are not being spent where they're truly needed."

I looked down at my hands.

"What are you thinking about?"

"Vincent and I have been talking on the phone."

"Is there any chance of——"

"No. I don't think so. We're just not ready to let go completely. Dr. Thatcher, I want to talk about Mother."

"Okay."

"I've been thinking a lot about her and remembering when she was young. I want to share my stories with Dr. Leu and perhaps he'll be better equipped to help Mom talk about her troubles. Maybe she'll talk to him this time."

~

After leaving Dr. Thatcher's office, I went to visit Mom again that afternoon. She was overjoyed to see me twice in one day.

"This is my daughter," she told the nurse who let me into the ward.

"Hi Mom, the flower stand wasn't open this morning. That's why I came empty-handed earlier."

"They are so beautiful, Ruby. Yellow flowers. I want to put them here at the nurses' station so everyone can see them."

"But they're for your room. They're some kind of miniature mums. They'll cheer the room up."

"No. I'm not in my room much. I want everyone to know that you brought me flowers."

"You look good, Mom."

"Dr. Leu gave me two pills. One for my appetite and the other for sleep."

"That's good, Mom."

"Your sister has been calling every day. I told her not to spend her money on long-distance calls. I wish she wasn't in Philadelphia. It's so far away."

"I wish that too, Mom. But she's made a place for herself and she's happy."

"You should get some fresh air, Ruby. Go home. Get some rest."

"I will. Mom, before I go." I took a deep breath and stroked her sleeve. "I want to say that I love you very much."

I saw the astonishment on Mother's face as she processed my words.

"I love you," she responded with a childlike quality in her voice.

In all our years as mother and daughter, I believe that was the first time we exchanged those simple words.

I hugged her and she hugged back. My tears fell on her shoulder. They were warm happy tears. I wiped my eyes dry with one hand.

"See you tomorrow, Mom, after work."

"Okay. See you tomorrow. Thank you for the beautiful flowers, Ruby."

"You're welcome, Mom. See you tomorrow."

She escorted me to the double doors, and the nurse let me out.

I walked out to the parking lot and sat in my car. Having said those little words to Mom made me sentimental and reflective, and made me think about an incident when Mother and I switched roles.

~

We were still in Hong Kong and I was seven years old. Mother had taken me to a restaurant to celebrate my being Number One Student in class. My heart was going pitty-pat-pitty-pat as I followed my mother into the restaurant. The waiter showed us to a round table where other people were eating their soup and reading newspapers.

Mother and I sat in the two empty seats. I studied my mother's face as she looked at the menu. I liked the way she pulled her hair into a bun. She had soft-looking skin and a heart-shaped face. Scanning the room, I decided that my mother was definitely the prettiest. I wished in silence that I would grow up and look just like her.

When the waiter came to our table, she ordered only one bowl of noodle soup. I wanted to ask her why just one bowl, but the voice in my head stopped me. Little children do not ask questions, the voice reminded me.

The man behind the steamy counter was churning out bowl after bowl. As soon as he put one bowl on the countertop, a waiter would rush it over to a customer. Seconds later, Mother's noodle soup was delivered to our table. She wiped off a pair of chopsticks and a spoon, and pushed the bowl in front of me.

"It's hot. Eat slowly," she said to me.

"Aren't you eating, Mama?" I asked, ignoring the voice in my head.

"I'm not hungry," she answered. "Eat."

I knew Mother must have been hungry because I'd had breakfast and she did not. In my clever little mind, I thought of a way for Mother to eat lunch.

"I am so hungry, Mama, I'll need two bowls of noodles." I had told the other voice in my head to keep quiet so that my mother would not go hungry.

"Are you sure?" Mother asked, talking to me as if I were an adult.

"Oh, yes, one is not enough."

So she ordered a second bowl and when the bowl was delivered to the table, I exclaimed, "I'm getting full, Mama. I cannot eat anymore."

"Why did you make me waste money like this?" she raised her voice. The men behind the newspapers looked up, but when they saw that it was a case of a mother disciplining a child, they went back to their reading.

I was scared. What if she didn't have money to pay for two bowls. I kept still.

Mother sat there, looking at the second bowl of soup. I thought she was going to stand up and walk away, leaving me behind. But instead she wiped another pair of chopsticks and a spoon. She scooped some chili sauce into her soup and started to eat. Turning to me, she said, in a gentle voice, "Eat."

After drinking the last spoonful of broth, she thought out loud. "That was good and hot."

You did the right thing, I told myself. Someone needed to take care of Mother.

~

I had a meeting with Dr. Leu the next day. "Dr. Leu, Mother thinks the two medications are for appetite and sleep. Did you tell her that?"

"No. She knows what they're for. It's all right that she says they are for something else. The most important thing is that she's taking them. She feels much better when she takes them."

"She was doing so well, Dr. Leu. Can you tell when she got off her medication?"

"Probably a few months ago. Your mother can see what happens when she doesn't take her medications. She gets confused and she doesn't know why. She told me she stopped taking her medication because she didn't like the side effects. She said she felt lethargic, not interested in doing anything, not even in watching television. I have changed her medication."

"She told you all that, Dr. Leu?"

"Yes. Maybe your mother feels more comfortable talking to me this time."

"Thank you, Dr. Leu, for everything. But I feel that 'thank you' is not enough."

"It is enough, Ruby. This is my job. Now tell me, how have you been?"

"I'm fine. Do you remember you had recommended that I join a support group three years ago? Well, I've been seeing a therapist and she's a wonderful person."

"I'm glad for you. I know coping with a parent with mental illness can be very frustrating. Your mother will be released in a few days. You can always call me if you have any questions."

"Thank you, Dr. Leu."

"Good luck, Ruby."

Why couldn't Mother have married someone like Dr. Leu?

~

"Emily, I think this time it's going to be different. I think this time Mom really listened to Dr. Leu. He also told me that she gave him

244

her full attention when he explained to her how these episodes make her loved ones worry."

"Sure is good news. Sis, I'm coming out for a visit. Is it okay?"

"Is it okay? What kind of question is that? Will it be longer than a weekend this time?"

"Oh, yes. One full week."

"I can't wait, Em."

~

"Dr. Thatcher, would you mind if I talk about Mother today? I don't feel like talking about myself."

"You talk about whatever you like."

"Remember I told you her name used to be Alice?"

Dr. Thatcher had an unsure look on her face.

"Well, it doesn't matter. My point is she's changed her name three times since then. She called herself Susan after she saw Susan Hayward in *I Want To Live*. Then it was Linda because someone told her *linda* is the Spanish word for 'beautiful.' The year she saw *Gone With The Wind*, she became Vivien because of Vivien Leigh.

"That was also the year she told Father she would go to night class, English class that is, without him. She said he was fraternizing with female classmates and ordered him to stay home. 'I'm the serious learner,' she said to him in Chinese.

"Then one night she told him his ugly voice should not speak English. I was actually sad for my father. It was a miracle that he didn't beat her that night. Over the next ten years she excelled in her pronunciation of words, leaving Father in the dust. Sometimes, she drops her ed's, but she doesn't have an accent anymore. It's really a shame—Father hasn't mastered the language.

"Dr. Thatcher, I wish someone could tell me whether Mother had always been mentally ill and no one cared enough or was smart enough to see it, or did the marriage bring on the mental illness."

"Your mother has a chemical imbalance in her brain. We don't know when she first developed this imbalance. Without her medication, she cannot call up her coping devices to deal with sadness, anger, trauma or tragedy."

"I wonder if my divorce, in some way, caused her recent breakdown. I think she was feeling bad that she couldn't be strong for me."

"You can't blame yourself for your mother's breakdown. She had stopped taking her medication. You can acknowledge her love for you. She does want to see you happy. I'm sure seeing you unhappy makes her unhappy too. But don't blame yourself."

"I think Mother sabotaged herself by not getting angry enough to say to herself, 'I must stop living vicariously through my daughters' lives and start living my own life. I will live for me and I will make myself happy.'"

"Perhaps one day she will see that."

"I've been so harsh with her in the past, severing contact, ignoring her as if I were punishing her for the years of . . ." I couldn't finish my thought. Tears welled up in my eyes.

Dr. Thatcher handed me the box of tissues. "The years of chaos, Ruby. Your childhood years were a total chaos. You must forgive yourself, Ruby. Now that you're cognizant of your behaviors, you won't use those methods of communicating. Be yourself and let your mother be herself. That's all you can do for anyone—accept them for who they are."

I looked down at my hands. Dr. Thatcher did not interrupt my thoughts.

"I wish someone would make her understand that she needs her two little pills. Why can't she see that?"

"Because your mother wears very special glasses."

"What?"

"Your mother wears a pair of funny glasses which have been tinted by her personal experiences. They're her special glasses to view and cope with the world."

"Dr. Thatcher!" I gasped. "All these years of talking about Mother's mental illness and reading about it, I still couldn't accept it, and now, just now you've made it so clear for me."

In all the sessions I'd had with Dr. Thatcher, I would say that that afternoon was worth all the other sessions put together.

~

Mrs. Nussbaum brought me dinner that night. I asked her to eat with me because I needed to be with someone gentle and nonjudgmental.

"Mrs. Nussbaum, my mom's in the hospital, again."

"Where is she, which hospital?"

"San Francisco General, again. Dr. Leu is still there. I hope this will be the last time she'll go into the hospital. But I think the biggest lesson for me is that if Mom does get into trouble again, I know I'll be there for her and we'll get through it just like all the other times. Each time with less drama, less anguish, even less guilt."

"You're a wonderful daughter, Ruby. Your mother knows that. A mother is lucky when she has a loving daughter. A daughter brings youth to a mother's life."

"I wish I could do that for my mom. Make her feel young again. She's not even close to sixty. But she says she's old. She won't rinse the gray out of her hair. She won't buy new clothes for herself. Her pants are all worn and tattered. That's why I'm sewing her a few pairs. Look, Mrs. Nussbaum. Do you think she'll like these colors?" I held up the pieces of fabric.

"She'll love them, dear. Do you have patterns already?"

"Just one pattern. She likes an elastic waist which makes it easy for me. I used to make pantsuits for Mom, but that was a long time ago."

"Ruby, you need sewing notions? Don't buy any. I have everything."

"Do you like to sew too?"

"I can't anymore," said Mrs. Nussbaum. "My hands. They won't cooperate."

"Does it hurt?"

"Sometimes. It's being old, my dear."

"I just had a thought, Mrs. Nussbaum. I can't do anything real fancy, but I would very much like to sew something for you if you pick out the pattern. I'm a tidy seamstress. You won't find hanging threads or crooked seams."

"We'll go look at patterns when you have time, after you sew those pants for your mother." Mrs. Nussbaum went into the kitchen. She liked eating meals in the kitchen; she said the dining room was too formal.

"It'll be fun, Mrs. Nussbaum. I need to have some fun," I yelled from the living room.

"Come eat, dear. Dinner is ready. Chicken pot pie."

"Coming."

~

That night, while laying out the pattern pieces onto the fabric, I remembered a time when my mother was happy. It was the year she had a job. One day I stopped by her workplace.

"What a good looking pantsuit, Vivien," her coworker, Nancy, remarked.

Mother was wearing the lemon yellow suit.

"My daughter," my mother boasted. "I choose the pattern and my daughter, she make it. I have four more pantsuits like this one, pink, light blue, light purple, apple green."

"You have the figure for tailored clothes, Vivien," Nancy said. Her tone was sincere.

"Oh no. I'm not a girl anymore." My mother blushed.

The year that Mother worked was the happiest year of her life. She was one of the breakfast-line ladies at a cafeteria on Columbus Avenue. Mother was hired when the restaurant owner needed an extra pair of hands to serve meals to a building crew of thirty men working at a construction site down the block.

"Ruby, it's wonderful. The construction workers are so happy to see me in the morning. Between seven and eight o'clock, they come in. When I see a customer wearing a hard hat, I always give him a big scoop of hash browns or more scramble eggs. Construction workers work hard, you know. Remember your uncle? He was a mover. Remember how he ate? Ruby, guess what time I get up in the morning? Four-thirty! Every morning. Never late! Oh, I get fifty percent off on all the food. So, next time you come, I'll have a feast for you. You like turkey? Mashed potatoes? They roast a big turkey every day."

That year went by too fast. It was a normal year, or as normal as it could get for us. I was living on my own. John had already gone away. Emily was in high school, still living at home.

When Mother first told me she had found a job, I took her to the fabric store to look at patterns for pantsuits.

"Mom, the pattern says: 'suggested fabrics—crepe or jacquard.'"

"No! Cotton. Lightweight cotton. I don't want to wear expensive fabric to work. Cotton is practical. Ruby, look! Pastels on sale, only ninety-nine cents a yard!"

Mother wanted only two new outfits. She said, "Like uniforms, like your gym clothes. Wash the dirty one, wear the clean one." The next day I returned to the fabric store to select three more pieces of cotton fabric. Five pantsuits, one for each workday. Nothing elaborate. They were tunics with elastic-waist pants.

Mother's happiness did not last long. A year later when the twenty-story office building was erected and the construction crew left, my mother was laid off. I was sad to see her sad.

"Mom, why don't you apply for work at another restaurant? You have experience now."

"It's not the same. That was luck that came my way. It won't come again."

"Sure it will, Mom. How about this? How about if we drive around town to look for big construction sites and go into nearby restaurants and see if they need extra help?"

"No, Ruby."

Why, Mother? Why, I asked myself. *Why is happiness only temporary? Why won't you go find it instead of waiting for it to find you? I don't understand, Mother.* I was screaming to myself.

Later, whenever my friends asked about her, even though she no longer worked at the restaurant, I found myself telling them not how my mother was presently doing, but how she had been doing "that" year. I needed to describe her with words like independent, fulfilled, and confident. I couldn't let go of the fact that happiness is temporary.

Years later, I still pictured her getting up early in the morning to go to work. As if to allow me to fantasize about her work life, Mother continued letting me make a new pantsuit for her each year until pantsuits went out of style.

"Mother, dresses are in. I saw some beautiful patterns for long dresses below the knee. You would look great in them!"

"No. No. I cannot wear dresses. I am not young anymore. Too old to wear dresses. I use to have a figure like yours, Ruby. You were too little to know what a figure was."

But I remember when I wasn't too little to know what she meant. A week after we bought our first family car, my mother took me with her to The Dress Barn. Never having bought a dress since we'd been in America, she was able to figure out her size from just eye-balling the width of the garments. She picked out three dresses, all of them combinations of black and white, and we went into the dressing room together. I sat on the chair in the fitting room as my mother undressed. In her bra and panties, my mother had a figure that resembled one of the models in the lingerie section of the Montgomery Ward catalogue. I could not take my eyes from the reflection in the mirror as she tried on her dresses. The first one was an A-line in white chiffon, sleeveless, with a black bow just below her bosom. It was so elegant. The second one had a square neckline, sleeveless again, white bodice and a black flounced skirt. The third dress had a white-with-black-polka-dot bodice, ruffled sleeves, and a full black skirt. The wide neckline showed off Mother's collarbone, and the dress made her look like a dancer. She bought all three! *Maybe we're rich after all. Three dresses in one day. And last week our first car. Could it be that we have become an average American family? Yes. And I do have a beautiful mother.*

I soon found out why Mother bought those dresses.

"Why don't you take us out more?" my mother asked my father. So he did. He took us out to restaurants. "Why did you flirt with that waitress?" she would ask quietly, at first.

"I was just being friendly," he defended himself.

"Why aren't you friendly with me?" My mother's voice grew louder.

Then he would give her the silent treatment and drink his tea, and her agitation would increase. The three of us children looked at each other, wishing we were home watching television. Even our little sister could see trouble was ahead.

"I see the way you flirt! You can't fool me!" my mother cried. She didn't look beautiful when she curled her upper lip.

The waitress, whose blouse seemed too small for her, delivered our food, at which point Mother would tell her to stop talking to Father. "Can't you see he's married and has children!" she scolded in Chinese.

It was a nightmare to see my mother carry on like this in public and a living hell to see my father beat my mother when we were home. There were times when, after having been humiliated in public, he did take us home with the intention of going off on his own but she would not let him. "No, you will not go out and leave us here. You will not go out and have fun with some waitress!" she would screech. Those nights were the worst. At times, I thought he would kill her.

One day she took the three dresses and jammed them in the back of the hall closet, where we kept hand-me-downs from relatives. The following year she was hit by a car. Even though no one could see the scars running down the center of her back, and she remained a beautiful woman, my mother never wore a dress again.

Finally she packed the lovely dresses and donated them to Goodwill. And she no longer preferred black and white. She wore pants, the kind with elastic waistbands. I saw the glamorous mother, the one in the store dressing room, no more.

CHAPTER 21

Let Sleeping Dogs Lie

If Monday's child is fair of face, and Tuesday's child is full of grace . . . I am Friday's child. So is Emily. Friday's child is loving and giving. *Am I?*

~

"Hello, Ruby. How is your mother?"

"She's fine, Dr. Thatcher. She moved into her board-and-care home already. She likes it. Same neighborhood. Outer Sunset. Nicer house. Bigger too."

"I'm glad to hear that."

"Dr. Thatcher, I had a dream a few nights ago."

Dr. Thatcher took out her writing tablet and pen.

"I dreamed that Vincent and I were invited to an intimate dinner by his parents. 'Just the four of us,' his mother says on the telephone. We arrive, but his parents are not home. Vincent goes to the garage to see what latest project his father is working on. I go to the seat at the windowsill, in the enormous living room that has sectional sofas along two walls.

"Then one by one, Vincent's relatives come into the room. They file in like soldiers marching to a funeral. They begin to seat themselves on the sofas. There must be forty or fifty of them. Not one of them looks in my direction. They each hold a scroll in their hands and they bow their heads as if in prayer.

"This is to be an inquisition. Each one of these people has a charge against me. I am being tried for betraying a Chinese family. The crimes committed are as follows:

- Not granting the wishes of her in-laws;
- Not agreeing with her husband's beliefs;
- Not conforming to the way of the Yaos.

"I remain seated at the windowsill and examine each person's face. Do I stay and argue my case? Do I try to reason with unreasonable people? 'No! I'm leaving this court of ignorance,' I say to myself. As I rise to leave the room, an old gray-haired woman in a wheelchair rolls herself in front of me. Her face is familiar yet I don't know her. She's wearing a red shawl. She looks up and speaks to me. 'Let no one judge you, my dear.'

"As I open my mouth to speak, the old woman smiles and steers her wheelchair around. I follow her down the hallway and out the side door, but she disappears into the garden. End of dream."

Dr. Thatcher put down her tablet and pen. "Tell me more about the old woman in the wheelchair, Ruby. Do you know anyone who uses a wheelchair?"

"No. Mother used a walker for a few months after her accident, but never a wheelchair."

"You said her face looked familiar."

"Yes. I've seen her before, somewhere."

"Have you been talking to Vincent lately?"

"No. It's very awkward. Saying goodbye on the phone to a man who doesn't want to be my husband anymore isn't healthy."

"How are you, Ruby?"

"I'm okay. I have a good cry now and then. You know. The kind that makes your eyes all puffy and your nasal passages all blocked. I'm weird. I like to have a good cry sometimes."

Dr. Thatcher smiled at me. She doesn't hug in these sessions, so her smiles express her warm and caring ways.

"I think the wise old woman in your dream was you."

"Me?" I asked.

"Yes. She was wearing a red shawl. I've seen you wear red many times."

"That's why her face was familiar to me!"

Dr. Thatcher smiled again.

"We often give ourselves other faces in our dreams. We might dream about people who have our characteristics, but we're really dreaming about ourselves."

"Wait until I tell Emily about this one. She's coming for a visit."

"Will you be able to get some time off work?"

"I've arranged it with coworkers already. I won't be spending every minute with her. Actually, I need some time to myself. You know . . ."

"I understand, Ruby."

"Dr. Thatcher, thank you for a very special session. For helping me analyze that dream."

"You're welcome, Ruby."

We spent the last twenty minutes talking about how excited I was that Emily would be visiting.

~

At work, I reminded Chad about my vacation request.

"Ruby, is it next week? I thought it wasn't for another month or two." Chad wrinkled his forehead.

"No, Chad. It's next week. Marilyn has offered to cover for me. Clyde and Cheryl will take over some of Marilyn's events. Everything is covered. You won't even know I'm gone."

"I'll know, Ruby. It's never the same when you're not here giving attention to details. I wish you had reminded me about this. It's a packed week. Can't you bring your sister to the evening functions? She'll enjoy seeing her sister in action."

"I can't ask my sister to come to work with me, Chad. She's on vacation."

"All right, Ruby." He threw his hands up. "It's not like you to disappoint me. Your performance evaluation is coming up soon."

"I know, Chad. It's been a great year and I've worked very hard. I don't have to tell you that. You're not the kind of boss who is blind to his staff's hard work." I couldn't believe I said that, but I did. Confronting Mrs. Yao had given me the strength to be assertive.

"Oh, I know my staff is a talented team of young people." The telephone ring interrupted his thought. He picked up the call. "Chad Hamilton," he answered gruffly. He looked out the window as he talked.

I left his office. Marilyn intercepted me in the hallway. "Is he giving you a hard time?"

"He's trying. He's reminding me that it's performance review time."

"What a creep. Didn't he okay your vacation request?"

"He said he forgot."

"Well, that's his problem. You take your vacation. We've got it under control, Ruby. What does he care? He's never there to do the work anyway."

"Thanks, Marilyn. I owe you one."

"You don't owe me anything. Don't come in. You hear me?"

"I hear you. Thanks. You're a pal."

~

A week later at the airport, while waiting for Emily's flight to arrive, I heard someone calling out 'Daughter.' Intrigued that other people would use the word 'daughter' as a pronoun, I turned to see who the caller was.

"Daughter! Daughter!" It was my father.

"Oh! Father, what are you doing here? I didn't know you were coming to the airport too."

"I told your sister. I tell her, I get to see my oldest and youngest toogeder. I take you and your sister to lunch."

"Lunch?" I had to get over the shock of seeing him.

How many years has it been, I asked myself. He looked older, shorter and smaller. The lines on his face were deeper and his hair had more gray.

"How are you, Daughter?" He always called me that, but it sounded different just then. The noun 'daughter' did not have that string attached to it, the one about my being firstborn and fulfilling my obligations. Perhaps the way he said it had not changed; but the way I listened had.

"I'm fine, Father. And you?"

"Oh, my knee is *vely* bad. *Vely* bad. How is your mother?"

"She's quite well these days."

"Are you being a good daughter, visiting your mother?"

"We enjoy each other's company when we get together. It's not quantity, but quality these days." I was not trying to be flippant; merely expressing the new me.

"Emily is a good girl. She remember to call me. She say it's cheap for her to call me. She say she got a good deal from the phone company. She's a smart girl, your sister. Always thinking. I keep telling her, 'start your own business.' She say she don't want to work so hard. I tell her she's young, she has energy." I watched his lips move. "I *werlie* about my children . . . save money . . . your cousin, Elaine making one hundred K . . . still not *mellie* . . . must save money." His lips finally stopped moving.

"Cousin Elaine? No, I haven't seen her. Please say hello for me. I wish her well."

"Are you still renting, Daughter?"

"Yes. A beautiful apartment. A wonderful neighbor. She's like a grandmother to me"

"Do you need down payment for a house? Don't be shy if you need down payment. I do not charge *intrust*," he chuckled.

I wanted to tell Father to drop his charades, but I didn't.

"Thank you for the offer, Father. I'm not ready to be a home owner. Not just yet."

"Foolish. You make someone else rich."

"Look! There's Emily." Saved by the *belle*. "Sis," I waved.

Emily had a surprised look on her face. She hugged Father, then me.

"Daughter, do you know the restaurant on San Mateo Avenue?" asked Father. "We meet you there."

"Actually I can't. I was going to drop Emily off at my place and take care of some business. So, you two have fun. Em, I'll see you later. Here's a spare key."

I gave Emily another hug, and she whispered in my ear, "Sorry, Sis. I'll explain later."

I winked at her. That was my code to let her know that the situation at hand was under control. To avoid the awkward goodbye with Father, I took one of Emily's carry-ons, and made a joke about how heavy it was as I waved goodbye. Father had a disapproving look on his face. Oh, how that look used to make me feel insignificant and unworthy of his approval. Not today.

I had lied about having business to take care of. In my opinion, it was a white lie to save myself from an hour of insults. It was a way to save face. Father and I would get nowhere, with his advice-giving and my defending my choices. Little did my father know that I had all the intentions of buying a house someday. But telling him would not have made him change his mind about me. I was a lost cause for him—his oldest child who had ignored his wisdom through the years. Emily told him about my wedding after the fact. He had a glimmer of hope when he heard that I had married a Chinese man, but of course both his glimmer and my marriage turned out to be short-lived.

So, while my sister and father were having lunch, I went home to eat and read the newspaper which I rarely did. I checked my answering machine, and sure enough Emily had left me a message the night before, telling me that Father insisted on being at the airport because that would be the only time he could spend with her. Apparently one of his cousins in Los Angeles had had a heart attack and Father wanted to drive down and help the family for a few days. That's the way he was—driving a great distance to help someone whether or not his help was needed or wanted. In the past, he would have had red envelopes with him, one for each unmarried person. Friends and relatives always welcomed the envelopes, which were usually stuffed with a twenty dollar bill. I wondered if the man-without-the-envelopes would be welcomed this time.

I thought about the day I accompanied him to the car dealer. He was brave—buying a big ticket item and not knowing how to speak

English. We made a good team—like the characters portrayed by Tatum O'Neal and her dad in *Paper Moon*.

~

Two hours later, Emily came back by herself. Father had dropped her off in front of the building. I knew he wouldn't come up since the elevator wasn't working and he could not have climbed three flights of stairs. Not with his bad knee.

Emily plopped her bag in the front hallway. "Ruby, I'm sorry about that. I thought you would have stayed away from the airport after getting my message."

"My fault. I didn't check the machine last night or this morning. Let's just say what happened at the airport was interesting for me. Em, he hasn't changed. His twenty-minute speech about stupid people renting has been condensed to twenty seconds but the message is still the same."

"You're right, Ruby. When he dropped me off at the front door, he had to say, 'Good looking building. I would buy it, rent out the top floors and live in the lower one. You can get more income renting the top units. Your sister is paying someone's mortgage instead of taking care of herself—' At that point, I said to him, 'Oh, Dad, there you go again. Renting has its advantages. If it were that easy to be a landlord, you'd be one yourself.' "

"Emily, you have a way with him. You always did. You can say anything to him and he'll chuckle. If I say it, he would call it being disrespectful to one's parent. All that doesn't matter anymore. He's getting old and if he's happy being the way he is, then I say let him be. But I don't have to be there for the insults."

"Deep down, Sis, I think he's proud of you even though he would never say it. At lunch, he thought out loud, 'Ruby must be doing well to be living in Pacific Heights.' He wants us to be happy and of course being happy to him is to have plenty of money. He lost his and he's miserable, but he won't show it."

I folded the newspaper and added it to the recycling pile. "At the airport, he said he worries about us. Why do parents use that word instead of saying they care? 'Worry' has a negative connotation for me. He makes it sound like I can't take care of myself. But I suppose that's his way of saying he does think about me."

"Don't let it bother you, Ruby. He thinks I waste my money traveling, and that the smart thing to do is to save up my money and go around the world after I retire. Damn, who can wait that long? I want to enjoy it now."

"And speaking of traveling, you must be tired. My room is all ready for you. Go take a nap. See you in a couple of hours. I have a surprise for you later."

Emily gave me a hug before heading down the hallway. She turned around to say, "You're the best, Sis."

"Sweet dreams."

~

That evening, I packed the surprise into a picnic basket and took Emily to Baker Beach. It was Indian Summer in San Francisco when the evening temperature drops to a perfect seventy-four degrees. Other people had the same idea. We were surrounded with coolers and portable barbecues. But we found a spot, spread out the beach blanket, and unpacked the basket. The breeze felt good.

"Surprise, Em! Your favorite meal—*pad thai*, chicken in yellow curry, spicy eggplant, jasmine rice, and yes, there's Thai iced tea in the Thermos."

"Wow! This is the life. I've never eaten a Thai dinner at the beach before." She kissed me on the cheek.

Emily poured Thai iced tea while I spooned out rice onto the plastic plates. The basil in the eggplant was aromatic—I attacked that dish first. Emily went for the *pad thai*.

"So, what are you up to tomorrow?" I asked. "Wanna use the car?"

"Nah, I can hop on the bus to visit Theresa and Evelyn, then go see Mom for dinner. Hey, are you sure you don't want to join us for dinner?"

"I think it'll be better for the two of you to catch up, one on one. The three of us can do something together before you fly back."

"Ruby, do you and Vincent see each other at all?"

"No. We still talk, on the phone. It's very awkward. Besides, something spooky happened the other day after I dropped Mother off."

"What kind of spooky?" Emily asked.

"Wrong word. Not spooky. Weird. My car stalled near the Great Highway. I wasn't blocking traffic, but was I frustrated! I tried starting the engine. Nothing. I sat there for a minute with the blinkers on. I swear, I didn't know whether to laugh or cry. I couldn't make out the street sign—the tree branches at the corner hung so low. I knew I had to give triple A an address, so I got out of the car to read the street name. I crossed the intersection and stood under the sign. The glare from the sun was so strong, my vision blurred. Guess what street I was on?"

Emily shrugged her shoulders.

"The sign said VICENTE and above it, instead of a number and an arrow, the word END. It was the end of Vicente Street."

Emily swallowed a mouthful of *pad thai* and gulped. "What did you do?"

"I walked back to the car, sat there like a dummy. Then something said, 'put the key in the ignition.' I did, and the car started."

"That *was* spooky. Any chance of reconciliation, Sis? Maybe over time?" Emily scooped curry chicken onto her plate, then mine.

"I don't think so. I think we gave it our best shot. At least I don't have parents hounding me about giving them grandchildren. He does, and his biological clock is ticking."

Emily giggled. "Are you serious?"

"Sure I am. Men have their biological clocks too. I had to go and marry one with an alarm but no snooze button."

"You're a crack-up." Emily laughed. I laughed too.

"I do miss him though. I thought I found the answer to my future—to be with my own kind. But the truth is . . . we come from different worlds."

"It's old world versus new, huh, Ruby?"

"Yeah, it's important to know the difference. I forgot about honoring your elders without questioning their intentions. Tell me, Em, how does a woman compete with that?"

"We don't. We take it or leave it. I think people misinterpret tradition. I believe in respecting and honoring the elders, but I don't have to agree with everything they say and do everything they suggest. There are meddling old people too, you know. Being old doesn't automatically make people smart or wonderful human beings. Being young doesn't automatically make a person modern either."

"Did anyone tell you that you're wise?"

"Yeah, the smart ones," answered my sister.

The tea was strong but sweet.

"His parents never gave us a chance to make a go of our marriage. Such hypocrites—they didn't honor their parents when they eloped—"

"They eloped? Really?"

"Yeah! That's what they told Vincent. Why can't they understand that maybe their own son might want the same freedom?"

Emily shrugged her shoulders. "Maybe they feel guilty for having disobeyed their own parents, and stifling their son would be atoning for their sin. Sis, what if Vincent doesn't want that much freedom?"

"He obviously doesn't."

"Are you gonna avoid Chinese guys like the plague now?"

"I don't know, Em. I can't think about it right now. You know, it worked for Vincent's oldest brother and his wife and they've been happily married for ten years. But then, they do live thousands of miles away from his parents and hers."

Two surfer-type guys walked by and one of them winked at me. I didn't smile back. *Is it all right to flirt when one's getting a divorce?*

"Too bad his parents didn't meet ours," said Emily. "Father could have knocked them out with a one-two punch. In-laws should duke it out and leave newlyweds alone."

I pictured Father in shorts and boxing gloves. "No, Em. Mrs. Yao would have taken Father down in the first round."

My sister suppressed a laugh.

"Vincent said his family is like a big circle and that they wanted to embrace me, making it a bigger circle. I kept on saying I wanted to create a new circle with him and start new traditions. We even drew two circles on a piece of paper, showing the overlapping area. I thought I was so smart. It was all theory. Let's change the subject, Em. Save room for dessert. There's fried banana back at the apartment."

Emily leaned back and braced herself on her elbows. "There's something about the beach, Ruby. Not a care in the world; feeling the breeze on your face and watching the waves roll and tumble. This brings back memories. I used to come here with Evelyn and Theresa every time the sun came out and we would bake our bodies until we were golden brown. Nowadays, I don't leave the house without sunblock. Look Ruby, those kids over there. Don't they look like us when we were little?"

I looked at the two girls and a boy playing in the sand. "They look like they're really happy. Remember your plastic pail and shovel?

And all the Popsicles we had to eat so that we could save the sticks for building our sand castle?"

"John did most of the eating, not that he liked Popsicles. He wanted our castle to be the biggest and the strongest. Remember he used to call other kids' castles 'sorry ass mounds' and I would laugh until my stomach hurt?"

"You were such a cute kid, Em."

The Golden Gate Bridge was majestic. In the sunlight, it looked as if it were rising from the sea and reaching for the sky. The beauty took my breath away.

"Ruby—"

"Huh?"

Emily's voice cracked with emotion. "Sometimes, I picture John as a beach bum."

"Em, that wouldn't be so bad. I used to think about him all the time, hoping he might have joined the Army or the Marines."

"No, not the Marines. He was too thin." Emily dabbed her eyes with a napkin.

"You're right. Not the Marines."

"I'll never forget the day, Ruby. You were in San—" Emily stopped mid-sentence. She must have seen the furrows in my forehead.

She continued, "John came home, marched into his room, came out with a duffel bag, and stormed into the kitchen where Mom and Dad were both sitting. I didn't see it, I only heard it. 'I'm leaving this hellhole. Go fuck yourselves.' I stood in front of my room, shaking. I thought he was going to hit Dad. From the hallway, he yelled to me, 'Little Sister, if you're smart, you'd get the fuck out too.' I went into my room and closed the door. I heard the slamming of the front door—the apartment shook. There was no dinner that night, but I didn't care. I didn't have the heart to see Mom and Dad's faces."

"Em, I'm sorry you had to stay in that house alone with them. How did you survive high school with their constant screaming?"

"I did my studying at school or at my friends'."

"Do you ever wonder if John resented us? Especially me. I was the oldest and I didn't help him when Father—"

"Didn't? You mean couldn't." Emily was tearing up again. "Ruby, we were caught in a web. You and I were witnesses to atrocities. Even though we weren't physically abused, we were still victims."

My sister saw my look of admiration for her. She sounded like Dr. Thatcher just then.

"That's why I moved three thousand miles away," she continued. "That's why I majored in psychology. Sis, I think a lot of psych majors go into the field so they can treat their own neuroses."

I poured myself some more tea. "The guilt and the blame stacked so high, it felt like a mountain was crushing me. I remember plotting in my teenage years—rehearsing in my head, picturing going to Mom and telling her the three of us kids were gonna jump Father the next time he laid a hand on her. But when the next time came, I drowned myself in the stereo and didn't do a damned thing. Then the one time I did something brave, picked up the phone to dial 911, Mother slapped me."

Emily leaned close to hug me. "No kid deserved such burdens," she whispered.

I hugged her back. My tears fell on her shoulders.

It was my turn to dab my eyes with a napkin. "I blamed Mom for tolerating violence, for not protecting her kids, for being weak. Then when John got so big, and Father knew better than to mess with him, I began to blame John for not helping Mom."

"Not only did John not help her, Ruby, he was starting to terror-ize her. I was so grateful he left. One time he threw a pail of water on her bed when she told him to get a haircut. It's all senseless."

"Em, why didn't school teach us to stand behind the little guy? A bunch of little guys can wipe out a bully."

Emily shook her head. I guessed what she was thinking.

"I know, Little Sister. It doesn't work that way. Peace doesn't grow out of violence."

We both looked over to where the three children were playing. They had built a sand castle. Their construction looked more like igloos in a line.

Emily looked into my eyes. "Ruby, I have a confession to make. Stay calm."

"Ooh, I don't like the sound of that."

"Ruby, listen. A few months ago, I was in Chicago for a conference. By coincidence, I found a John F. Lin in the phone book. So, I called the number but no one answered, and there wasn't an answering machine. No address was listed with the number. When I returned to Philly, I tried the number again. Each time no answer. So I called up a friend who worked for the phone company and persuaded him to help me find the address. It took him awhile, but he was able to get the information for me. I sent a note to that address and used my friend's post office box as my return address. I was very careful, just in case the listing belonged to some pervert. I kept the letter short.

> Dear John,
>
> If you are the John F. Lin who was born on June 1, 1961 and went to Washington High School in San Francisco, this is to let you know that your sisters are concerned and would like to know how you're doing. Please respond to this P.O. Box.

"Emily, you're scaring me."

"I was cautious, Ruby. I didn't leave my name."

"Well, what happened?"

"A month later, my friend got a letter in his P.O. box. There was no return address, but the postmark was from Chicago. It was handwritten. It said,

To Whom It May Concern,

I am not your brother. But here's a piece of advice: leave people alone and mind your own business. Some people don't like to be found.

You're probably nice folks, but don't go bothering people.

No signature. Ruby, here's the strange thing. Remember how John signed his name? The way this guy wrote his letter 'n'—in the words 'concern' and 'own'—the 'n's had the spike tail, exactly the way John used to make 'em."

"Maybe it was John. Em, why didn't you tell me about this?"

"I didn't want you to tell me 'Don't do it.' "

The sun had begun to set. We packed up the basket, shook the sand from the blanket and folded it. As we walked toward the car, I stopped to give my sister a long hug. The two of us made a pact that we would respect our brother's wish to be left alone. Then, I said a silent prayer that John F. Lin would take good care of himself wherever he may be.

~

Emily's visit was too short, as always. A week later, I took her to the airport. I sat with her at the boarding gate.

"Well, Ruby, next time your turn."

"Okay. Hey, how about if we meet somewhere like New Orleans or Atlanta? Wouldn't that be fun?"

"I'd like that."

The announcement for passengers to board echoed around us.

"Oh, Emily, I can't help it. I'm going to cry."

"That's all right, Sis. I'll cry with you." She kissed me on the cheek. "I think we turned out okay, didn't we, Ruby?"

"I know we did. Love you, Little Sister."

"Love you too, Sis."

Chapter 22

No More Pretending

"Ruby, will you come into my office." That wasn't a question from Chad. It was an order.

"Hello Chad," I greeted him.

"I'll get right to the point. You were out all week, after I told you that I needed my team here. This doesn't look good, Ruby. If I let you get away with dismissing my orders, then everyone else will be doing it."

"Chad. First let me say thank you. Because you are a decent human being, you approved the change in my vacation request. Then you forgot about it, and yes, I could have reminded you, but as you know I just went through a divorce, and this you didn't know, my mom was hospitalized again. If I weren't a strong person, I would have had a breakdown myself. But because I take pride in my work, I've been doing my job as usual. When you approved my vacation change, you did it because you have a heart. No one is going to say you're less of a boss for being human. I know my performance review is coming up. I'm not worried, Chad, because I know you'll do the right thing. Marilyn wants to go over some accounts with me and I don't want to be late for Managers' Meeting." *Wow. All that came out of me, without Bette Davis or Joan Crawford.* I didn't need to play out a movie scene anymore.

"I'm sorry to hear about your mom, Ruby. And I'm sorry about the divorce." He looked me in the eye to say that.

"Thanks, Chad, I'll see you later."

"Yes." He walked me to the door.

~

"Dr. Thatcher, I'm running out of classes to take. I suppose I could take Algebra or a Science course, but I really don't feel like it."

"Do you have to take a class?"

"No. I don't have to. I've been taking classes to undo something I've done in high school."

"What do you mean, Ruby?"

"Dr. Thatcher, no one knows about this. I'm not a high school graduate."

"I thought you finished high school before moving out on your own."

"No. I didn't graduate."

"What happened?"

"I couldn't put up the pretense anymore by the time I was a senior. My friends called it senioritis, you know, slacking off the last year, preoccupied with class rings, parties, the prom. I felt that too, but the truth is I was at the breaking point at home. My friends, Kristie and Bonnie, had applied to U.C. Berkeley. I wanted to go to college too, but how could I? I wanted to move out right after graduation by getting a job. I couldn't stand it at home anymore."

Dr. Thatcher listened, nodding her head.

"That year, the straight A student stopped studying and even cut

some classes. No one noticed. Not the teachers, certainly not my
parents. I purposely didn't show up on the day they took pictures for
the yearbook. I didn't want to be remembered. I just wanted out.
But in order to get 'out,' I had to pass the mandatory swimming test.
Seniors were warned: If you do not pass the swimming test, you will
not receive your diploma.

"Two weeks before graduation, in front of Mrs. Williams, the
Girls' P.E. teacher, I swam the width of the pool, back-floated and
swam back. I saw her checking off my name on her clipboard that day.

"A week before graduation, at rehearsal, the principal read off the
list of names of those who had not taken their swimming test. He
warned us for the last time, 'If you do not take the test, you will not
receive your diploma.'

"I sat on the bleachers with my friends. The principal called out
the names: 'Albert Bertolucci. Wayne Fong. Ruby Lin. . . .'

"No. It cannot be. I passed the test, I said to myself. 'Ruby, go tell
him you took the test last week,' my girlfriends jabbered. 'Tell them
they've made a mistake.'

"I sat on the bleachers and held back my tears. It was nothing to
cry about. Mrs. Williams made a mistake. Why should I correct
someone else's mistake? Besides, I didn't give a damn about a diploma. I told myself it was just a piece of paper. And so, on graduation day, when they passed out diplomas in the room behind the
auditorium, there wasn't one for me."

"Ruby, you didn't talk to Mrs. Williams?"

"It was too late. It was over. One thin piece of paper to show for
years of hard work."

"Ruby, have you ever thought about going back and talking to the
principal?"

"Many times. But what would I say? Those teachers are gone. It's
probably a new principal."

"You'll never know until you try, Ruby. I want you to think about calling the school and getting this resolved. Do it for yourself. Will you think about it?"

"Yes. Maybe that's why I wanted to tell you about it. To get encouragement from you. I was such an angry girl—turning the anger inward—couldn't speak up."

"I'm right behind you, all the way."

"I know. Thanks, Dr. Thatcher."

~

That afternoon, I went home with a sense of relief. All those years of hiding the shame about the diploma seemed less of a tragedy after telling Dr. Thatcher.

In the lobby, Mrs. Nussbaum and a group of people were coming down the stairs.

"Ruby, Ruby," Mrs. Nussbaum called out. "These are my friends. This is Olga. This is Ida."

"Hello ladies, nice to meet you." I shook their hands.

"Hello Ruby, you're the sweet girl we've been hearing about," said Olga.

"These are my grandchildren," said Ida. "Emma, Liza, say hello to Ruby." The girls buried their heads in Ida's skirt. "They're shy," Ida apologized.

"That's all right. I was a shy little girl myself. Where are you all going?"

"Shopping," Mrs. Nussbaum answered. "Ruby, come with us."

"Thanks. But I better not. Next time, okay? Have fun."

"Ruby, I have something for you. Come by later or tomorrow." Mrs. Nussbaum had her arm around me.

"Okay. Bye everyone. Have fun."

"Bye, Ruby. Nice meeting you. Bye," Olga and Ida called out while the little girls waved their little hands.

"Mrs. Nussbaum, don't forget. We're going fabric shopping this week," I yelled.

"Okay, dear," she answered.

~

I had the urge to clean out another closet that afternoon. I had something to look for—an old address book. In the box marked "journals and class notes," I found the book. I turned to the page for 'R' and there it was. The address to Vonn Ruiz in San Diego.

Seeing Ida's little granddaughters made me remember Vonn's little girls. I'll never forget Vonn.

~

I was in San Diego that year. I was nineteen. That was the year I lived out my biggest lie. At the job interview, I told my prospective employer that my fiancé had accepted a promotion to be the regional marketing manager for his firm and that his territory would be all of southern California. As I talked and walked the story of a young woman with a bright future, Don White gave me the job. He was a nice man.

Monday through Friday, I was one of the "eager to please" junior catering assistants at the Westin Hotel. The only part of my life that wasn't a lie was my work ethics. In the first two weeks, I had proved to my employers and coworkers that they had found a dependable gofer.

This was another world. A world where people paid a sum equal to my paycheck for a small dinner party; a world where professionals flew in from all over the country to attend conferences. First class service was synonymous with our hotel and in a short time, I had learned how to troubleshoot any situation.

Among my new coworkers, one woman, Vonn Ruiz, made extra

efforts to help me. She was thirty, the accounting manager for our division, a wife and a mother of two little girls. She had photographs of her family, proudly displayed on her desk. Every morning at seven forty-five her husband, Pete, dropped her off at the office, and at five-fifteen he picked her up. He was a shipping manager at our warehouse.

Vonn was the only coworker who took an interest in me. Never prying, she gently asked personal questions.

One day in the lunch room, Vonn asked, "How do you like San Diego, Ruby? It must be lonesome to move to a new town and having to make new friends."

"It's all right," I lied.

"Why don't you and your fiancé come over this Friday night for dinner? Nothing fancy. It's fish and chips night at our house. Perhaps we can all go to the ice-cream parlor afterwards. Think it over, Ruby. It'll be fun."

"Thanks, Vonn. I'll check our schedule."

There was no fiancé. Just a boyfriend, a mean lying bastard who couldn't keep a job.

Vonn didn't look surprised or disappointed when I showed up by myself that Friday night. Vonn greeted me with a warm embrace. "Ruby, perfect timing. The grandmas need help in the kitchen. Pete is helping the children with their homework. I'm trying to fix the washer before we have a flood in the garage."

Fish and chips never tasted so good. Both grandmas lived with them. Pete's mother did all the cooking and Vonn's mother did the housecleaning. The little girls were named after their grandmothers, Margaret and Cassandra. Maggi was seven and Cassy was five, two well-behaved little girls who liked to talk. Cassy reminded me of Emily when she was that age. Bright-eyed and curious about everything. Maggi was tall for her age. She had her mother's features: soft eyes, thin lips and a delicate nose. She made sure I knew that there was no "e" in the spelling of her name. "My grandma doesn't have an 'e.' I don't have an 'e' either."

Having recently learned the word "probably," Cassy used it in every other sentence. "We'll probably go out for ice cream later. After we wash the dishes. And probably I'll order Rocky Road."

I did very little lying that evening. Mostly, I watched this family treat me like a dear friend who had come to dinner. I assisted in clearing the table and helped the girls put on their jackets.

"Ruby, here's your lunch for tomorrow. We always eat leftovers for lunch." Vonn had packed a generous serving for me. We piled into their station wagon and off we went to get dessert.

Over ice cream and sundaes, Pete told the story of how he and Vonn met.

"She wouldn't give me the time of day. At a company picnic, she thought I was one of the hired hands at the barbecue. I saw her in line holding her paper plate and I said to myself, 'What a cutie!' When she came up to me, I gave her a big grin and a 'How ya doin?' She must have misinterpreted my friendliness because in a cold voice, she said 'I'll have one of those medium cooked burgers.' A month later, she called me to verify an invoice, of course not knowing I was the charming guy who gave her the burger. On the phone, she put the voice and face together when I asked her how she enjoyed the picnic. I took the opportunity to ask her out, but she had a policy about not dating coworkers. So that was that. Three months later, we ran into each other at a collaborative church function. Vonn probably thought it was okay now to date me since God approved. Married a year later. It'll be ten years in June, right, honey?"

Vonn stroked her husband's face. "Yes, dear. Eat your ice cream. It's melting."

"Yes, Daddy. It's probably melting," Cassy chimed in.

What melted that evening was my heart. I felt safe. I felt as if I had finally met a loving family who were not television characters. They invited me to subsequent visits which were the happiest times spent in my nineteen years. Never had I felt so comfortable with people who barely knew me. The girls started calling me Auntie Ruby and I wanted to be a good role model for them. I wanted to tell Vonn the truth—that I was the great pretender, the great liar.

If I had confessed to her, she might have said, "You don't have to pretend with us, Ruby. We like you just as you are. Our door will always be open to you because we believe in you." I can almost hear her voice saying those words.

I left San Diego nine months after I had arrived. I couldn't bear to say goodbye to her. I sent Vonn a note without leaving a return address and flew back to San Francisco.

~

I've often wondered how Vonn and her family were doing. So many years have passed, I wouldn't recognize the girls if I saw them. That afternoon, I addressed an envelope to Vonn and started a letter that was long overdue.

Feeling good about myself, I called up Mom.

"Hi Mom, I know it's late notice, but can you break away to have dinner with me?"

"Of course. When?" I heard the thrill in her voice.

"In an hour. Is that okay?" I asked.

"Yes. I'll get dress."

~

I took Mom to a little Thai place in her neighborhood.

"Order *pad thai*, Ruby, and hot rice." Emily had introduced *pad thai* to Mom.

"Yes, Mom. And eggplant and tofu, mild?"

"Yes." Mother sat up like a kid at McDonald's.

"Mom, Emily and I have this great idea. She'll be taking pictures of herself, a couple of shots a week, until the roll is used up. Then she'll send us the pictures and we're supposed to do the same. That way, we'll get to see each other in between visits. What do you think? I brought my camera."

"Let's take one here." Mother was beaming.

"We can ask the waiter to take it for us."

An hour later. "Mom, I'm stuffed."

She took out her plastic Ziploc baggie, the one containing bills. "I'll pay, Ruby."

"No, Mom. I invited you. I should pay."

"No, Ruby. I want to pay. I'm very happy you called."

"Okay. Thanks, Mom." I said those words without strain. It was that simple. Okay.

Mother scattered three one dollar bills on the table. I didn't re-arrange them. I just let them be, scattered on the table to show the waiter that Mother had left him three, not just one or two, bills. After he took a picture of us standing in front of the beaded elephant on the pedestal, I went back to the table and added another dollar bill.

~

Next day after work, I went up to Mrs. Nussbaum's.

"Ruby, the door's open," Mrs. Nussbaum yelled from inside.

Rashi greeted me.

"Rashi, I've got something for you. Go ask your mom if you can have it."

He waddled into the kitchen and wagged his tail. Mrs. Nussbaum was tossing a salad.

"Hi Mrs. N." I gave her a kiss on the cheek.

"Hello, dear. What did you bring?"

"A chef's special. The chef at the hotel cooked this today. It's called *poulet jubilee*. He says the Queen had it when she stayed in the hotel."

"Fancy schmancy, as my Herman would say."

"And I got this for Rashi. It's a variety pack of doggie snacks."

"Thank you, Ruby. I'll give him one later. Can you help me set the table?"

"My pleasure."

We talked about my job, my mom, my sister, her friends, their friends. We laughed at Rashi. He came into the kitchen every five minutes to see if Mrs. Nussbaum would open the pack of snacks.

"I don't know what I would do if he weren't around. Such a joy, he is."

"It must be nice to have someone to take care of," I said.

"He takes care of me, Ruby. He gives me a reason to go out twice a day." Mrs. Nussbaum opened the bag of treats and gave Rashi one. He wagged his tail happily and went back to watch television.

After dinner, we sat in the living room. Mrs. Nussbaum went into her bedroom and came back holding something in her hand.

"Ruby, I want you to have this. Open it."

I unwrapped the layers of white tissue to expose a bracelet that had delicate pieces of gems embedded in the gold. The gems sparkled under the living room lamp.

"Mrs. Nussbaum, this is the most beautiful thing I've ever seen. I can't take this. This is too valuable."

"Don't be silly. I want you to have it. Here. Let me put it on for you. It's very old. My mother gave it to me. I was going to give it to Isabel for her eighteenth birthday."

"Mrs. Nussbaum, I'm speechless." My hand was shaking as she inserted the clasp and adjusted the safety lock chain.

"Ruby, don't cry. You've given me joy and I want to say thank you. And you're going to sew that dress for me. There. It looks beautiful on your wrist. Such a little wrist."

I hugged her close and she stroked my hair.

"I'll take good care of it. I promise."

"It's yours, dear. To enjoy. Now, come. I have dessert. Your favorite."

I folded the layers of white tissue and put it in my pocket. The wrapping would be kept in a safe place, next to my grandmother's birth certificate.

We said goodbye that night like grandmother and granddaughter. I slept soundly in my apartment.

~

Winter in San Francisco can be breathtakingly beautiful. Store fronts were dressed in festive colors. The air was cold and crisp. The lobby at the St. Mark was adorned with red and pink poinsettias, each plant regally set on a pedestal.

It's the season when I move my little heater from room to room. The central heating in my apartment works, but the unit clinks and clanks like an auto mechanic's shop.

Walking down Vallejo Street, bundled up in my long wool coat, my scarf, and my gloves, I was thinking about how cozy Dr. Thatcher's office would be. As I opened the front door I felt the sensation of entering a house for the first time. In the waiting room, I peeled off my gloves. Unwrapping the scarf from my neck, I looked up and saw, for the first time, the ceiling trimmed with carved roses.

Later, sitting in my wing chair, I noticed that Dr. Thatcher's office had the same molding. Why hadn't I noticed things like that before? Where had I been?

~

"Dr. Thatcher, I had such a wonderful week. I saw Mom Saturday night. We had a great time eating Thai food. Then Mrs. Nussbaum gave me a beautiful bracelet that she had saved for her daughter. And I did it. I called up the high school principal on Monday and I saw him on Thursday."

"Tell me all about it." Dr. Thatcher's silver earrings sparkled.

"He's the new principal. Mr. Tom. Very nice man. When I got to his office on Thursday, he had my transcript on his desk. Guess what, Dr. Thatcher, you'll never guess?"

Dr. Thatcher leaned forward and gave me one of her smiles.

"I'm a graduate!"

Her smile grew bigger.

"Mr. Tom showed me, in black and white. There was a check mark in the box labeled 'Graduated.' He explained that because there were no records of my passing the mandatory swimming test, a diploma was not issued. He was so nice. He said, 'Since you had completed all the required courses, you are a graduate as the records clearly show. All those years, Ruby. You thought you did not graduate because the diploma was withheld. I'm so sorry.' Then he said, 'Also, I must apologize for the negligence on the part of the counselors and teachers, because looking at your grades over the three years you were here, I see a dramatic plunge in your GPA. You came to this school with straight As, but look at the grades in your senior year. Cs, even one D. Someone should have noticed, Ruby.' He shook his head. 'Had there been a disturbance at home?'

"Doctor Thatcher, when he asked that, I felt like someone had taken ten pounds off my chest. I got teary-eyed. He was so nice. I told him he was a caring principal and that his students are very lucky. He gave me a copy of the transcript. See?"

Dr. Thatcher took the paper and looked at it for a long time. "I'm so proud of you, Ruby."

"Now I'm really going to cry."

Dr. Thatcher handed back my transcript.

"After I thanked Mr. Tom and said goodbye, I wanted to skip out of his office like Dorothy on the yellow brick road in *The Wizard of Oz*. Then I wanted to run back to his office to tell him that the tears were tears of happiness, but I didn't. I told myself it was enough that I knew, and I enjoyed the moment."

"This is such wonderful news."

"And I have you to thank. Thank you for encouraging me to seek the truth."

"You're welcome, Ruby."

Later, walking out into the street, I watched a teenage girl and her Welsh corgi coming towards me. Dorothy and Toto, I said to myself. The dog stopped to sniff the patch of grass in front of a house, as the girl dropped the leash and sighed. Her breath lingered in the cold air. I passed them and turned to look at the dog. If I were Dorothy, then I've found the Scarecrow and Tin Man. All I need is the Lion.

CHAPTER 23

The "A" Paper

Saturday was blustery. I held my portfolio tight to my chest. In front of Dr. Thatcher's office, the wind was blowing piles of raked leaves into the street, clogging the gutters. The bougainvillea looked petrified; its magenta paper-like bracts were gone.

Suddenly I thought about *The Flying Nun*, how Sister Bertrille used her gift of flight on windy days. Explanations about her weight and the shape of her starched cornet did not convince me, for I believed there was another reason for her ability to fly. She was able to do what the other nuns could not because she was not afraid to soar.

"Dr. Thatcher, have you ever had one of those dreams when you know you're dreaming?"

"Yes."

"The other night, I had one. I can't remember the details, but I think I actually said to myself in the dream, 'You're dreaming.' Isn't that weird?"

Dr. Thatcher smiled.

"Well, in this one, I was being chased by something, someone, but

I flapped my arms and flew a few feet off the ground. Then I gave up, saying to myself, 'Humans can't fly' and I plopped to the ground."

"Were you hurt?"

"No. The dream ended."

"Who or what do you suppose was chasing you?"

"It's *who*, Dr. Thatcher. I know who it is. I've known it for years, but was afraid to talk about it. I'm no longer afraid. May I tell you now?"

"Of course, Ruby."

"Actually, I have something to read to you. It's from Emily. This is one of the reasons why we're so close. May I read?"

Dr. Thatcher nodded.

I pulled out the contents from my portfolio. "Emily sent this to me for my twenty-sixth birthday. She was in Philly already. A few days before my birthday, a carton was delivered, and inside was a box wrapped in gold foil and tied with ribbons of red, purple and blue curled at the ends. I opened the box and sitting on some tissue wrapping was a note that read:

Dear Sis,

    I took a chance in sending this to you. It's a paper I wrote for Psychology Class. Well, it's actually the first draft, what I used for the scenario in a case study. I didn't hold back, I had to get it all down on paper. I did change names for the final paper and by the way, I got an "A" on it. Please don't be angry with me.

Love you very much,

Emily

"I unlayered the tissue wrapping and reached in. Paper. A few sheets of paper stapled together."

I looked up to see Dr. Thatcher nodding for me to continue.

"The paper is dated March 19, 1984. Emily's name is at the top right corner and the title is . . .

Secondhand Violence

The birthday celebrations of our youth, my sister's, my brother's, and mine, all started with balloons, streamers, and a thawed, store-bought cake, but ended with name calling, ill wishes and violence between our parents. Just like a script that could not be changed, our mother would not cut the birthday cake until our father came home; and he always managed to come home late. She would accuse him of betraying his family by wasting time with his "lowlife" friends; he would tell her to go to her grave so that he could live in peace. Most years, we, the children, took our birthday cake to the living room and turned up the volume on the television set while our parents exchanged verbal and physical blows in the kitchen.

All that hatred our parents felt for one another. Where did it come from? Why didn't they reserve the hatred for the people who committed atrocities during wartime or for people who could not tolerate poor folks or those who cheated them? Did they hate themselves for carrying around so much hatred?

My sister, Ruby, left home right after her high school graduation. I heard her talking to a friend on the telephone the day before she moved out. "I won't have to listen to the goddamned fights anymore," she told her friend. I was twelve at the time, and I could not understand why she wanted to leave home. Yes, it's true that our parents fought, and she would no longer have to listen to their cursing and screaming, but had she forgotten one thing? Had she forgotten about me? She was the one who blasted the radio to drown out the screams. Who will turn up the radio now?

Perhaps her moving out was for the best since she had been harsh with our mother the past few years. On three occasions, Ruby told our mother that she was stupid for tolerating physical abuse from our father. "You're a fool. If someone were to hit me, I would leave," Ruby boasted. I was afraid to say anything to Ruby since she was the older sister, plus, I was afraid she would tell me that I was stupid.

I couldn't sleep the first night she was away from home. Wasn't she scared to live by herself? She came home the following weekend; she walked in like a visitor. She sat in the living room and did not go into the kitchen until Mother announced that dinner was ready. Then her visits became less and less frequent.

A few months later, she brought a man with her. He scared me. He had cold eyes and he never smiled. Mother didn't seem to mind. I had never seen my sister kiss a boy until she brought this person home. He was no boy. He was ten years older than she.

For Ruby's nineteenth birthday, I planned a surprise party. I invited all her friends to her studio apartment, instructing them to bring food or gifts and I would buy the biggest birthday cake I could with my allowance. I had told her that I wanted to cook her a birthday dinner to show off what I had learned in home-making class. She said "Yes, Little Sister. I get off work at six. Should be home by seven if the bus is on time." That's what she said two days before her birthday.

All her friends arrived on time to hide in the bathroom at a quarter to seven. Seven o'clock came and went. Half past seven and still no sign of her. Eight o'clock—still no Ruby. We were concerned by now. I called the store where she worked and there was no answer.

Nine o'clock. The telephone rang. It was Ruby, but I could hardly hear her. "Hi Emily, sorry for the mix-up. We're on our way to L.A. for the week. I completely forgot you were coming over tonight. I'll make it up to you when I get back, okay? Love you. Bye."

She didn't even let me get a word in. She hung up before I could tell her that all her friends were there, and we had been worried sick for the past hour. "It's not like her," one of her friends commented. "Oh, she must be having fun. Give her a break," someone else said.

I did not see my sister until three months later and that was a disappointing visit because she told me that she was moving to San Diego with her boyfriend. I was angry with her that day. Again she said that she would make it up to me for forgetting about my going over to cook her a birthday dinner. How was she going to make it up to me by leaving? And so my sister left for San Diego. Her boyfriend never came into the house to say goodbye. She said he was waiting in the car. "We couldn't both come up and leave the car unattended, with all our stuff," she explained.

At first she called about once a month. Then we did not hear from her for three months. We telephoned the last number she had given us but strangers answered the phone. "There's no one here by that name," the woman said.

I called all her friends and no one had heard from her. "Your sister has changed ever since she started dating that man," her friend Kristie said to me. "She doesn't talk about anything anymore. I just hope she's all right."

Then we started receiving cards from Ruby. Beautiful greeting cards with short personal messages from her: "Dear Family, Everything is great. We moved—closer to my workplace. Decided not to get a phone since we're never home. Love you all, Ruby."

Exactly a year and one day after she had missed her surprise birthday party, she called. Mother spoke briefly with her, and the next day Ruby was home. She had a small suitcase with her. She had come back to live with us. I did not know how to greet her. What do you say to a sister who shows up one day after staying away for so long? We hugged, but she did not look at me. She had lost weight and her face was different. She had on a lot of makeup.

Two months after my sister moved back home, Mother announced that we were moving and getting a new telephone number. I asked why but Mother would not tell me. "And after we move, don't answer the door unless it's one of your friends," she said. Just that summer, John, our brother, moved out, and our father was living in a hotel. Perhaps Ruby might not have come back if Father was living at home.

Ruby lived with us for six months. She was like a boarding house tenant who showed up for the evening meal and afterward went straight to her room. She slept a lot. The light from her bedroom was out every night by eight. She went to work Monday through Friday and slept day and night on Saturday and Sunday. When Mother announced that Father was coming home, Ruby packed her bags again.

Three years later, I moved to Philadelphia to go to college. It seems that Ruby and I became closer when we were three thousand miles apart. We swapped telephone calls, she flew out to see me, and I went home for the holidays. There were times when I wanted to confront her about her mysterious behavior that year while she was in San Diego and why we had to move when she came home to live with us, but I could never bring myself to ask.

Three months ago when I was home for Christmas I ran into

Ruby's friends, Kristie and Bonnie, who were also Christmas shopping at Macy's. They invited me to have a snack with them. Over chocolate cake and coffee, they talked about jobs and men. I talked about school. Then one of them mentioned San Diego. I knew that if anyone would know what had happened to Ruby during that year, these two women would. Appealing to their sense of friendship and sisterhood, I persuaded them to tell me the whole story.

For the next hour I listened to these two women. I found out that on the night I had planned a surprise birthday party for Ruby, she had stopped off to see her boyfriend. When she arrived, he told her that he had just been laid off. She started to console him, but he told her that he was sick of her always trying to fix everything. They argued. He told her to leave. She wouldn't. They argued some more.

Suddenly he was out of control. He slapped her. She stood there and heard herself saying, "I don't believe this is happening. This isn't happening." He slapped her again. She repeated her denial and he kept slapping her until she screamed.

"If you don't believe this is happening, you'd better take a look in the mirror," the vile man said to Ruby.

She ran to the bathroom and looked in the mirror. She saw a bloated face with two eyes that looked like tiny round beads engulfed by the swollen head. She covered her face with a cold towel, but when she removed the towel and looked in the mirror again, she saw the same hideous sight in the reflection. She heard her boyfriend crying in the living room. That's when she called and told the lie about going to Los Angeles for the weekend.

She told herself it was a bad dream and she went to sleep while the guilty man sat in the living room.

But it was no bad dream. Ruby spent the next two months

hiding in his apartment because her face had bruised to the point that she would have been unrecognizable even by those who knew her. She lied to her employer that an aunt was very ill and she had to fly out immediately to take care of her affairs.

During those two months, he told her repeatedly that he was sorry and that it would never happen again. Another month later, they moved to San Diego.

He lied. That was not the last time. Having seen how she bruised so easily and that people would detect the signs, he administered his "disciplinary" doses in other ways.

Ruby wore long-sleeved sweaters to work. She pretended that she was happy. She lied to coworkers that she was engaged to be married. In her private moments, she told herself that she had deserved every horrible day of her life; that she was being punished for calling our mother a fool; and that this was to be her destiny.

Ruby's love for this bad man had turned to hatred. But she could not leave. He had threatened to harm her family, and she started to fantasize about escaping and warning her loved ones. She fantasized for a month. But her mind would not let her follow through with her plans of leaving. "I'll kill your family if you ever leave me," he had warned her.

On her twentieth birthday, they were on their way to the shopping mall to buy her a present. It was seven o'clock in the evening. He became irritable in the car, telling her that she did not deserve a birthday gift. The name calling began. She knew what was going to happen to her that night behind closed doors. He made a turn onto the main thoroughfare and started to speed up. He slowed down again when he saw a police car on the other side of the street, parked in front of a large apartment building. He did not want to be pulled over for speeding.

Ruby also saw the police car, with an officer sitting in the driver's seat. She felt as if she were in the chase scene of a movie.

Ruby looked over at her boyfriend, then at the police car. She felt numb. He drove for another three blocks before realizing he was going the wrong way. So he made a U-turn and they were now on the same side of the street as the apartment building.

As the car approached the block where the police car was parked, Ruby looked at the passenger door next to her. She had only a second to make up her mind.

As the car crossed the intersection and Ruby saw the police car only twenty yards away, she reached for the passenger door. When her boyfriend heard the click of the door handle, he tried to grab her arm. She jumped out and felt the sensation of concrete moving under her feet. She stumbled, fell, but picked herself up and ran towards the police car. The officer got out of his vehicle. Her heart was pounding as she ran; and she heard her boyfriend's final words, "I'll kill you, you bitch." She collapsed in the officer's arms.

Ruby pressed charges that night. First, the police officer took her to the medical department at the precinct. "What is your name?" asked the nurse. "Ruby Lin," my sister answered. "Your date of birth, Ruby?" asked the nurse. "August 22, 1958," said Ruby. "August 22nd? That's today! My dear. I'm so sorry." The nurse hugged my sister.

Every person Ruby met that evening was kind to her. The doctor who examined her took pictures of her arms, her chest and her abdomen. He also took x-rays of her rib cage to check for internal damages. "Ruby, you're twenty years old. You have a whole life ahead of you. No one has the right to do this to you.

I hope you know that. I have a daughter who is going to be twenty next year," said the doctor. He must have felt a paternal closeness to Ruby. If circumstances were different, this could be his daughter.

My sister slept at a shelter for battered women that night. No one drilled her with questions. A woman named Kate showed her to an empty bedroom, and told my sister she would be safe there and wished her a good night.

In the morning, Kate gave Ruby some statistics: In America, one out of every two women has or will experience some form of violence. Thousands of abuse cases are never reported. The odds are high that a woman will go back to the offender.

After hearing Kristie and Bonnie's story about my sister, I felt as if a wall between Ruby and me had come down. Kristie and Bonnie told me it was my decision whether or not to let Ruby know that I had heard the story from them. When I saw Ruby that weekend, I did not mention to her that I had run into her friends.

I understood now—why she slept so much when she came home. She had told her friends that she had to sleep because every waking hour haunted her. She knew she would go back to him if she had enough waking hours to forgive him.

Kristie and Bonnie also told me that the wicked man was released from jail two months after my sister had pressed charges. The judge had let him go with the stipulation that he would not contact Ruby, her relatives or her friends. So that is why we had to move. He was probably the type who would want to hurt Ruby because she had pressed charges. She must have been terrified that he would come back for her and take revenge on us.

Ruby started working two jobs soon after. She seemed carefree whenever I saw her. She always dressed beautifully, probably to pamper herself the only way she knew how. She talked only about her jobs. She said she did not have time to date. It's all clear to me now. She did not date because she was afraid of men.

Time and distance had saved my sister from going back to the bad man. I don't know if she ever forgave herself or acknowledged her own courage. I went to a lecture last year about domestic violence and the speaker made a comparison of exposure versus nonexposure.

The speaker said, "Let's say you grew up in a loving home where you never witnessed any form of violence among family members. If someone were to come up to you and raise a hand as if to strike you, you would reject the interaction because raising of the hand is not a familiar message. However, if you did grow up in an environment where violent behavior was routine, then not only would you be more likely not to reject the interaction, you would probably engage in it. Many women who were never physically abused as children, but whose mothers were, find themselves involved with abusive men. It is like secondhand smoke. The exposure can be deadly. Those little girls who witnessed their fathers assaulting their mothers are victims of secondhand violence. They were conditioned for violence. In many instances, they were witnessing their own futures."

Knowing what she had experienced, I saw my sister in a different light that Christmas. Over five years have passed since that horrible year. It's March now, and I have been waiting for an opportunity to tell Ruby that I am proud of her, that she should be proud of herself for having jumped out of that car on her birthday in order to save herself from further harm. I know I will find just the right time to tell her all this. And I will remind her that we have a special bond between us—the bond that started more than fifteen years ago when we found Pebble and Mimi for Christmas.

The end.

I put down the paper and looked up. Dr. Thatcher was wiping her eyes with a tissue.

"Dr. Thatcher, are you all right?" I asked, wanting to leave my seat and give her a hug. But I didn't. We'd never hugged before. I would have to ask for her permission.

"Yes, Ruby. I'm all right. Are you?" She blew her nose, causing her earrings to jingle.

"I'm okay. When I read this the first time, I cried and cried. Then I called Emily. We cried and cried. It's really strange, Dr. Thatcher, this horrible nightmare, it doesn't have the same power over me anymore. You did it. You've given me the tools to forgive myself. I can live with this now." I put Emily's gift back in my portfolio. The tears were falling now. I had finally forgiven myself.

"Ruby, by allowing the darkness to come out into the sunlight, you have cast out the fears. I am so proud of you."

"You always are. I'm so lucky to have found you, Dr. Thatcher. I've learned so much, especially this last year. Forgiveness, gentleness, acceptance. For others. For myself. For Mom."

Dr. Thatcher blew her nose again.

"How I used to hate my parents. I hated Father for having been the abuser, then I hated Mother for accepting the abuse and setting me up to follow in her footsteps. I even hated John for leaving, even though I had left home first. The one I hated most was me—for living the same nightmare that I was running away from. I don't hate my parents anymore. I certainly don't hate myself. As a matter of fact, I like myself these days."

"I liked you the moment you sat down in this office for your first appointment."

"Even though I was here to sign you up as my mother's doctor?"

"Yes. I knew you cared about your mother."

"Just think. Maybe, since I got secondhand violence, I thought I could deliver secondhand psychotherapy."

Dr. Thatcher smiled.

"I haven't seen Kristie and Bonnie in years. When I found out they told Emily everything, I was relieved, at first. Then I was ashamed. Every time they called, wanting to get together, I made up excuses that I had to work. I thought that if I saw them, that would open up the ugly past. I didn't even invite them to my wedding. But I think it's time I reclaim the good things in life, like friendship with these two women."

Dr. Thatcher nodded.

The tiny clock said 3:00.

"Oh my gosh!" I jumped out of my chair.

"Ruby, do you remember that I'll be on vacation the next three weeks? Will you be all right?"

"Yes, I'm fine. You have a wonderful time."

"Thank you. I'll see you when I get back. Don't forget you can always call my answering service. They'll know how to track me down." Dr. Thatcher walked me to the door, stopped, took a step closer, and hugged me.

"Thank you, Dr. Thatcher," I told her.

CHAPTER 24

Beginning

The following Saturday morning, I went up to Mrs. Nussbaum's floor. Her knee had been bothering her. I wanted to let her know that the elevator wasn't working and that I could walk Rashi for her.

I rang the doorbell. No answer. Perhaps she and Rashi had gone out already. As I was about to leave, I heard a scratching sound. Rashi was whimpering and scratching at the door. I rang the doorbell again. Still no answer. A scary thought entered my mind. I had a feeling that Mrs. Nussbaum was in trouble.

I rang her next door neighbor's bell. Mrs. Craft opened her door. She was in her pink cotton robe.

"Mrs. Craft, I think something is wrong. Rashi is scratching at the door and Mrs. Nussbaum doesn't answer the doorbell."

"Come in, Ruby. I'll call her." She dialed, and waited. "No answer," she said. "She's always out of the house by this time in the morning. I'm calling 911."

I went back to Mrs. Nussbaum's door. "Rashi," I called out. He came to the door and scratched it. "Rashi, everything will be okay."

~

Two policemen and two firemen showed up almost immediately. One officer rang Mrs. Nussbaum's bell and knocked hard on the door. Rashi barked frantically from the other side. "Ladies, we'll need to go in through the fire escape," said one of the firemen. My heart was racing. Mrs. Craft showed the men into her apartment. She was shivering.

The two firemen climbed out her dining room window onto the fire escape. Seconds later we heard their footsteps on the roof. Mrs. Craft and I went back to the hallway and waited with the police officers.

Standing close by me, Mrs. Craft whispered, "What's taking them so long?"

It just seems long, I wanted to tell her. Instead, I rubbed her arm. Breathe, I told myself.

One of the firemen opened the door. The officers went in first; Mrs. Craft and I followed them. The men walked towards Mrs. Nussbaum's bedroom. Rashi was hiding under the hallway table, shaking and whimpering. I picked him up and carried him with me as Mrs. Craft and I walked down the long cold hallway.

They had found Mrs. Nussbaum. She was still in bed. One fireman checked her pulse. He checked it again. He shook his head. Mrs. Craft and I were standing outside the bedroom looking in. Mrs. Craft grabbed my arm when the fireman looked up and said, "I'm sorry, folks." Rashi whimpered in my arms.

Mrs. Nussbaum looked peaceful, as if she were sleeping.

The police officers asked us to sit in the living room. They asked us all kinds of questions. It was a big blur.

I looked up Olga's and Ida's telephone numbers and called them. They came immediately. Olga took Rashi from my arms. "Ruby, would you mind walking the poor thing. The poor thing." She stroked his hair.

"Oh, I didn't think of it. Poor Rashi." I put his leash on, grabbed a biscuit off the kitchen counter and took him out.

Once outside the building, Rashi knew the route. Rashi led me around the corner and down four or five blocks. I heard Mrs. Nussbaum's voice in my head. "He takes care of me, Ruby. He gives me a reason to go out twice a day." It felt like half an hour later when I found myself standing in front of the apartment building. Rashi had taken me home.

In Mrs. Nussbaum's apartment, only Olga, Ida, and Mrs. Craft were there. The hallway was warm. The tea kettle was whistling. The ladies had gathered in the kitchen.

I took Rashi into the bedroom. Mrs. Nussbaum had a sweet look on her face. I kissed her cheek. It was stone-cold. Wiggling in my arms, Rashi slipped away from me. He licked Mrs. Nussbaum's face. We both said goodbye to her.

In the kitchen the ladies were drinking tea. Olga pulled out a chair for me. She and Ida looked like they'd been through this before. Ida said arrangements had been made long ago. Mrs. Nussbaum had made them herself.

"She went in her sleep, like an angel," said Olga.

Mrs. Craft picked up Rashi onto her lap. The five of us sat in the warm kitchen in silence.

~

I called Emily that afternoon. I couldn't cry one tear. Em and I didn't talk long. I just needed to hear her voice, to know she was there, alive and well. "Get some rest, Sis, I'll check up on you later," she said in her sweet little voice.

That night, I looked inside my refrigerator. I had not eaten all day. Sitting on the top shelf was half a turkey loaf that Mrs. Nussbaum had given me. Instead of eating in the dining room, I stayed in the kitchen just as Mrs. Nussbaum and I used to do. In my head, I heard her say to me, "Eat, dear. Eat."

~

Vincent called a week later. I told him Mrs. Nussbaum had passed away.

"I'm sorry, honey. I know she was very special to you." He was still calling me "honey." It felt good hearing it. He asked to meet me for coffee the next day. I said "yes." "Seasons Cafe?" he asked.

"No, let's not. Too many memories. How about Carmen's Bistro?"

"Okay, Ruby. Take care of yourself."

"I will. See you tomorrow."

~

Vincent was at a window seat when I walked into Carmen's Bistro. Just like old times, he rose to greet me with an embrace. We ordered two coffees and the waiter delivered them immediately.

"How are you, Ruby?"

"Okay. And you?

"So-so. How's your mom?" he asked.

"She's doing well. Thanks for asking."

"How's Emily?"

"She came out in October. She looked great. I miss her so much." We sat there, both quiet.

"I miss you, Ruby."

I was happy to hear those words. "I miss you too."

He took my hand into his.

I looked into his eyes. "We did the right thing, didn't we, Vincent?"

He nodded. "But I'm still not sure what went wrong? I've been asking myself that question."

"I think we were looking for what was missing in our individual lives. I wanted to be part of a family, but when I found out I was just a private first class enlisted in a platoon with the generals already in place, I resented the whole system, especially you. I wanted to blame you for not having warned me."

"You make it sound so terrible. My family is not that bad, Ruby."

"I know. Just like my lifestyle is not that bad either. I need to know that whatever choices I make I don't have to clear them with anybody's parents, including my own."

"In time, Ruby, my parents would have come around. They just needed to know that their daughter-in-law loved them as much as they loved her."

"So many kinds of love. Have you ever thought about that? I love my mother but I know I could never live with her. I even love my father. He's getting old and I suppose if Mother can forgive him, so can I. I think I was hoping that our marriage would redeem my parents'. I know how ridiculous it is now. Plus, I was enchanted with the idea that we were from the same culture. It was like finding my roots."

"But we're not from the same culture, Ruby."

"Was that an insult?" I took my hand away.

"No, not at all. Earlier, you said we were attracted by what was lacking in our lives. You were right. You were the self-sufficient, confident woman that I couldn't resist, but I thought that because you're Chinese, your parents must have brought you up the same way my parents raised me."

"You didn't know I was raised by black-and-white movies, did you?"

"Movies are not real, Ruby."

"It was a joke. I know movies can never replace real people, but that's all I had growing up. I have plenty of healthy role models now."

"I know. You're a great role model yourself."

"Thanks for saying that."

"I mean it." He said it with sincerity.

"I know life isn't a two-hour movie. You've helped me realize that. I had my script all written, but then so did your parents. It was unfair to make you choose which script."

There was an uncomfortable minute of silence.

"I was so angry with you when you rejected my folks. I didn't mean all the nasty things I said. I'm sorry."

"Me too. I'm sorry for having blamed you for my own actions. Perhaps if we had dated longer, we would have seen the conflicts. But I have no regrets, Vincent. I married you because I loved you. I'm sad that I had to find out that love doesn't solve all problems. I'll always wish you well. You know that."

He took my hand again. "It's not going to be easy. I wish there was a way to start all over again. Before you came along, I never thought too much about responsibilities. Then it all came at once. I wanted to be a husband and father. My folks . . . I never knew how generous they were until I showed them I was ready to start my own family."

"The right woman will come along for you and your folks, and I'm not being facetious. Everyone should have the life they want. I've learned a big lesson about marriage. It's not negotiating with just one person. There's a much bigger picture."

"Do you think we can be friends, Ruby?"

I took a deep breath. "I don't know about that. As confident and self-sufficient as I may be, I'm not the kind of woman who can turn a divorce into a friendship and go on double dates."

Vincent nodded. His face was solemn. "Bad idea," he muttered. We sat in silence for a few minutes.

"I know I'm going to cry, Vincent, if you say those damned words, 'have a nice life.' So don't say it. Just let me sit here alone for a minute, okay?"

"But I don't want to walk away first."

I took his other hand into mine. "It's okay, Vincent. Really."

He squeezed my hands, then let go. "Everything will be okay." He stood up, hugged me one last time, and kissed my temple. As he gently pulled away, his chin quivered as if he were about to cry. He nodded at me. I watched him walk away for the last time. He never turned back.

~

All week I fantasized about Vincent running back to tell me he had a dream and the dream guided him to Ruby's world. But that scene would be as ludicrous as Rhett Butler running back to apologize to Scarlett.

Friday night I cried long and hard. The next morning I bundled up in two thick sweaters and walked down Buchanan, turned on Filbert, and continued towards Scotts Street. I saw joggers, walkers, and young people at Laundromats. At the Marina Green I had my choice of benches. The sun came out, warming me. I sat there until a quarter after one. Then I walked to Dr. Thatcher's office.

"How was your vacation, Dr. Thatcher?"

"Very nice, Ruby. How are you?"

I told Dr. Thatcher what had happened while she was away. "Two people out of my life. I miss them so much."

"I'm sorry, Ruby."

"You know what I realized last week?"

Dr. Thatcher shook her head. She wasn't wearing earrings, but a gold necklace with a diamond charm.

"I thought that by having Vincent around, he would chase away the scary dreams. But I created those dreams, whether or not Vincent was there."

"Yes, Ruby."

I took a deep breath.

"Ruby, are you really okay? Mourning two losses."

"Yes, I'm not fibbing. Mrs. Nussbaum will be with me always. I can hear her voice, like the other day at the grocery store, someone sounded exactly like her."

"It'll take time to heal, Ruby. Be gentle with yourself."

"I will. Dr. Thatcher, will you see me through this? I mean, I would like to wrap up my work here in a couple of months. What do you think?"

"We haven't really talked about your father or brother in great detail."

"I will, in due time. I know what it feels like now, to have some peace of mind, how to let go, well I suppose that's a lifelong lesson. How to take care of the business at hand, but not forget about the self. You taught me all that."

"I wish you all the happiness, Ruby. Also, remember to enjoy moments of pleasure. Don't forget to have fun."

"Thank you, Dr. Thatcher. I'll try to remember all your golden advice." I looked at the tiny clock: 2:49. "Mrs. Nussbaum's memorial is this afternoon. It's not a wake. Her buddies are giving her a special memorial, a celebration of her life."

"Take care of yourself."

"I will. See you next week."

~

The memorial was held at a community center on California Street. The place was packed with people of all ages. They were eating and drinking. Lovely flower arrangements filled every corner of the room. At the center table was a large framed photograph of Mrs. Nussbaum wearing her small pearl drop earrings.

"I took that picture last year at my house," said Ida as she came up beside me. "What a sweet little face," she said affectionately.

"Yes. A beautiful face," I said, feeling the tug in my heart.

Also on the table was a huge photo album. "Ruby, you can look at that later when we take it back to the apartment. I want to show you something now. Come." Ida took me by the hand.

She led me into a side room and closed the door behind her. It was a cozy little room with a floral print sofa, end tables, and two oversized chairs. The fragrance from a vase of peach-color gladioli, white roses and pink stock filled the air.

"Dear, please sit down," Ida pointed. She sat beside me and took out an envelope from her pocket. "Ruby, this is for you. No one will disturb you while you read it. I'll close the door." She handed me the envelope, patted me on the arm, and left the room.

The onionskin envelope had my name on it. I peeled off the seal and took out a letter. My hands were shaking.

Dearest Ruby,

By the time you read this, I will have joined Mr. Nussbaum and Isabel. How are you, my dear?

There are a few things I want to tell you myself, before Ida and Olga, my executrixes, formally tell you. The reading of the Will will be boring. I want you to hear it from me, this way.

Ruby, you are the granddaughter I never had. I want to give you something useful. There is a piece of property on Geary Blvd. I own it. I want you to have it. For your hearty food restaurant, remember? I'm also leaving you my mother's recipes. Remember what I told you? All plans start with talk. You talk it over with people you can trust. Use the property however you like. Trust your judgment. Always trust your judgment, dear.

Also, Ruby, it's okay to tell everyone now. I own the apartment building. I kept it a secret because I didn't want everyone to think I am a rich old lady. I am not. Mr. Nussbaum and I worked very hard for many many years. We were lucky. I have instructed Olga and Ida to extend the existing leases for fifty years so that no one will lose their apartments. At first, I was going to put in my will that your rent is to be paid by the trust, but I know you are a proud girl. I can see you with your chin up, saying "I don't need a handout." Am I right?

One more thing, Ruby. That beautiful gift you gave me. I want you to hang it in your hallway. That beautiful 'oy.' I want you to keep it so that I'll be watching over you just like Mr. Nussbaum and Isabel watched over me.

Rashi. I'm giving Rashi to Ida. She gets lonely when her grandchildren don't come to visit. She needs Rashi. But will you go visit them when you have time?

This letter is getting long. I will end it here. Don't let anyone change you. I love you, little Ruby.

Always,
Mrs. N.

The tears that had been collecting since the morning of her death came down like a gentle rain. I put her letter back in its envelope and slid it into my pocket. The fragrance from the flowers was like a lullaby. I thought about the fabric Mrs. Nussbaum and I picked out for the dress I was going to sew for her. It was a golden-colored rayon with speckles of purple. "Too young-looking, Ruby," Mrs. Nussbaum said at the store. "Never too young," I said. "Okay," she had agreed.

I curled up on the floral print sofa and fell asleep.

~

The next day I met Mom at Mel's. Nat King Cole was playing on the jukebox. She was already sitting in a booth.

"Hi, Mom. You look great."

She stood up. "Look, Ruby. I'm wearing one of my new pants."

"Great, Mom. There's this piece of fabric; I think it'll look beautiful on you."

Her smile grew big. She whipped out a single red rose and presented it to me. "Look, Ruby. It's in a tube of water."

"Oh, Mom. It's lovely." A rose from my mother. I wanted to cry.

Before sitting down, she reached over to stroke my hair. "Your hair is getting so long. So beautiful. Like silk."

The waiter came over and took our order.

"I remember you used to say that my hair was like gold thread in the sunlight. When I was little, remember?"

"I remember. You had fine hair and fair skin. Do you know why?"

I shook my head.

"Because I ate egg whites while I was carrying you. That's why."

"Oh, Mom. It's your genes. Did you know I was envious of you when I was a teenager? My girlfriends always referred to you as 'Ruby's pretty mom' and I didn't like the fact that I looked like Father."

"You did look like your father. But you are starting to look like me. Both you and Emily are starting to look like me. My genes are stronger."

I laughed. "I think you're right, Mom. Your genes are strong and they're not afraid to take chances in life. Mom, I have good news. I'm thinking about leaving the St. Mark and starting my own business."

"Starting your own business? That's so much work. Are you going to open a hotel?"

"No, Mom. No more hotel business for me. Don't worry. I'm planning every step. I won't rush into anything. I'll tell you all the details in a few months. Don't worry. I'm happy just thinking about it. It's exciting, Mom."

"I'm happy that you're happy."

"I know, Mom. Speaking of that, how's your appetite and your sleep?"

"Good. I told the doctor the new pill makes me wide awake at nighttime, so he said, 'Take it in the morning, then you'll have energy.' I take it in the morning, and he was right."

"I'm so proud of you, for talking to the doctor."

Mother noticed my bracelet. I was wearing the one that Mrs. Nussbaum gave me.

"What a beautiful bracelet, Ruby."

"Isn't it? Mrs. Nussbaum said her mother had given it to her and she was going to give it to her daughter. Mom, she passed away three weeks ago."

"So sad. No grandchildren?"

"No grandchildren. And her daughter died as a little girl."

"I don't have anything to give you, Ruby."

"Mom," I sighed. "You've given me so much. You taught me to be generous and kind. You gave me your good looks, your strong genes. You gave me my name. Those are all valuable things that money can't buy. Also, Mom, I've been meaning to tell you how thankful I am that you and Father came to America so that we could grow up here. You were both very brave to do that—pick up your world and come here, not knowing a word of English. I am proud of you."

"Do you know why I named you Ruby?"

I shook my head again. Our food had arrived.

"Because you were my firstborn. You were precious to me. Rubies are precious and red is good luck."

I was astonished at those words; I swallowed hard. "I never knew that. You never told me that."

"I didn't tell you many things. I remember many things now."

"Mom, since we're on the subject of memory . . . I found Grandmother's birth certificate in the gray tin box. Is it okay if I ask you about it?"

"You can ask, but I might not know the answers. You know who would know the answers? My uncles, if they're still alive. Do you want the address book? I don't want it. If you want it, I'll look for it."

"Yes. I can't believe this. I'm really going to have a family tree. And you're the one who's going to give me that treasure. What about Grandfather, Mom?" Mother's expression changed.

"Mom, sorry. I'm asking too many questions."

She smiled. "Eat, dear. Eat," she said.

I looked at her lovely heart-shaped face.

She had changed. So had I.

I drove her home. As she was getting out of the car, I reached over to hug her. "I love you, Mom."

"I love you, Ruby," she said without hesitation. She waved good-bye as I drove away.

~

Monday at work, I pulled Marilyn aside. She was a blonde again. I complimented her on the change; she informed me it was her natural color.

"Marilyn, this is strictly confidential. I'm leaving. I'm giving Chad notice today. He's going to have to find someone to replace you because we both know you're going to be the one to be stuck with my job."

"Ruby, are you and Vincent getting back together?"

"No. I need a change. I wanted to leave a long time ago. I want you to have my evening gowns, so don't say no. I won't need them where I'll be working. No more high heels either."

"Where are you going?"

"Let's say it'll be a place where I can serve matzo ball rice porridge."

"What?"

"I'll explain later, Marilyn. Thank you for everything. For all the times you've covered for me."

"That's what friends are for, Ruby."

"Let's go to Managers' Meeting. It could be my last one." We walked down the hallway arm in arm.

~

That evening, I called Emily.

"Little Sister, remember all those times you said I could have gone to Europe if I had been less frivolous with my money? Listen to this. I'm going to Italy. I'm looking through brochures as we speak."

"Italy? For how long?"

"A month. That's about right, isn't it. The travel agent gave me tons of material to read. I'll have to take out my Italian books and start cramming."

"Wow, I can't believe it, Ruby. I want to go too."

"You can. Let me look through all this stuff and give you some choices. Okay?"

"Okay. Can't believe it," my sister said again. "You're taking a vacation!"

"An overdue one."

"I talked to Mom today. She was in a good mood."

"I have so much to tell you, Em. I'll call this weekend when the rates are cheaper."

"Am I talking to Ruby Lin? She cares about cheaper rates?"

"You'll be surprised to hear that your sister has saved up enough money for a year of living expenses."

"Wow."

"I'll need it when I come back from the trip. Let's just say your old sister is about to make a career change with an angel's help."

"What change? What angel?"

"I'll tell you everything this weekend, *mia sorella.*"

"Tell me now, Ruby."

"No, Little Sister. It'll take hours. This weekend. Hey, what am I saying? We can really talk person to person in Italy. It'll be a walking, talking, and eating trip."

"Ooh, I like that."

"*Ciao,* Emily. Love you."

"Love you too. Bye, Sis."

~

Before retiring for the evening, I hung the framed *'oy'* in my hallway. Mrs. Nussbaum wanted me to do that. Love, made of heart. Under the *'oy,'* I hung old photos of Emily, Mother, Father, and John. I left space for two other photos. I would ask Mom for Grandmother's and Ida for Mrs. Nussbaum's.

~

At my last session with Dr. Thatcher, I brought her a bouquet of yellow roses in a vase. I had noticed in the past she had only a bud vase on her desk.

"Ruby, for me? They're beautiful." She moved the tiny clock on the round table to make room for the vase. "There," she said. "This way we can both enjoy them while we chat. Thank you."

"You're welcome."

That's exactly what we did. We chatted. No dreams to analyze.

No problems to solve. No complaints to make. I took a good look at the room.

"I've been sitting in this chair for over three years, Dr. Thatcher. Has it always been blue?"

Dr. Thatcher burst into laughter. I did too.

"Yes, Ruby. It has always been blue."

"That tells me I've been focused in here. So focused I never noticed the color of the chair I sat in. I've been a good student."

"You've been a wonderful student. You've taught yourself well and now you're graduating."

"No. You've taught me. You've showed me. You've encouraged me. This is one graduation I will cherish for the rest of my life and I won't need a diploma to make me feel good."

I told Dr. Thatcher about my upcoming trip to Italy, my leaving the St. Mark, and the business plan I was working on. She listened and she smiled.

The tiny digital clock said 2:44.

"I'm going to miss you so much, Dr. Thatcher."

"And I'll miss you, Ruby. My Saturdays will not be the same without seeing you."

"Is it okay if I leave five minutes early today, being the last day and all. You know, like the last day of school?"

"Yes, Ruby." She walked me to the door. We hugged. I smelled the fragrance in her hair.

"Bye, Ruby. Good luck."

"Bye, Dr. Thatcher. Thank you."

And with those words, I waved goodbye for the last time.

AUTHOR'S NOTE TO READER

Thank you for letting me share Ruby Lin's story with you. Many readers have asked what the characters in the novel have done for me. My answer is this: I've learned that behind every face is a compelling story.

Please remember me as a writer who says YES! to compassion for mental illness and NO! to domestic violence and child abuse.

Who is Mrs. Nussbaum? She lives in all our hearts. Just as we have the "child within," we also have the "wise elder within." May you always embrace your compelling story and allow your Mrs. Nussbaum to embrace you.

Sincerely,
Teresa LeYung Ryan
www.lovemadeofheart.com